Deep in the Hollow

Brandy Nacole

Ponahakeola Press
www.horri-fi.com

Edited by J. Cameron McClain
Cover design by Melissa Stevens
www.theillustratedauthor.com

Manufactured in the United States of America.
First Edition September 2015
Second Edition March 2020

www.brandynacole.com

*This book is dedicated to all those who speculate on what's real and
what's not real.
You guys rock and help keep the creative wheels turning!*

Prologue

July 11, 1972

Once again, I've fallen prey to MaryAnn's pleading. I follow her out the window, my stomach churning with dread, a contrast to her excitement. I don't know why I let her talk me into these things. She's always getting us into trouble, has been since we were little. Yet, here I am, still following her after seven years of mistake after mistake. There's something about her that makes me unable to say no. I've always thought of her as my sister, not my cousin. We were born only two days apart and look alike. We've been mistaken as sisters our whole life. Still, even sisters tell each other no occasionally. Not me. This time though, I should have.

Our tiny flashlights give off a bright beam in the dark forest, mine unsteady as it shakes in my hand. Thorns scrape at my skin and I look back, hoping to see a light in the cabin on and my grandfather coming out to see where us girls have run off. No such luck. The small, two-bedroom cedar cabin is dark. Its frame nothing but an outline against the trees around it.

"I think we should go back," I whisper, my voice trembling.

"Will you quit whining, Ester? This is no different than walking through the woods during the daylight."

I beg to differ. During the day, the green leaves look welcoming, not over-powering and creepy like now. I don't feel trapped and afraid when walking these familiar woods when the sun is shining bright. Tonight, I do.

"Grandpa said—"

"He was just trying to scare you," she hisses, as she shines her light on a raccoon scavenging for food. It rushes off to hide from what he perceives as danger and we continue through the thicket.

No matter what MaryAnn says, I know she's wrong. I saw the fear in our grandfather's eyes as he told us the story of the thing that haunts these woods. MaryAnn had been enthralled as she sat by the fire, her eyes bright, her body unmoving as she absorbed every word. I had been terrified. Our grandfather has never been a skeptical man, always saying rumors and legends are nonsense. "What you don't see with your eyes, don't witness with your mouth." To see the fear in his eyes as he witnessed the story he told us tonight is enough to convince me he was telling the truth, and not just telling a tale to scare his grandchildren.

An owl hoots overhead and a chill slowly creeps up my back, making me shiver.

"I think we should wait. I don't have a good feeling about this."

MaryAnn ignores my pleas, knowing I won't go back alone.

The leaves rustle as a slight wind picks up. I can no longer see the outline of the cabin. I don't know if it's my fear getting the best of me, but our flashlights seem to be growing dimmer, making the darkness feel as if it is weighing down on us.

A small clearing comes into view, with timber laying hazardously along the ground.

"We are almost there," MaryAnn whispers. "This is where grandpa and his workers have been logging close to the overlook."

Good. Once we reach the overlook and she sees it's the same during the night as it is during the day, we can go back to the safety of the cabin. I can already feel the relief of being back under my blankets, eagerly waiting for morning, with the fresh smell of biscuits baking in the oven and bacon frying in the pan filling the air.

Whoosh.

"What was that?" I ask, panicked, and spin around in a circle, my flashlight shaking with more force.

"Ester, please stop this nonsense. I'm sure it was nothing."

Once on the other side of the clearing, we start the mile hike up the incline and again I wish we had stuck to the main road instead of taking the shorter path through the woods. The ground is slick from the rain we had yesterday, and with every step I take, I lose two as I slide back down.

MaryAnn grabs my hand, steadying me as we both use our weight to climb the impossible hill.

Whoosh.

"Did you hear that?" she asks, her voice a bit higher than before.

I close my eyes, my stomach tensing. *She better not be playing any games with me. I will rat her out in a heartbeat if she is.*

"Yes. What do you think it is?"

Before she can answer, a strange mist builds in front of us. I examine it closely and point it out to MaryAnn, but before it takes on a shape, it's gone.

Whoosh. Whoosh. Whoosh.

A strong wind spins around us, and not caring about what MaryAnn thinks, I let go of her hand and tumble back down the hill, scared for my life. My feet are unsteady as the land levels out again and I fall over a log. Seconds later, MaryAnn lands on top of me.

"Come on!" she screams, terror in her voice. "We have to get back to the cabin."

"What did you see?" I demand, as I race after her, dodging fallen limbs. She doesn't answer. She keeps running, looking back to make sure that I am close behind her.

A strong force comes from behind me and I'm shoved into MaryAnn's back, making us both lose our footing.

Whoosh.

Tears pour down my face as we scramble to our feet, our flashlights lost in the darkness. We try our hardest to run through the darkness with no light to guide our way. MaryAnn grabs my hand, our sweaty fingers clinging as tightly as they can while we try to make out where we are.

When MaryAnn screams, her body jerked away from me, I feel as if I can't breathe. Something is trying to take her from me. My grip on her hand tightens, my small twelve-year-old frame pulling as hard as possible against whatever is trying to tug her away.

A movement behind her catches my eye as we struggle, but I can't make out who or what it is. It's shrouded in a black cloak, practically invisible under the blanket of night. I do make out the grey mist behind it, as if it's drifting and waiting for its prey.

My heart thrums, feeling as if it's trying to escape out of my chest, and my throat grows tight as I choke on my tears. MaryAnn screams, begging me not to let go of her as our fingers begin to slip.

Why can no one hear us? We have to be close to the cabin.

A sharp pain explodes in the back of my head, and I pitch forward, disoriented. My legs slip out from beneath me, and I can feel myself losing consciousness. MaryAnn's fingers slip out of mine as I land against the damp leaves on the ground. The last thing I hear is her pleading for me to save her.

Chapter One

Squinting against the bright red digits of the clock, I groan and swat it until the blaring stops. Then comes the contemplation game. Should I get up? Should I skip out this year and stay home, finish my senior year online? Probably, considering what's waiting on me. Then again, I'll have to deal with Tyler and all his older brother angst. That's even more dreadful and gets the win every time.

"Jo, you awake?" Speak of the angsty monster and he shall call your name.

I fumble for the light switch. "I'm up," I holler and hope he hears me. What's he even doing up anyway?

Looking down at the pile of clothes laying on the floor, I scratch at my messy bun and contemplate what to wear. If there is one thing I miss about my low-life, good-for-nothing mother, it's this. Laundry. She always made sure my clean clothes were folded and put in their place. Never did I have to worry about what was clean and what was dirty. Then she flaked and I lost my will to care.

I reach down and grab the first pair of jeans my fingers land on and grab the last shirt hanging in the closet. The reflection that greets me when I enter the bathroom makes me flinch. *Man, how I've let myself go.* All of yesterday's mascara and eyeliner has smeared into a nice raccoon look around my eyes.

With a quick clean up, I plaster on a fake smile and head out to the kitchen. Tyler is standing at the stove, finishing up breakfast.

"Morning," he mumbles and turns to put eggs on a plate. He's already out of his work clothes and in his pajama pants and a plain t-shirt.

"I'm surprised you're not in bed yet," I say in way of greeting, though I'm really not. The dark circles under his eyes is a normal look for him. Ever since our parents decided to skip out on us this past spring, Tyler has taken it upon himself to make sure I'm cared for. Problem is, Tyler working double shifts at the mill, while also being a volunteer first responder, isn't cutting it. Not for my guilty conscious and not for his mental state. Sure, the bills are paid and there is always food in the fridge, but what about him?

"I made you some eggs and sausage."

"Thanks, but I'm not hungry." His face tightens with anger. I don't blame him. He did stay up to cook for me instead of going to bed. It was thoughtful, but after the restless sleep I got last night, thinking about eating makes my stomach lurch. Showing his frustration, he throws the fork down onto the plate.

"Fine. I'll eat it." His eyes narrow as he takes me in, again. I feel like we do this scrutinizing dance once a week. "When was the last time you ate?"

"I had dinner at the diner last night."

"Jo..." he starts, worry thick in his tone.

"Here, I'll take this granola bar. Happy?"

The sigh and defeat that makes his shoulders drop causes my stomach to hurt worse. "Whatever," he mumbles and takes a bite of the eggs.

He turns back to the stove, but I don't miss the expression on his face. It's one I'm used to. I've put this family through a lot this last year, which is supposedly one of the reasons my parents bailed—awesome parents, right?—but no matter how many speeches I get, it's the sadness in his eyes that gets me.

Me and Tyler have been close our whole lives. We liked the same sports, played on the same teams, and loved hanging out at the end of the day to talk. That night one year ago changed everything. I've changed. He knows everything there is to know about what happened that night, but no matter how much I try to explain why I am the way I am now, he doesn't get it. He doesn't understand the nightmares. The despair. The darkness that clouds my mind. It's the only time in our lives we have never seen eye to eye, and I hate it.

"How did you sleep last night?" he asks, turning back toward me, coffee cup in hand.

I try not to flinch as I answer. "Same as always."

"Have you thought anymore about what I asked you the other day?"

"About what? The shrink?" It's not that I don't think counselors are good for people. They are. They're just not good for me. They wouldn't believe a word I would have to say, therefore, I'd be lying every single session. Kind of a moot point. "I'm not doing it."

He hangs his head, as he leans his weight on the counter. *Oh boy, here it comes. The guilt trip.*

"Jo, I'm just trying to help you. Why can't you see that?"

"I do see that," I reply, trying to keep from yelling. "But why can't you see that I can handle this on my own?"

"Because you're not," he yells, the first to lose his temper.

Tears start to burn at the back of my eyes. Taking a deep breath, I step back and gain control of my emotions. This will never end until I find a way to make him understand or I become a better liar. Avoidance is the game for now. "I gotta go."

I grab my bag off the back of the kitchen chair and head out the door before he can argue. Glancing down at my phone, I see I still have a few minutes before Millie gets here.

Taking a seat in the white rocking chair on the porch, I lean back and close my eyes and try quelling the nerves rumbling through my body. *I can do this. It's just the first day of senior year.* The coaching does little good. Never did I think I would look at my senior year with so much dread. I've known my classmates since kindergarten. They used to be my friends, not my enemies.

My stomach rolls. *Yeah, that pep talk is nothing but a lie.* The truth is I've been dreading this day and every day until graduation. No one, not even the loners, are going to let me forget about what happened last year. Sure, I can handle myself while I'm there, but what about the nightmares and the despair I feel when I'm alone? They don't realize how much they bring it all back to the surface and how I come home and deal with it alone. I should have been the one to run away, not my parents.

A blaring horn brings me to attention, and I jump out of the chair as Millie comes to a screeching halt.

"Get in girl, we're going to be late!"

Here goes nothing. I close the gate and hear the lock pop as it slides home, the white paint looking worn. It hasn't had a fresh coat of paint in quite some time. Neither has the house, which is visible from the road. Chunks of paint are missing here and there, and the original wood is showing. The red shutters my grandmother picked out the last time they renovated look worn. I wonder what my great-grandparents would think of the house now. Every dime they had went into building this house. I'm sure they wouldn't like the fact that two teenagers now occupy it. Tyler almost being twenty doesn't change the fact our parents ditched us and left him to raise their seventeen-year-old daughter. I'm sure they would be proud.

Millie hits the gas as soon as my door shuts, her Jeep lurching as she lets out on the clutch too soon. "I'm still trying to get the hang of it," she says, her cheeks a little pink from embarrassment.

I laugh, thinking about all the times her dad tried to teach her to drive a manual. She didn't know it at the time, but he had already bought the Jeep for her, and wanted to make sure she could drive it before he gave it to her. She almost gave up until one day she walked out and there sat the Jeep, with a pretty pink bow on top. Now, she's determined to master the craft of driving a manual. She asked me once to show her, but I refused, having vowed never to drive anything that reminds me of that night. My hands begin to sweat with the memory of my shaking hands on the cold metal of the gear shift and I shiver.

"Don't laugh at me. I'm getting better." She sweeps her straight black hair out of her face while her blue eyes narrow on me.

"Sorry." I bite back my laugh and look out at the neighborhood.

The streets of Dover are busy with morning commuters, dedicated mothers taking their children to school while their fathers go off to work. American flags line the streets, while bows of school colors hang from front doors and mailboxes. Before long, they'll be replaced by fall decorations and fake scarecrows.

"Jo?" Millie snaps her fingers in my face before reaching down to put the Jeep in first gear while a line of buses pass.

"Yeah?"

"I said, how are you doing? You okay?"

My mouth goes dry. She's fishing. "I'm fine," I reply with the standard, not feeling the conversation right now.

It's been a few days since I last talked to her and I know she's wondering if I've made the decision to see a counselor. After Tyler asked me if I would be willing to see someone, I had been furious and went to Millie's thinking she would find it as crazy as I did. I was wrong. She agreed with Tyler and urged me to talk to someone. We haven't talked since, minus the 'will you pick me up for school' text.

Seeing that I'm not going to give her an answer, she changes the subject. "Guess what," she says with excitement and lets off the clutch as the last bus passes. "There's a new guy starting school today."

"Poor sap. I'll be sure to say an extra prayer for him tonight."

Millie sighs, her excitement deflating faster than a balloon. "Jo, maybe you should, I don't know, quit being so sarcastic and snippy all the time. This is a fresh year, full of new beginnings. Embrace it. What happened last year was awful, but you know this isn't what Bryce would want for you."

Like a fast-moving rollercoaster, my stomach drops, my heart racing, as my vision begins to swarm. I can feel the bile rising in my throat as I gasp for fresh air. How dare she go there. "If I'm such a burden to you, then why do you still hang out with me? I'm fine on my own, you know." She, of all people, knows how hard this is for me. At least I thought she did. Bringing up Bryce like that was a low blow.

"Don't say that. I love you. We've been friends for as long as I can remember and no matter what those other shits say, I'm not giving up on you. I'm only trying to help, just like Tyler. That's what friends do, Jo. I don't want you to ruin your life over something that wasn't your fault."

"It was my fault, Millie!" I yell, losing my temper and hating her for bringing this up right now. I was having a hard-enough time dealing as it was. This isn't helping at all.

Millie reaches over the console and places her hand on mine. "I'm sorry."

A tear slips down my cheek and as soon as Millie sees it, she pulls over. A van behind us honks as they pass, but we pay no attention. There's too many emotions flying around the Jeep to care.

Millie pulls me into a hug. "I didn't mean to upset you. I'm so sorry." She rests her cheek on my shoulder. "I just hate seeing you so sad. I want to help."

"I know, that's what Tyler says. Every. Single. Day." I emphasize the words, hoping she gets that I'm tired of hearing it.

Millie pulls back and settles in her seat but says nothing. I'm a puzzle everyone wants to figure out. Some want to take pieces and change the game. Other want to put the pieces together to make me whole again. I just want to be left feel and deal on my own.

I look out the passenger window and see we are parked next to the church by the football field. My heart aches at seeing that green field. The memories. The laughter. I'm quick to turn away from it all and put on my best smile.

"Look, I'm fine. Yes, I'm dreading this school year and all the asshats I'm going to have to face, but I'm okay."

"That's what worries me the most, Jo. You say you're okay, and you believe you're okay," she pauses with sadness in her eyes, "but you're really not okay."

We drive the last half mile to school in uncomfortable silence. I hate fighting with Millie, not only because she's my only friend, but because I know she's right. But just because I know she's right, it doesn't make it any easier to move on, to get over the feelings holding me down. Someone saying 'get over it' sounds simple, but it's not, yet they don't seem to understand why.

We pull into the senior parking lot, after having to stop every five feet to let someone rush by as they hustle into the building. Lord knows it'd be a sin to miss those burnt biscuits and runny gravy.

"I have to get to the office. You going to be okay?"

"Peachy, Sugarbugs."

A small smile forms on Millie's face at her old childhood nickname.

"Meet me at lunch under the oaks. Okay?"

"The oaks. Got it."

Grabbing the strap of my bag, I take a deep breath and get out of the Jeep. The determination I'm holding onto deflates when I spot my other nightmare. Kirk. I was hoping to avoid this until, I don't know, never. Seeing how that's never going to happen, I straighten my shoulders and get ready for the insults.

Kirk spots me instantly and without pause, strides in our direction. His familiar eyes send a pang through my heart. I have to remind myself he is nothing like Bryce was, maybe once, but not now. Now he is a major jerk and goes out of his way to make my life a living hell. Once we were friends, but that ship sailed the night I killed his brother. Can't say as I blame him for the death glares.

"Hey Millie, glad to see you're still alive."

Sure he is.

"Could we not do this now?" Millie asks, coming back to stand by me.

"Why? Now is a perfect time," he replies, his eyes narrowing at me.

"Whatever you have to say, say it," I tell him. There's no use in arguing with him, he's going to do and say whatever he wants. Even if I walked away, he'd follow me, taunting me with every step.

The hatred in his eyes is clear. He wants revenge. "I've been wondering, with homecoming getting close, who's on your hit list this year?"

"Kirk," Millie warns, but I say nothing. He's not finished.

"I'm curious so I know the facts and can give you a believable alibi."

"Screw you, Kirk." Not an effective comeback, but it's all I can think of as flashes from last year assault my mind. The skeptical looks from the cops and Bryce's family as I told them what happened. The whispers from my one-time friends as I walked by. They all believed I was lying, though until the day I die, I will stand by my word.

"You would like that, wouldn't you? Then after that, you could reunite the Rowan brothers."

I lurch forward, my fist tight, but Millie grabs my shoulders to stop me. For him to say such a thing stings. He knows me — or at least knew me — better than that. I am so sick of everyone insulting me about Bryce's death without realizing how much it hurts me. It hurts to my core, and I hate every single person who keeps ripping at the wound.

"You free Friday?"

"Jo!" Millie scolds, looking horrified that I would say such a thing.

"What? He offered. I'd hate to stand him up."

"You stupid little b—"

"Kirk," Millie warns, stepping in again and placing her hands between us to defuse the situation. "Jo is already having a bad morning, how about you back off?"

He smirks. "More like a bad life."

Choosing to let it go for now, he turns and saunters over to his goons. They all high five him as he struts his stuff, acting as if he showed me who's boss. *Please. If those posers only knew how much I ruffled his feathers in return.*

"What were you thinking, Jo? Why would you say something like that to him? He lost his brother and is trying to deal with it. This was their senior year."

Wow! How about what I've been through since the accident? I lost someone too, and it's not like Kirk wasn't throwing out his own line of insults. Yet, I'm the bad guy?

"You're right," I snap, my gaze roaming the crowd. "Tell you what, I'll go apologize and give him a big fat kiss to heal his wounds."

"Jo—"

I wave her off, not caring to hear what she has to say. I've had it with excuses and explanations. I get it, I can be an ass at times, but how can I not be angry? Almost everyone has treated me like crap since that night a year ago. I'm sick of the double-edged sword.

Passing group after group of friends, all chatting about their summer and only pausing long enough to stare at me as I walk by, I have the urge to turn around and walk back home. I don't think I can put up with this for a whole year. Why can't they pretend I don't exist and pay no attention to me as I walk by? Instead, they treat me as if I'm about to pull out a gun and shoot up the place.

All those years spent on the squad, rallying our boys as they got ready for a game, petitioning for more creative group funding, attending school meetings, working on school dances, all of it gone and forgotten by the very students I helped. Now, I am nothing more than an eye sore to them. Which is fine, I deserve nothing more. I hate being here and being bashed by those I don't care about anymore. I do it to myself enough, I don't need anyone's help.

I toss my bag against the oak tree in the front quad, still having ten minutes before the bell rings. My stomach gives the slightest of grumbles and I unwrap the granola bar I'd grabbed this morning. Taking a bite, I search through my bag for my favorite charcoal pencil, its tip rounded and worn from the abuse I put it through, and turn to a fresh piece of paper in my sketchpad. I've always enjoyed drawing, but this past year it has become a deeper part of me. While some write out their feelings and troubles in a journal, I let curves and shading take mine away.

Considering the morning I've had, I'm surprised when the first image that my hand responds to is one of a happy time. It's not dark and full of anger, nor is it depicting some monster from my nightmares. I begin with an outline of Bryce's face, including the swollen cheek he got that night at the game, before moving to his eyes.

His eyes had been intense as we sat under the stars, talking about anything and everything. We weren't only celebrating homecoming that night, but also our two-year anniversary. Seems silly now, but I thought it was the biggest deal at the time. There seemed to be a secret in his eyes, something he was nervous and excited to share with me.

As I'm filling in the shading around his pupils, a shadow casts over my sketch. Figuring it's Kirk or one of his buddies, I brace myself for the insults and words about to exchanged. Looking up, I'm surprised to find it's not one of my tormentors. It's someone I've never seen before.

"Hello," he says, his voice smooth with a slight southern accent. His smile is broad as he stares down at me. This must be the new guy Millie was trying to tell me about. He stares down at me, his green eyes searching mine, as he digs his hands deeper into his jean pockets.

"That's some great shading. You have talent."

"Thanks."

Not wanting to give him the new best friend vibe, I focus back on my drawing and put my pencil to use. His shadow moves again, his foot coming into view as he fidgets. From his movements reflecting over me, I can tell he's nervous, and is fussing with his bag strap.

"So..." he stammers, obviously grasping for more to say. "Can you tell me where the office is?"

Seriously? Raising my head and showing my annoyance, I point at the office sign to our right, plain as day and only twenty feet away.

"Oh. Thanks."

Just when I think he's going to move on and be done with trying to make small talk with me, he pauses. "By the way, I'm—"

"Look," I snap. "I'm sure you're a nice guy and all, but I could care less what your name is. And as you can see," I indicate my sketchpad, "I'm busy."

Throwing his hands up and taking the hint, he turns and heads for the office. As he pulls open one of the double doors, he looks back at me and there's a small smile tugging at his lips. I have a strange feeling that won't be our last encounter.

Chapter Two

I slam my locker door and head out toward the front quad, stopping by the library's snack machine to get two packages of crackers on my way. I'm still pissed about my encounter with Caylee and Amber after third period, so there's no way I'm going to the cafeteria to see what crap they're passing as food today. I knew before I left the house this morning that I would be enduring taunts until everyone became tired of me, but I don't have to deal with them over dry hamburgers and cold fries.

Running into Caylee and Amber as they made their rounds to collect ballots for homecoming queen hadn't been a surprise, nor were their lame attempts at mocking me. *But I swear, if those girls don't back off, I will make their lives a living hell.* Whether they like to remember it or not, I was the queen bee not long ago. I know their secrets after spending many nights listening to them spill their guts once they were wasted. I'm also the one who designed the cheers they still use to this day. I've got enough ammo to make any of them squeal like a pig.

The sad part, though, they'll never understand what's really important until it's too late and all that's left is the despair. I sure as hell didn't.

I toss my bag on the ground next to the tree trunk, thankful for the shade it provides. It's scorching hot outside; the August weather in full, sweaty bloom. Taking out a bottle of water and opening the crackers, I close my eyes and take in the silence. Not many come out during lunch because of the smothering heat, which is fine with me. Makes for a peaceful break.

As I'm digging out my sketchpad, I see Millie come walking out the side door. I know it will take her a few minutes to come out here. She can never go two feet before being stopped by someone to chat. Many have asked her why she's still my friend. It's something I wonder myself. No matter the answer, I will never forget her loyalty to our friendship, even if something changes in the future.

A few seconds after Millie steps out into the sun, the door opens again and out walks the new guy. I groan, hoping he isn't following her. But, as my luck would have it, he is.

"God it's hot out here," she remarks and takes a sip of her water.

I agree, and turn my attention back to my crackers, hoping not to have to engage with the new guy, who walks up behind her. Of course, she's not going to let that happen.

"Have you met Cooper?" she asks.

I glance up and squint against the blaring sun. All I can make out is his black hair against the light blue sky, and god that smile. It's back, and wider than ever.

"We've met," I reply dryly.

"I'm showing him around and thought I would introduce you two."

"Good job. Now we've met. I'm sure there's more you have to show him, though. There's the oh-so-awesome coke machines on the other side of the quad, or how about the cool gym lockers they just put in. The possibilities are endless," I mockingly reply, then rifle through my bag to find my pencil, hoping she gets the clue I'm not interested.

Pulling out my pencil, I go on about my business as if they aren't there. I'm sure the new guy is interesting and all, just not to me. I want to finish senior year and then blow out of this town like it never existed. Looking up at Millie with the plan on my mind makes my stomach knot. Another hard day I'll have to conquer.

"Don't mind Jo. She's always got her nose in that thing," she says, pointing to my sketch pad.

Great! Now she's making excuses for me.

"I don't mind at all. I think her artwork is amazing."

I'm not sure if it's because of the mood I'm in – thank you Amber – or if it's because I don't want some strange guy looking at my private drawings, but I shove the sketchpad back in my bag and jump to my feet to head inside.

"Jo, where are you going?"

"I've got stuff I need to do," I snap, and keep walking.

"Jo!" Millie calls after me, but I wave her off and head for the art room. There's still ten minutes left of lunch but I'm sure Mrs. Adley won't mind me coming to class early. Out of all my teachers, she is the only one who hasn't babied me. She doesn't give me the sad eyes like the others, but instead encourages me to connect my art with my emotions.

As expected, Mrs. Adley is at her desk in the back corner of the room. Her lunch sits beside her, the lid open but the food untouched. She's flipping through a new art supplies catalog, with a list beside her of the supplies we need. Considering the art departments low budget, she has to take extra time out of her schedule to look for the best deals.

I place my bag on my desk, the one closest to the board, which snags her attention.

"Oh, hi Ryleigh. You're a little early to class."

I used to try and insist she not call me by my first name when we first met in ninth grade, but I quickly learned she called all her students by their full names, so I tolerate it. She's the only one I tolerate it with. I've always hated the name Ryleigh and prefer Jo. It's laid back, easy going.

"It's hot outside so I thought I would come in and finish my latest sketch."

She nods and goes back to her magazine. No more questions asked. *Good teacher.*

I flip through the pages until I reach Bryce's intense eyes, still unfinished, and grab my pencil. The tip hovers over where I need to finish the shading, my hand shaking, as tears sting my eyes. This morning I had been so inspired to start this sketch, being back here had brought our memories into the open. After the morning I've had, I have no inspiration to finish it.

He should be here, right beside me, with a smile on his face and those intense eyes staring at me as I finished some other sketch. It's so unfair that his life was cut so short.

Feeling overwhelmed, I slam the cover shut and shove it aside. Mrs. Adley looks up from her desk, her eyes trained on me, but she says nothing. The art desks are arranged in a square u shape so every student can see what daily project we will have on the board. I picked the desk at the front, on the same side as Mrs. Adley's desk, so I'm closer to the storing shelves behind me. The problem with this spot is that I can see her watching me as I work, and sometimes it unnerves me. I'm not sure of what she sees when she watches me, but it never seems to be dull for her. Like now, her head is tilted and she looks as if she sees something I can't.

I spend the next few minutes staring out across the room, my mind spacing, until the bell rings. Students start pouring into the room and I go to retrieve my daily sketchpad from my cubby. It's full of our daily projects from the end of last year, but there are still plenty of pages left for me to use. Mrs. Adley puts away her magazine and picks up a stack of handouts. Like most my other classes, I'm sure it's the class guidelines for the year.

The chair beside me scoots out, and then I see that bright smile. The one from this morning and lunch. I groan, fighting the urge to run from the room screaming with frustration. *Is he intentional seeking me out?*

Mrs. Adley stands before the class and starts her greeting for the new year. Cooper's attention remains on me, though, and I do my best not to fidget as he stares. Once the handouts are distributed, the class is directed to the bowl of fruit sitting in front of the marker board and I smile. It's the same assignment every year on the first day of school, even though I've advanced every year from Art_1 to Art_4.

"What are we supposed to be doing again?" Cooper asks, his breath tickling my hair as he leans over.

"If you had been paying attention," I whisper hoarsely, "you would know."

"I was paying attention," he defends.

"Yeah, but not to the teacher." I meet his eyes with my narrowed ones. "I'm not the lesson today."

He mumbles something under his breath that I don't catch, but don't bother asking either. He's entitled to his opinions just like everyone else.

"Can you please tell me what we are supposed to be doing?" he asks again and looks around at the rest of the students getting out their art supplies.

I sigh. "You see that bowl of fruit?" I gesture toward the center piece and he nods. "You need to draw it on the first page of your daily sketchbook, be sure to put the date at the top."

"I don't have a sketchbook."

I rip out a page from my pad and put it on his desk. "Get one before tomorrow and then tape that on the front cover."

"Thanks," he says and stares down at the paper. "Umm, I know I'm being a pain," he says, smiling up at me, "but where are the charcoals?"

Not taking the time to explain it to him, I get up and go to the storage bins to grab a pack of charcoals for him. When I turn around, I lose my grip on them and they fall to the floor. Bits of dust cover the white tile as they break apart but my attention is focused on Cooper's hand as it flips through my personal sketchpad. I rush over to him, crushing the charcoals in the process, and snatch it away from him.

"What do you think you are doing?" I ask, my voice high. I can feel the other students staring at us, but I ignore them. *Who does he think he is? Has he never heard of respecting others privacy?*

Holding his hands up, he looks mortified. "I'm sorry. I didn't mean anything by it. I really like your drawings."

A year ago, I would have smiled at the compliment. Now I'm on the verge of tears. No one is allowed to look at this. No one.

"I don't care if you're sorry, or if you feel you need to be coddled because you're new, stay the hell away from me!" I yank my bag off the back of the chair and storm out of the class, my sketchbook tightly clutched to my chest. Waves of emotions assault me and I run to the bathroom, feeling the bile rise in my throat.

The rest of the day only gets worse as talk of my art class meltdown become the talk on everyone's lips. Of course, as the rumor spreads, the words get twisted more and more. Some say I threatened to kill Cooper, while others say I tried to claw his eyes out in class. *Classic.*

When the last bell rings, I bolt out of my chair and head straight for the parking lot. Millie is already outside. Having office aid as her last period class gives her a head start on the crazy storm of rushing students. She's leaning up against the Jeep, with her arm resting on the hood as she talks on the phone. Seeing me coming, she says she has to go and puts the phone in her pocket.

"Hey, I heard about what happened. Are you okay? I tried finding you after 5th."

"I'm fine. It's just a bunch of bullshit." I shrug and toss my bag into the front seat. Together, we put down the top before climbing inside. With the scorching afternoon heat, we're going to need the air.

"I know it is. I didn't believe a word of it, although I did question the part about scratching his eyes out. I could see you doing that."

"Haha, funny."

She starts the Jeep but pauses before putting it in gear. "I did talk to Cooper."

Of course she did. "Did he explain what a total ass he was being?"

"Not in quite those words," she says, chuckling.

"Do me a favor, will you? Keep him away from me. I may go ahead and try to rip his eyes out if I see him anytime soon."

We pull out onto the street and make the two-block drive to the diner. With Tyler working the late hours he's had lately, and me not wanting to cook, eating at the diner has become a daily ritual for me. The only time I eat at home is when Tyler and I have time to cook dinner together, which is never. Having skipped breakfast and lunch, an early dinner is a must.

"I'm not going to be able to stay today. Mom needs me at the shop," Millie informs me as we pull into the parking lot. "I can come back and get you, though, if you need me to."

"That's okay. A walk will do me some good."

I get out of the Jeep, grab my bag, and head for the diner. I'm almost across the parking lot when my feet skid across the gravel and I come to a halt. Cars honk as I stand there, scowling at the familiar vehicles parked front and center. Looking through the front window and past the large yellow McAllister's Café sign, it's easy to spot Kirk and his buddies in the corner booth. Another car's horn blares and I start to turn for home when my stomach growls in protest as the smell of fresh cooked food assaults my senses.

Oh, what the hell.

Straightening my shoulders, I walk inside and go to my usual corner booth. Kirk and the others sit on the other side of the small café, but as loud as they are, they might as well be sitting right next to me.

A few minutes later the doorbell jingles and in walks Caylee and Amber. *Great.* I guess this is going to be the after-school hangout now. It used to be Pirate's Pizza down the street, until old man McAllister got smart and installed free Wi-Fi. Maybe I should switch my taste from American to Italian food. Picking up the menu, mouthwatering as I skim over the burgers, I'm not sure that's possible. I do like a good burger.

"Hey, Kirk. The party still on for Friday night?" Caylee asks from the bar as Amber puts in their order to go. There's some good news. At least they're not staying.

"Sure is," he replies.

"Do I need to bring anything?" she asks.

"Just that pretty smile." He smiles and winks at her, making my gag reflexes respond.

"I think it's so great you're having a memorial party for your brother. We all miss him so much."

Memorial party? I shift in my seat to get a better hearing angle.

"The overlook is the perfect place. It was his favorite spot," Amber adds.

A warm flush floods through my body and my vision swarms. My stomach tensing. *No. No. No. This cannot be happening.*

The waitress walks over and asks if I'll have my usual, but I shake my head, losing my appetite. With shaking hands, I pick up my bag and rush to my feet. I need to get some fresh air. Now.

"Hey, freak!" Kirk calls out as I'm heading out the door. I stop, a cold chill running over my skin as I gasp for air. "Whatever you just heard, erase it from your memory. Because I promise if you show up, you will regret it."

I burst out the door, gasping lung full after lung full of the humid air. This cannot be happening. Not there. Not ever. Kirk wanting to honor his brother is understandable, but not there. Not at that place.

Chapter Three

The week passes in a blur, with the hot topics being homecoming and the after-party. Of course, I'm reminded several times that I'm not invited. The thing that pisses me off, though, is through all the excitement and loud chatter, not once did I hear Bryce's name. Sure, that doesn't mean they didn't let his name slip when I wasn't around, but instead of smiles about remembering Bryce, it was all for the beer and who was going to be there.

It's Thursday night and I've been pacing my room for hours, tossing between problems. I haven't said a word to Tyler or Millie about the party, or how I plan to attend. They would try to talk me out of it, saying I would be hurting no one but myself. I already know this. Going up to the overlook is going to be hell. It's been the scene of my nightmares every night for the past year.

They'll also warn me about the others who don't want me there. If they see me, all hell will break loose, and no amount of pleading will ever convince Kirk I'm there to help. I'll be the one receiving the brunt of it. There will be no one to stop the onslaught. It's also why I don't plan on being seen.

The front door slams shut and I jump, my nerves on edge. I feel like something is going to happen, that another nightmare is about to begin. It's strange. It could be my mind playing with me, but deep in my gut, I know it's not. Driving myself crazy and needing someone to talk to, I walk out to see what the fuss is about. Tyler rarely ever slams a door.

In the kitchen I find Tyler leaning over the sink, his head hanging. I don't even get my mouth open to say hi before his harsh tone stops my steps.

"When were you going to tell me?"

Okay... What have I done now? Nothing comes to mind. "What are you talking about?"

He swivels around, hurt in his eyes. "I thought we told each other everything. You said—no, you promised—you wouldn't keep anything from me. That you trusted me."

I don't know if it's his tone or the swarm anxiety of things to come, but I snap. I snap hard. "I did trust you," I yell. "Get that word? Did! That is until every time I talked to you, you judged me and started throwing that counseling crap in my face. I don't need to talk to some stranger for advice, Tyler. I need you, but you don't seem to get that. Instead, all you do is judge me."

Tears burn my eyes, my anger and emotions getting the best of me. A few fall down my cheeks, but I'm quick to brush them away as I turn to head back to my room. Tyler is quick and rushes around the bar. He grabs me by the shoulders and pulls me into a tight hug. I don't mean to, but I lose my hold on my emotions and soak his shirt as I sob in his arms. The emotions and fear too much right now.

I gasp for air, trying to get myself under control, trying to get my barriers back up. This day – no – this week has sucked and I've done my best not to let it get to me. I guess this is what I get for holding back: a total meltdown. Once the sobs have subsided to a small sniffle, Tyler pulls back to look at me.

"I'm so sorry, Jo. I guess I have been kind of crappy here lately. It's just... I don't know what to do anymore."

I nod, knowing this all along, and wipe at my face. "You shouldn't have to deal with all this, with me. I wouldn't blame you if you walked out the door and never came back."

"Hey," he says, his tone firm, "I am not like them. I won't leave you. *Ever*. I can't change what our parents did, but I sure as hell can make sure I never do the same."

Running my hands over my face, I take a deep breath and clear my throat. "Thanks. Whether I show it or not, I appreciate all you do for me. I worry about you too." I run my finger through my hair and rest my head in my hands. "Here lately, I've felt so out of control and going back to school hasn't helped. I feel like everything I say or do is going to be used against me."

"That's my fault." His beeper goes off, but he silences it. Minutes later, his fire department-issued radio goes off. "Don't worry about it," he says, and grabs my hand to guide me in the living room. We both plop down on the couch, a sigh leaving us.

"You know, I meant everything I said. I'll never abandon you, Jo. But...."

There it is. The wonderful but.

"I also don't know how to handle this anymore."

"You mean me," I whisper.

"I just want to see you smile again. I can't imagine what you've been through, and I know being back at school isn't helping, but there are healing stages after grief. You haven't reached that point yet, although you should have.

Sure, you are always going to feel sadness and longing when it comes to Bryce, but it shouldn't consume you like it has. The only reason I suggested you see a counselor is because I don't know how to help you move on."

I stare up at the mantel. The girl he wants to see again looks back at me from a dozen pictures. Tyler had been nice enough to remove the ones with our parents standing beside us and replaced them with ones of just me and him. I want to be that girl again, if for no one else but him. The problem is, I can't get over what happened that night. It haunts me. The screams. The horrifying sounds and images. The blood.

"I honestly try and do the best I can," I finally whisper, and cast my gaze toward the floor, no longer able to look at the pictures. "I'm just so freaking angry."

"I know." He grabs my hand and gives it a good squeeze. Seconds later, he's removing his hand and shoving my shoulder. "You little rat, how did we go from me being mad at you to you sobbing in my arms and me petting you? I don't think so. I may be older than you, but I'm not that old, or stupid."

"It's all about being smooth," I joke before sobering up. "Let me hear it. What's word on the street?"

"Kirk's having a memorial party tomorrow night?"

I pause to make sure I heard him right. "Wait a minute, you're mad at me because I didn't tell you about some party?"

"It's not just any party, Jo. It's for Bryce."

All the resentment that's built up in me this week over the party rises, causing my answer to come out harsher than I mean. "It's not for Bryce."

"Jo," he says with caution. "Kirk talked to me about it. He said it was a memorial service."

"Oh yeah, and what a memorial it will be. I'm sure Bryce will be touched by the endearments made by drunks and idiots having meaningless sex."

One thing I always admired about Bryce, he partied but never drank. He never said anything to Kirk when he got wasted, but I could tell it bothered him, what with having a drunk for a father and all. He didn't want Kirk to end up on the same path as their dad.

"I know this is going to be hard for you to accept, but everyone has their own way of celebrating life and those they miss, whether you agree with it or not. Just because they aren't crying their eyes out and lighting candles in his memory doesn't mean they're not mourning his loss."

"You believe that line of bullshit?" I do understand how grief is dealt with in different ways. But this, it doesn't feel right. Not to mention it's not safe. Am I pissed I wasn't included? Hell yeah, but that has nothing to do with how ridiculous I find all this. I'd still find it stupid, even if I was graced with an invitation.

"Wait a minute, did you say Kirk talked to you?" I ask.

All the concern leaves Tyler's face as he tightens his fist. "Yeah, I talked to him or I guess you could say he talked to me. I didn't get much say in the conversation."

"Let me guess, he warned you to keep me away."

"Something like that," he replies and looks away.

Knowing Kirk, I'm sure there was more BS spat about how insane I am and how he should have me committed. Better yet, how proud Tyler must be to be aiding a murderer.

"Are you going anyway?" he asks.

I contemplate telling him the truth but can't gauge whether he will agree or disagree. Freaking Tyler and his stupid ability to sound unbiased until he gets an answer, then he flips a switch and lets his true opinion shine forth. Even if this is a trap, it would be nice to have someone know where I am in case something was to happen. Right as I get up the nerve to spill the truth, my phone rings. Seeing Millie's name flash across the screen, I say, "Hang on a sec," and tap the screen to answer.

"H—"

"I need a huge favor," Millie rushes before I can even say hello.

I tense. "What's going on?" Terrible images flash behind my eyes and I squeeze them shut while I breath through the panic. Crazy how bad my anxiety has become in the last year.

"I have a ton of things I need to finish in the morning for homecoming. I was going to do it tonight, but my mom needs me to work until closing. Can you...?" She pauses, probably rethinking this whole favor thing.

"Just ask me. I can't say no if I don't know what it is you want."

"Haha. Funny. Can you pick up Cooper in the morning for me? Please."

"No! No flipping way," I reply without hesitation. Since the incident in the art room on Monday, Cooper has made sure to stay away from me. It didn't keep him from staring at me though. I could feel his eyes on me, like a heavy weight, and every time I felt it, I looked up to see him staring at me. It unnerved me, though I tried to hide it, not wanting him to know he was getting to me. No way am I going to endure being in a closed space with him.

"Please, Jo," she begs. "It's supposed to storm in the morning and I noticed he walks to school."

"Let me guess, you offered him a ride."

"That was before I knew I had to work tonight. Mom has orders coming out of her butt for homecoming and Mrs. Jones' funeral is this weekend."

"I hate you."

"I hate you too," she replies, all sweet and hopeful.

A bell rings in the background and Millie yells at her mom to come to the front. I can picture her mom, glasses halfway down her nose, with ribbon wrapped around her shoulders like a shawl, scowling at Millie before plastering on a smile to talk to her customer. Laura's Flower Bouquet has been a family business that was started in the early sixties by Millie's great-grandmother and grandmother. Millie swears she's not going to be the next Thompson to take over, but I disagree. She knows the business and loves this small town, and she's dedicated to her family and friends. Proof from what she's put up with from me and the huge favor she's asking me to take.

"Please Jo!" she begs again. "I haven't asked you to do anything for a long time, but I'm asking now."

And there's the nail for the coffin. Sighing, I look over to Tyler. "Can I borrow the truck tomorrow?"

"Sorry. I have to work a double shift tomorrow."

"It's Friday." He usually has Fridays and Tuesdays off. He shrugs and throws up his hands in a 'what can you do' gesture. "Sorry Mills, but I don't have a—"

"There is another vehicle you can drive," he says, interrupting.

I almost drop the phone and sweat instantly begins to gather at the nap of my neck. "I can't," I whisper.

"Are you talking to me?" Millie asks, but I don't answer. I meet Tyler's eyes, and allow the vulnerability to show.

"I know, no matter what anyone says, that you are going to go to that party tomorrow night." He smiles. "I know you. If nothing else than to watch and make sure everything is ok." I open my mouth to argue, but he rushes forward. "And you'll need a ride. Ever think about that?"

"Jo, are you there?" Millie asks, as the blip of the cash register dings with every item she rings up.

"I'll call you back." I hang up, ignoring her protest.

"Tyler, I don't think I can do it. That car...." I trail off, unsure of how to put my feelings into words.

"It'll be okay. It's time. Besides, we can't afford to buy you another car and you can't be chauffeured around the rest of your life."

Damn him and his logic.

~

With sweaty hands, I take the keys off the hook by the back door, grab my bag, and walk out into the garage. There, taking up most of the space, sits my dream car. A slick black 1967 Shelby Mustang. A classic. It had been my grandfather's until after years of begging and wishing, he finally handed the keys over to me. It had seemed so unreal, and unlikely. This car, a present from my grandmother who had passed away two years before, had meant so much to my grandfather. I never thought he would part with it. It wasn't until the illness took his life two month after he gave it to me that I understood. He needed someone to take care of her. I can only hope he knows that I still love and cherish the car, even though I've neglected her.

Running my shaking hands over the hood, I walk around to the driver door but stumble over a box. The lid is loose and all the contents inside tumble out, including a teddy bear that's holding a picture of me and Bryce inside of a red plush heart. I remember the Valentine's Day he gave me the bear. Hugging it tight to my chest, tears stinging my eyes, I get in the car, leaving all the other clutter where it lays.

Taking a deep breath, I start the car, loving the sound of the engine and how well it sounds. It's a sound I've missed. Of course, if it wasn't for Tyler taking the time to start her up occasionally, I probably wouldn't be going anywhere. Engines do tend to lockup and batteries die from lack of use. I'll have to remember to thank him, once again, for taking care of it for me. Putting the car in reverse, I pull out of the garage, the heavy rain hitting the windshield and making a thunderous roar erupt inside. Man, Millie wasn't lying when she said it was going to storm.

Before I pull out of the driveway, I look at the text Millie sent me of Cooper's address after I told her I would take him and then pull out onto the road. The wipers are set on high but are barely able to keep up with the rain.

The teddy bear rolls across the seat as I make a turn, and I look over to see Bryce's smile pointed right at me and I can't stop the onslaught of memories.

"So where do you want to go now?" Bryce asks, wrapping his arms around me as we lean against the car.

"What about Kirk?" I ask, knowing he likes to keep an eye on his brother.

"He'll be fine. You, woman, are all I want tonight." He leans down and runs his hands through my hair, then wraps his fingers around the back of my neck and draws me closer. His lips meet mine with intensity, a passion igniting between us. He pushes me up against the car, his legs pressing against mine.

When he pulls back, both of us breathless, there's something more in his eyes that I haven't seen before.

"God, I love you," he breathes, sending a shiver over my skin.

"I love you too," I reply, wrapping my arms tight around his neck.

"So where will it be?" he asks.

"The overlook," I answer, smiling with the magic of what could happen tonight.

"So be it. I'm driving."

"I don't think so," I argue. He knows better. No one drives my baby but me.

"Oh yes, I am. Because if I don't, we will never make it there."

I laugh, a blush spreading up my cheeks. I relent and give him the keys, although intrigued by the idea of what would happen if I didn't. Once inside the car, he leans over to kiss me again, then leans his forehead against mine.

"I'm so glad you're my girl."

I pull over, my chest heaving as tears stream down my face. Unable to sit still, I get out of the car, getting soaked instantly, but uncaring. *It was my fault. I'm the one who took him to his doom, picking the place that would be his last.* I kick the tire, feeling overwhelmed and unable to breathe. *He trusted me. How could I do that to him?*

"Jo?"

I turn to see Cooper running down the street. That's when I notice I'm only a few houses down from where I was supposed to pick him up.

I turn my back, trying to regain control of myself, but I can't. All I can see are Bryce's intense eyes and hear the chill of his screams. I kick out at the tire again, screaming, as tears mix with rain.

Cooper's hands grab my shoulders and pull me away from the car. I try wiggling out of his tight hold but do little good. He spins me around, keeping me at arm's length, but his grip still tight. Thunder rumbles overhead, drowning out my sob and my knees buckle on me. Cooper doesn't expect it and collapses with me onto the road.

"I killed him. It was my fault," I weep, while beating at the hard pavement with my fist.

"Jo, stop," Cooper yells and grabs my hands. "You're going to break your hands." He stands, pulling my dead weight with him and opens the car door. I slump inside, my chest heaving. I'm so cold inside.

Cooper rushes to the other side of the car and jumps in. His breathing is heavy as he assesses me. What does he see? A wild girl out of control? Someone he should avoid at all cost? The broken girl I've really become?

Slowly, he asks, "What was that about?"

At this point, after all my breakdowns, I'm really regretting not choosing to homeschool.

"It's nothing."

"How about that," he says astonished. "I always wondered what you called a hysterical girl in the rain. Nothing. Glad I have the title now."

I smile despite myself. "I can be helpful when I need to be." I wipe the water off my face with my shirt, not that the soaked material does much good to get rid of the moisture.

"Jo, I think there's—"

"Look, we don't know each other that well and personally, I'm not one for sharing with complete strangers. I appreciate what you did, ya know, bringing me back to my senses and all, but that's as far as that road is going."

Cooper looks as if he's wanting to finish what he was about to say but sensing a negative outcome if he does.

"Fine," he says, and leans back to look out the windshield. "Nice car by the way."

"Thanks," I reply and put the car in gear.

Chapter Four

I drop my keys and curse, hating my anxiety. This day has flown by, the excitement of the party – or should I say "memorial service" – still a hot topic all around me. I stayed under the radar as best I could, not needing any reminders that I'm not invited or how tonight's party wouldn't be happening if it wasn't for me. This proved to be a harder task than I thought when it came to Millie. That girl was relentless. Every corner I turned, there she was. Each time, I managed an excuse, stammering that I had to get to class or had somewhere to be. As much as I would like her by my side tonight, I know she would only try to stop me.

I wring my hands to try and stop the shaking, before picking up my keys again. I don't know what I'm more nervous about: the party or the flashbacks that I'm sure will assault me as I drive my car up the winding road to the overlook. With that double whammy, I'm sure to be a wacked-out mess.

I'm almost out of the driveway when a solid wall of maroon appears in my rearview mirror and I have to slam on the brakes. Millie gets out of her Jeep and throws her hands up in the air.

"Do you really think I'm that stupid?"

"Shouldn't you be at homecoming?" I ask, avoiding the question. I know why she's here, but no amount of her pleading is going to stop me from going tonight.

"Yeah, I should be, but since my best friend decided to avoid me all day, I couldn't get in the cheering spirit. Not to mention I know what you're up to."

I cross my arms over my chest, not willing to budge on my plans. "You can stop right now, because no matter what reasons you have as to why I shouldn't go tonight, I'm going anyway. I know the risks, not to mention the consequences I'll probably suffer later, but I have to do this."

"I know, goofball, which is why I'm going with you."

Wait, what? I'd consider her joking if it wasn't for the serious set to her stance. She's not budging.

"What about homecoming? You've worked so hard on it, not to mention it's your last one." I love the gesture Millie is making, it means more to me than she'll ever know, but I can't let her sabotage all her hard work. I've been there, I know the crap she's had to put up with as everyone either complained or hysterically screamed with excitement.

"Do you really think a game is more important than you?"

"It's not just the game. There's the announcement of homecoming queen, which will probably be you. There's the parade before the game, the dance afterward. You can't miss all that."

"Well, I am. You need me tonight more than they do."

I open my mouth to keep arguing, but Millie holds her hand up to stop me. "Say whatever you want, I'm not changing my mind, so either get in the Jeep and let me go with you or come to homecoming with me. Either way, you're my hip buddy tonight."

I scowl as she tightens her voice, and I calculate my chances of winning this argument. The results are not good. Hip buddies it is. I grab my bag out of the backseat and then hop in the Jeep, silent. Millie smiles as she gets in, satisfied by the win. *Turd*.

"What's the plan? Most people won't be there until after the dance, and that's six hours away."

"I was going to grab dinner at the café and then head up to Montgomery cabin."

Surprise crosses her face, but she doesn't argue. She came here knowing she wasn't going to talk me out of going tonight, and no matter how crazy my plans may be, she's here to go along. Going to Montgomery cabin isn't the brightest of ideas, but it's a good cover.

The cabin is a place most avoid. Others ignore the no trespassing signs and go in for a quick thrill.

For over a decade now, the cabin has been abandoned. Some say they can hear the shrieks of the woman who found her husband dead on the floor, his brains blown to bits. Others claim they can hear children screaming for help in the woods late at night, right outside the cabin. I've never been inside it, or even lurked around at the edges of the property hoping to hear something. Whether you've heard the screams or not, the cabin is creepy enough on its own, with its worn logs and broken glass, the thick, dark ivy that spreads up along the sides, grasping for the roof. The leaves dancing in the wind and casting eerie shadows at night.

My stomach tightens and my tension spikes at the thought of having to leave the Jeep parked behind the house and having to walk through the woods to stay hidden from the others. We have no choice. There's nowhere else to hide Millie's vehicle, and with the warnings from Kirk still fresh in my mind, I know better than to leave it where he or one of his friends might see it.

"You know what, I think I'm going to skip out on dinner."

"Changing your mind?" she asks, with what sounds like hope, and flips her blinker to signal she's pulling into the café's parking lot.

"No. Just not hungry."

Millie stomps on the brake, causing a car pulling in behind us to screech to a stop. They blare their horn and go around, giving us the one finger salute. I look at her like she's lost her mind.

"Are you crazy?"

"Maybe. Considering I'm going through with your crazy plan, I'd say so." She gives me a hard look that I return. We don't break the stare until she shakes her head and throws the Jeep in reverse.

"I know exactly what you need."

I ask her repeatedly what it is she thinks I need as we travel downtown, past the line of cars heading to homecoming, and head out of town. When she continues to ignore me, I sit back and enjoy the feel of the wind blowing my hair around. The smell of the last cut of hay wafts through the air, as the tires whine against the pavement. I throw my arms wide, the wind rushing around me. For a moment, I feel free again.

The Jeep sways as she makes a sharp right turn and I open my eyes to see a familiar sight, Old Huckleberry Road. As the pavement turns to gravel, I look over at Millie and smile. Past the few farmhouses and last cedar bush on the right sits a water reserve framed by hills and the glow of the sun as it starts to set. I collapse back against the seat and try recollecting the last time I was out here. Gawd, it must have been ages ago.

When the small lake comes into view, I gasp at its beauty, my hand already itching to get a hold of my pastels. The sky is clear, the water calm and reflecting the world around with perfect clarity. Some of the leaves have begun to die, their colors now orange and brown. The sun is still fairly high in the sky, but I know as it begins to drop, a mixture of reds and oranges will take over, before the somber blues darken to black.

"I'd say we have about an hour and a half before we have to head up the mountain. Plenty of time for you to unleash some magic," she says, smiling.

"You know me so well," I reply, grateful for her. Without needing any further persuasion, I dig around in my bag and pull out my sketchpad. I shuffle around through the flashlights, extra batteries, snacks, and loose paper, hoping to find my pastels. My mood isn't dampened, but I'm a little frustrated when I realize they aren't in there. I'll have to dig deep to bring about the beauty before me with only my pencils.

Finding a nice patch of thick grass under a weeping willow, I get to work as my anxiety fades away and I get lost in the lines. I start with the outline of the water and build up the hills around it. As the drawing comes to life, I deepen the shades of the trees on the ground but use lighter shades of their reflection in the water. As the sun continues to dip down, I leave it for last, waiting for the contours of color that will build as it gets closer to the horizon.

"One day, I'm going to be visiting you somewhere nice and fancy, probably New York or Paris, as your work is presented in front of thousands. It'll be the only time I'll get to wear the most elegant dress I've ever owned." Millie squeals. "I can't wait."

I laugh. "For which part? The dress or the art?"

"Definitely the dress. I get to see your amazing talent all the time, but I never get spoiled in elegance."

I look down at the different layers of shading. It's true that I get lost in my art and can spend hours escaping as the piece comes to life, but never have I considered using my talent as a career option. It's a therapeutic technique for me, one I've always had, but which has grown over the last year. I don't know that I want to take away from my escape by making it a job that I become frustrated with. Everyone needs a place to let go and unwind from life, mine happens to be where pencil meets paper.

I stand and close my pad. Like the snap of a whip, my nerves flare to life again. The tension isn't as intense as it was, but I can feel it building with each step we take back toward the Jeep.

"Feel better?"

"Yep." I smile, repressing the lie. If she had asked me that while the long reaches of the willow branches swayed above my head and my fingers gripped my pencil, I could have said yes with honesty. Now, it's back to the unnerving task of the night.

"Good. Change your mind?" she asks, hope in her voice.

"Nope." As nice as the small reprieve was, nothing can persuade me from going now.

"Let's get going then."

~

Montgomery cabin comes into view and Millie pulls off the side of the dirt road and into the grass outside the gate.

"Where should I park?"

"Hang on a second." I get out of the Jeep, taking my bag with me. My hands begin to shake again as I retrieve the lock cutter I found in the garage. *Come on, Jo, you've got this.* When the metal pops, Millie gasps behind me.

"Are you crazy? Do you know what could happen if someone figures out who cut that thing, or finds us on the property?"

What did she think when I said we would park behind the cabin? I thought that part was quite plain.

"We will be fine," I say and swing the gate open. "Just get your ass in gear and get off the road. I brought a backup lock."

Millie's expression mirrors her nervousness, but she does as I say and pulls through and around to the back of the cabin. After shutting the gate, I slip on the new lock and put the key in my zipper pocket.

"This place creeps me out." Millie walks out from around back, her arms folded over her chest, and her face twisted with worry as she keeps her eyes trained on the old cabin like it will come to life and swallow her whole.

"Why? Because of those stupid stories?" I mock. "Millie, this is a place where a family once lived, but that no remaining family wants. That's it. There's nothing creepy about that."

"That's crap. You know what happened in there," she answers.

"Like those things don't happen every day in normal neighborhoods. It's only because the house is in the woods that makes it scary."

Millie lets the subject drop as we start our hike up the road. Gravel crunches under our shoes, the small pebbles getting caught between the rubber lugs on the bottom of my boots.

"You know the others won't be up here until around eleven, right?"

"You've mentioned it." My breathing is rapid as we climb up a small incline. *I have got to get back in shape.* My life has consisted of art and avoiding everyone as I hid in my room. Not much of an exercise plan.

"Well, I still don't understand why we couldn't wait until ten or so." Her breathing remains slow and steady.

"We don't know when people will start showing up, and I don't want to be spotted. I'm just being cautious, and believe it or not, trying to be respectful in some way. I don't want to start anything tonight."

Once we are almost to the overlook, we head off into the woods to find a nice spot to hide, but where we can still see what's going on. The last bit of day lightens our way enough that we still don't have to use our flashlights. I warn Millie once we set up we will not be able to use any kind of lights, including phones. She groans in protest but doesn't argue.

Hours pass, with many complaints from Millie, and small talk—like catching me up on everyone's business. Fun times. The partygoers begin to show up and soon a fire is blazing, giving us better light than we had before.

Most sit on top of the rock wall that separates the overview parking and the cliff. Within an hour, cars line the road. I'm surprised word hasn't gotten out about the party going on, which is against the law. Wildlife officers do their best to dissuade anyone from partying here, but considering the ghostly stories and beautiful view, their attempts are futile.

Kirk shows up close to midnight, with most of the football team following. As another beer keg is opened, he gets on top of the rock wall and holds his plastic cup high and makes a toast to his brother. It's a hearty speech that's followed by a crowed cheer of Bryce's name.

Hot, angry tears sting my eyes and I clench my fists, feeling the bite of my nails digging into my skin. Bryce deserved better than this. He hated drinking and Kirk knows it.

He's dealing with it, Jo. It's no different than how you lock yourself away.

I jerk, causing a tear to escape, and search wildly through the woods. There's nothing but darkness but I could have sworn... No, it can't be. I'm imagining things. Bryce is dead. There's no way it was actually him, just my emotions playing with me. But that voice...

"Hey, are you okay?" Millie asks quietly as she gets to her feet and comes to stand in front of me.

"Yeah." My voice trembles. Inhaling and holding the air in my lungs for as long as I can, I let it out and turn back to the party. My stomach churns with uncertainty. "Maybe this was a bad idea."

"Jo," Millie says my name with caution. "I love you, which is why I came with you tonight, but you're right. This is crazy. I came with you so you could see nothing is going to happen. All you're doing is torturing yourself. I think it's best if we go."

A movement catches my eye as someone walks the perimeter of the crowd. Cooper. He scans the swaying bodies, his muscles tense. Something bulges under his shirt on his back, and I notice his hands are loose at his sides, as if he's waiting to jump into action. What is he doing?

"Jo?" Millie says, but my attention is on Cooper.

The temperature suddenly drops as a light wind rustles the trees. The fire swirls, but of course no one notices except me. My heart begins to race and that when I see Cooper reaching under his shirt as he looks off into the woods.

"Jo, you have to run."

I turn around at the sound of the voice and almost lose all control of my body. I feel like I can't breathe, and I dig my nails deeper into my palms, checking to make sure what I'm seeing is real.

This isn't real.

Standing in the shadow between two trees, a year after his brutal murder, is Bryce.

Whoosh.

The sound and movement that haunt my nightmares fills the forest. I swirl around in circles, trying to find the cause.

"Jo, I'm not kidding. Run. Forget the others. Get out of here."

I turn back to where Bryce is standing and stop, frozen. How can this be happening? How can I see him? I'm losing my mind.

Whoosh.

Bryce rushes toward me, his face full of panic. He reaches out like he wants to grab me, but his hands pass through my body and causes a deep chill to take root in my muscles.

"Jo, please. I'm begging you. Run!"

"Jo!" Millie screams, bringing me out of my stupor. "What's going on?"

Before I can explain, the creepy sound comes again, and a moment later the fire is extinguished. People begin to scream. I run toward them, searching for Cooper. What did he see? Bryce's warning screams in my mind, but I have to make sure the others flee as well.

I run out into the middle of their semi-formed circle. "Everyone run!" I yell, panicked. "It's not safe here."

No one takes heed of my warning. Of course, they don't. The light of a full moon casts shadows all around us, but I can see that all eyes are trained on me.

"What the hell are you doing here?" Kirk yells, and stalks toward me.

"Wait!" I yell, holding out my hands against the fury that is emanating from his face and clenched fists. "No matter how pissed you are that I'm here, you have to get them to leave. It's not safe here."

"Oh, here we go." He throws up his hands and turns to face the crowd. "Jo here thinks—"

Whoosh.

Before he can finish, a girl that's closer to the cliff screams, her cry of panic grabbing everyone's attention.

Whoosh. Whoosh. Whoosh.

Something flickers to my left and I turn in time to see a mist swirl off toward the darkness. To my right a black outline moves amongst the trees, heading away from the pull-off. I start toward it when someone spins me around, with a tight grip on my arm.

"We have to get out of here," Cooper states and starts dragging me with him.

I yank free of his hold and step back. Who does he think he is? I don't know him or trust him. He's too edgy—like he knows something and is trying to hide it.

Another scream rips through the air from close to the cliff.

Whoosh.

The white mist appears again, seconds before the crowd panics as a terror-filled cry for help rips through the air.

Oh god.

Chapter Five

When I think I can't cry anymore, another tear burns my eyes before it slips down my cheek to land on my ear. I'm not sure what hurts worse, believing I heard and saw Bryce or witnessing another death I think I could have prevented. I clutch my blanket tighter and try to get a grip on my sporadic breathing. My chest hurts from my sobs, but no matter how hard I try, I can't shake the images from last night. They mingle with the ones from a year ago, making for one hell of a horror flick behind my eyelids.

A soft knock comes at my bedroom door, followed by the hinges creaking as the door opens.

"Jo?" Tyler's voice is soft and laced with concern. My back is to him and I want to fake sleep so he'll leave me alone, but the shuddering breaths that wrack my body betray me.

The bed dips with his weight as he sits down and places his hand on my back. "I know you've been through a lot, but I need to know you're okay."

I squeeze my eyes shut, hating the weak state he's seeing me in. Again. "I'm fine," I croak, my throat dry and soar.

"Don't lie to me, Jo. Please. Talk to me," he pleads and begins running his hand up and down my back to comfort me, just like he did every night for two months last year.

"I don't know what to say, Tyler. What happened out there…" my voice catches as I try to grasp for words to explain what I'm feeling. "It doesn't make sense."

He stays quiet for a moment, I'm sure he's trying to come up with something to soothe me. "The chief is saying it was an accident, Jo. A stupid misstep that cost someone their life."

I roll over and look at him with disbelief. "That's not what happened. Have they even questioned the others? Didn't anyone tell him about what was out there? What took Kaylie's life?"

The inability to understand or help me cope worries a line into his forehead, and he takes my hand. "Jo, there was nothing out there except a bunch of reckless drunk kids."

I jerk my hand away and roll back over, hurt that he doesn't believe me. How can he not see the fear and truth in my eyes?

"Go away," I mumble, not up for an argument right now.

Tyler sighs. "I screwed up again, didn't I? That whole 'no judgment' rule keeps eluding me."

I huff, letting him know he's spot on.

"I'm sorry, Jo. If I promise not to disagree again will you talk to me?"

"Nope." Not right now anyway. I'm still trying to understand what happened myself. "Just let me think for a little while, sort it out."

The heavy silence filled with his guilt and worry weighs down on me, to a point I almost break down and cry again. I hold strong. I want to talk – need to talk to him – but I can't right now. I can't explain the feelings I've had since leaving the overlook last night. The one thing I do know without a doubt is this is not over. And if that's true, I'll need Tyler to be on my side because he believes me, not because he feels sorry for me.

I know that he hates this, me not talking to him. I hate it too, but not enough to break under pressure right now.

"You get some rest. The marshals wanted to come question you today, but I managed to put them off until tomorrow."

Great! The oh-so smart marshals. I wonder how twisted my statement will be once they're finished with it. Last time they interviewed me, I swear I saw them write Bryce and I had been intoxicated, when in fact we hadn't had a drop of alcohol. Taking what they think happened and writing it as fact is how this town's justice system works, why mess with it?

Before the door shuts, Tyler pauses. "I'll come check on you in a bit. Please, talk to me then. I promise I'm here for you, Jo. If I wasn't, I would have bailed a long time ago."

The door clicks shut and I flinch. To him he was just reminding me that he was here for me, but his statement echoes the fear I hold inside. Who would be left after I've pushed past the point of exhaustion, beyond the lines of selfish, causing nothing but heartache in my wake? No one, that's who.

I have to shake out of this and start trusting others so I have someone left waiting on the other side of sadness.

The day passes in a haze as I fall in and out of sleep, the light glowing and then fading as the sun sets once again. In between naps – nightmares, call them what you will – I search through my old sketchpads from the last year. Most are of ravens set with different backgrounds. One has a line underneath. It was a passage from one of my dreams.

Majestic and wise, trust the ravens whisper as it guides you through the darkness.

It isn't until my last nap when I wake up screaming, that I become truly desperate to find the drawings of the shadow. If I remember right, each one had been different and could hold some clue as to what is happening. At first, I thought it was a part of my subconscious interpreting what happened to Bryce, the shadow of death lingering until the end. After last night, I'm not so sure. Something real had been there lurking, watching, until the end.

While I'm scrambling to pull all my sketchbooks out of the black trunk at the foot of the bed, the door swings open and a wide-eyed Tyler looks around the room. "What the hell happened?"

"What do you mean?" I ask, still searching.

"The screaming. I thought…" he trails off, scratching his head, and then turns his gaze to the mess around my bed. "Never mind. What are you looking for?"

"A drawing."

"A little vague, but I should be able to help. Oh hey, yeah, here's a shit load of them. You're welcome."

"Aw, how cute. You think you're funny." I smile, finding comfort in our banter. "It's a drawing of a shadowy figure I thought I imagined… the night Bryce died."

I mentally high-five myself, proud that for once I'm able to say 'the night Bryce died' without shooting death glares, gritting my teeth, or bursting into tears.

"I think I saw it again last night. There are a few in my current sketchpad but most of them are in here," I say, indicating the trunk.

Tyler stands in the doorway, indecision on his face. Does he judge me or not? Running his hand over his face, he sits down on the floor with a sigh, his long legs cramped in the small space.

"Explain it to me, so I know what I'm looking for."

I smile, unable to help it. He's trying and that's all that matters. "I've drawn it several different ways, some in dark shades against white, or vice versa." My muscles tense, the familiar ache deep from all the tension that has built over night. There's a transparent face that looks deep into my eyes, baring my soul, right before terror consumes me and the image becomes a black mass of horror.

"It's presence… it's… terrifying," I murmur as I stare down at the mass of sketchpads, my vision unfocused. "I get this deep disturbing feeling, like I know something evil, something that wants to hurt me, is close but I can't see it. If I do see it, it's only a glimpse, but that one glimpse is enough to leave me sick… lost…" I shake my head, at a loss for words to describe the breath-taking apprehension that clenches at my lungs and seizes my muscles until all goes black and what's left is an unyielding fear. Even I can't grip how deranged this… what… *thing* is. Is that what I'm considering it now? Am I finally going to dare say, and believe, there's something out there in the woods besides my imagination, and accept that I wasn't the cause of Bryce's death? It might be possible, if I wasn't the only person willing to speculate it exists.

A tear lands on my cheek, startling me. I'm so out of it, I don't feel the burn of the tears forming or acknowledge the blur in my sight. Seeing my emotional state, Tyler pulls me to him and wraps his strong arms around me. He murmurs words of encouragement and safety repeatedly as he rocks me, holding me tight, but I can't hold on to his words. I can't believe them. He doesn't know. Doesn't understand.

"I'm here for you, Jo. Nothing is going to hurt you."

It already has. Whatever is out there has already taken Bryce from me, haunts my thoughts, and now it's back to continue its slaughter.

I pull away from Tyler and reassure him what feels like a thousand times I'm okay. I dry my cheeks on the sleeve of my shirt and try my best to push aside the fear crawling in my chest and shuffle through my drawings, with Tyler doing the same beside me.

It's Tyler, who, after hours of looking has about given up, pulls out the first drawing. I scream, unable to hold back the flood of terror that escapes me. With concerned eyes, Tyler pulls out more from the bottom of the trunk. Page after page of the shadows in an array of shading lie around us.

"Is this what you dream about?"

"No," I answer. "I don't ever see it in my dreams. I only feel it."

"You said you saw it," he says, confused.

I pick up the closest drawing with shaking hands. This one is done with a dark gray stone pastel, the texture smooth. "I thought I saw it last year, but I wasn't sure until last night. These drawings are from nights I couldn't sleep as images—or memories—assaulted me nonstop. I threw them in the bottom of this chest, thinking it was some stupid symbolic interpretation of the burden I carry, or something idiotic like that." I hang my head, feeling foolish. It could be a mixture of all of it.

"That's not stupid, Jo. I can see why you would think that. You've blamed yourself every day since the accident." He places his heavy hand on my shoulder, squeezing tight, before letting out a rushed breath. "You need to leave all that shit in the past and move forward. Find the truth, Jo. You may be the only one who can."

"Do you really think this is possible? That some..." I throw my hands up in frustration and bite out the word that has been itching at the back of my throat, "ghost is haunting the hollow."

Tyler shrugs. "It's a big world, Jo. Who am I to say what is and isn't possible?"

"Um, the guy who was in here hours ago, yesterday morning, last week, and many moons ago judging his ass off, and shaking his head at his poor little sister."

As nice as it would be to believe Tyler could so easily jump onboard with my theory, I know better. He's not the type of guy to shrug and say, "who knows". He might believe what he's saying now for my sake, but if push came to shove, he'd never admit to the possibility of something as farfetched as what I am suggesting.

"Okay, okay. Point. But I've been thinking about it after you kicked me out earlier, and I mean it, who am I to say you aren't telling the truth. After looking into your scared eyes, well, that's all it took for me to not only realize you are telling the truth, but that you're also terrified. I'd rather not win the bastard brother award this year, thank you very much."

"Too late, you've already been nominated. I'm told you're in the top five," I tease, as I arrange the pictures from lightest shadings to the darkest. "Do you see this?"

In the last drawing, the darkest of the bunch, there are small orbs of lights in the background.

"You mean those blotches?"

"Yes, 'those blotches'," I answer in a deep voice, mocking him. "And they're not just blotches, they're there for a reason."

"No offense Jo, but this could be anything, and since it's not a real picture how can you expect me to get chills from that? For all we know you blubbered like a baby while you were drawing this, and those are water stains."

"You're right," I mutter, though a feeling deep inside me screams it means something. Instead of pushing the issue with my now "open-minded" brother, I put the pages away in the top drawer of my black nightstand.

Tyler sighs behind me and I turn to find him staring a hole into the floor.

"What now?"

"I don't know." He shrugs. "I am here for you, sis, but be careful. If it gets to intense, drop it. No sense in putting yourself at risk over something that may not even be real."

Wow. Fifteen minutes. He held out longer than I thought he would with the 'be real' remark. "What time am I supposed to talk to doofus face?" I ask, changing the subject.

"You have one of two options. You can go down to the station bright and early around 8:00 or he can swing by here at 8:30. Your call."

"Wow," I say with enthusiasm. "Let's shake it up," I say sarcastic, although neither choice is appealing. Last time I sat in front of Chief Tucker, my tears meant nothing to him. For him, I had guilty written on my forehead and nothing I said was going to change his opinion. Nothing. We caught him doing drive-byes past the house, following us as we went to work or school and then back home, heck we even ran into him at the grocery store once. Sweat was thick and beaded on his forehead once he realized we'd caught him red-handed following us. Being in a grocery store, no buggy, no shopping list, and no items in your hands for over an hour – not to mention always being one aisle over – is a red flag stalker sign. And pathetic detective work if you ask me.

It had also been the last straw for Tyler. Never mind the creepy eyes peeking in our windows at night or following our every move as we drove around. No, that was all good, but stalking us in a grocery store? Line crossed, man. After several phone calls, Tyler was able to reach the county commissioner, and next thing I know, no more Tucker.

Factor in all the misguided feelings between us – me thinking he's an ass and him thinking I'm a murderer – the question stands: do I want to meet him on his turf or mine?

"I'll be ready by 8:30," is my answer.

Tyler's lips tighten into a, thin line. I can picture the wheels churning in his head as he thinks my decision over.

"If that's what you want," he says, the wheels starting to slow. "Either way it could be bad."

His phone buzzes in his back pocket and he retrieves it with a look of frustration. I'm surprised when I see that it is mine. "Here," he snaps, holding out my phone. "Don't you ever, and I mean *ever*, leave this out of your sight again. It has been going off all afternoon."

I take my phone and hit the end button, ignoring the call from Millie. Looks like she's called about a billion times. "Why didn't you turn it off?"

"I thought about that, but...." he pauses and takes a deep breath. "I wanted you to see how much we care about you. Me by pestering the crap out of you, barging in your room day and night. Millie by calling or texting every five minutes."

I nod, unable to say anything around the lump in my throat. Guilt sits on my chest as I think of Millie sitting at home, worried, and thinking god knows what about me. But I can't talk to her right now. She heard me say Bryce's name, saw the disbelief in my eyes. No amount of lying or excuses will convince her she was imagining things. All the proof I need is in one of the texts she sent me.

We need to talk.

The thing is, I'm not ready to talk about Bryce right now, and definitely not by text. How can you talk about something so casually when it has shaken you to the core?

Tomorrow? I send, needing a little more time to straighten it out in mind.

And I'm okay. I send two seconds later, knowing she's been worried. *You okay?*

I'll be better once we talk.

Tossing the phone aside and reassuring my brother I will get him if I need him, I'm left alone with my thoughts. Alone and staring down at the shadows etched on each piece of paper sprawled across my black quilt, I go back to the nights I've seen this creature. I know without a doubt it was never in a dream, only ever in my presence. My thoughts continue to spiral as I stack each piece of paper, having grown tired of looking at them, and place them in my nightstand. Can it—

I don't have time to shield myself as shards of glass from the shattering bedroom window fly past. *What the hell?* Reaching over and grabbing my wooden baseball bat, I somehow have the mental capacity to give a silent thanks for the socks still on my feet. Perspiration begins to build as my pulse rises, causing my hands to loosen on the wooden handle.

The door flies open at the same time Cooper's face appears in my now broken window.

"What happened?" Yells Tyler.

I take the moment to wipe my hands on my flannel pants and then tighten my grip on the bat, ready to knock somebody out. My body's already been on one heck of an adrenalin ride the last twenty-four hours. Add this minor heart attack, and I'm wired to dish some payback.

"I can explain," Cooper responds.

"That might be wise," Tyler warns, never taking his eyes off Cooper.

"I'm here for Jo."

Pretty sure that's not the best way to start a good, 'please don't beat me' explanation.

Chapter Six

"You want to rephrase that?" Tyler advances toward the window, taking the bat from my hands as he passes. Cooper's eyes go wide. I'm sure if it wasn't for his need to hold onto the windowsill, he would throw them up in defense.

"I... no, I don't mean as in I want her or... need her... I mean...." Exasperated, he hangs his head and curses under his breath. "What I mean is," he says, his voice steadier now, "I came to see if she's all right. I called Millie to see how the girls were doing after what happened last night, but she said she hadn't heard from Jo all day. Millie's parents have her on lock-down or she would have been over here herself. I told her I would drop by to see if Jo was okay."

What he's saying could be more easily believed if he wasn't trying to pitch it so hard, but his explanation seems to satisfy Tyler. "You had to break her window to do that?"

"Pure accident. I didn't think—"

"No, you didn't," Tyler scolds.

Throwing up his hands, Tyler looks at the mess around us. "Fine. Y'all can talk, but help her get this mess picked up." He turns for the door but before leaving turns with a warning in his eyes when they meet mine. *Ha. No worries there.* "Next time, know that we do have a working front door."

"Yes, sir," Cooper sputters, to which Tyler gives him a hard look.

"Okay, ease up there soldier," I say and take the bat back from Tyler. "I think you've made him piss his pants enough."

I toss Cooper a shirt to knock the last remaining shards of glass from the window before he climbs through. Tyler demands he replaces the window before going downstairs. Cooper and I work in silence to clean up the mess. Once I'm satisfied it's safe to walk barefoot again, I plop down in my worn-out recliner in the corner.

"So why are you really here?" I ask.

"Nice room," he remarks and takes a seat on the corner of my bed.

I look around at the mess I call my room, with the contents of my closet puked all over the floor.

"Spill it."

"I really did talk to Millie. I swear."

"But I bet she said nothing about you coming to check on me." Millie knows me, knows that I would want to be left alone and wouldn't send anyone over to chat, especially some new kid she knows I don't like. If I'm not talking to her, she knows I'm not talking to anyone.

"I suggested it, but then she warned me not to."

"Advice you decided to ignore."

His sheepish shrug is the only answer I get.

"Before you start, I want to know what you were doing at that party last night." My memories might be obscured by flashes of shadows and noises, but I haven't forgotten his actions last night. He wasn't there to party like the others.

"I was invited."

"The whole school, minus me, was invited. You were there for a different reason. What was it?" I demand.

"I'm not ready to get into that just yet," he says and stands to his feet.

"Oh, I'm sorry, does it look like I care what you do or do not want to talk about? You're the one who barged into my room, broke my window no less, and I want some answers."

"Where's your sketchpad?"

"My sketchpad?" I repeat, the question throwing me off. "Why?" I ask, not understanding the one eighty we've taken.

"It will help me explain."

Hmm, tricky situation we're in. I could refuse to show him my drawings and be done with this conversation and demand he leave. But what if he knows something? I can't get answers out of him without indulging him a little.

After thinking it over, my curiosity wins out and I retrieve my sketchpad from my bag. When he tries to take it from me though, I pull back.

"Demanding guy, aren't you?" My grip tightens on the pages. "Which one do you want to see?"

"Are you serious? Just let me see it." He goes to reach for it again. I take another step back.

"If you don't want to be slugged right now, I'd back off."

Murmuring under his breath, he steps back. "You know, I've seen almost every drawing in there. It would be easier if I flipped through until I got to the one I want."

"Yeah, but you did that without my permission," I snap. I look down at the worn pages, at the abuse it's been through over the last month as I carried it around, tossed it to the side, and gripped it through the pain. Never have I willingly let someone look inside to my secrets, let alone given it to someone to hold. These are my secrets. My feelings. My fears. Handing them over seems wrong, like I'm finally trusting someone to see inside of me. Still, I want to get to the point of why he felt he needed to come barge into my space.

With a shaky resolve, I hold it out. "Here."

Cooper takes the sketchpad, but before he opens it, he pauses and looks at me. "Thank you."

It's like he can see how hard this small feat is for me and he's thankful of me trusting him. It's hard, though. Oh, it's hard. I want to scream and tear the book away from his hands, maybe even run screaming from the room.

He sits back on the bed, flipping the pages until he stops at one midway through. My interest is piqued as he stares down at the dark shape surrounded in hues of purple and blues.

"Do you remember when you drew this?" he asks, not taking his eyes off it.

"No. Why?"

He sets the pad down on the floor, leaving it open to the drawing. "This is why I'm here," he says, pointing at it.

To say I'm confused would be an understatement. "Um, you came here for a drawing, as in tonight, or as in you moved here for my drawing?"

"No. I moved here to hunt this thing down."

He points at the drawings again, and although I get what he's hinting at, my brain refuses to process it. I don't know why. I've been thinking this thing is something real, although I've tried to refuse it, but still yet I can't believe it. Now someone is sitting in front of me saying it is real. *What is happening?*

"Don't look so surprised. I know you saw it last night."

My head snaps up. "You saw it too?"

"It's kind of my job." His arrogance is unwelcomed.

Still, I'm skeptical and keep up a charade. "You mean they pay people to act crazy? Where can I apply?"

"Don't," he snaps and gets to his feet. "Don't pretend you don't know what I'm talking about. Running from this thing does no good, trust me, so you might as well tell me what you know so I can help."

I cross my arms, not willing to give in, nor trust him yet. "And what is it you think I know, Cooper?"

He shakes his head and runs his fingers through his hair, frustrated. "You may not understand what you're seeing, but you see it. And apparently, you're the only one around here able to." Sitting back down, he places his elbows on his knees and interlocks his dirt stained fingers. "We call them chindi, but the popular term is 'ghost'." At the mention of my hidden fear spoken aloud, my eyes go wide and I start to protest, but Cooper cuts me off. "I know, I know, it's a little weird but the name has been passed down from hunter to hunter since this whole gig got started way back in the Navajo days. After some time, you get used to the names."

"Like a technical name is what I'm worried about right now." My legs give out from underneath me and I collapse on the floor, not even feeling the impact as my mind blanks out. I feel nothing, think nothing, as a haze takes control and my brain refuses to believe the unimaginable.

Snapping fingers bring me out of my stupor. "You with me, Jo?"

I nod and focus on his face but am still clueless as to how to continue this conversation. What does he expect me to say? *Ghosts? That is, like, so cool. I've always wanted to meet someone who thought outside the box and totally gets the whole spiritual realm stuff.* Not quite me, Cooper Man.

"I'm sure you didn't expect to hear me say any of this."

"Gee, ya think?"

"Honestly, I have never, nor have I ever planned on telling anyone my family secret. But after seeing your drawings in class the other day, among other things the last few days, and the chindi itself last night, I knew you would need some answers. If for nothing else but closure."

I look down, the tense edge of my nerves loosening. "So, you've heard what happened last year," I say, my voice breaking.

"Not everything. I haven't heard the whole story from you."

My eyes find his, my breath catching. If he only knew how long I've waited to find someone who wanted to hear my story, and who truly believed what I was saying. As my parents looked at me with worry in their eyes while Tyler paced behind them, I knew they wouldn't believe a word I said. How could they, when I couldn't even believe what I thought I saw? It wasn't hard for me to wash the images from memory and replace them with second-guesses, guilt, and self-blame. That was easier for me to grasp and believe, as it was for everyone else in this godforsaken town.

Now here is this stranger, telling me he hunts what I couldn't even begin to fathom as real, and wanting to hear what no one else has asked me without already having their version in mind. He wants to hear my side, the truth. The question is, do I even know what that is anymore?

"It's okay," Cooper prompts. "You'd be amazed at all the things I've seen."

"Maybe you should tell me a few stories, for inspiration."

"You need inspiration from a guy you hardly know, to tell me about *your* past, something I know little about?"

When he puts it that way... "Hey! I'm not the one talking crazy here, yet. If I heard a little about your past it might help convince me you're not playing some game."

Calculating with a tilt to his head, Cooper concedes. "This would be easier if we went back to my place." The look of caution on my face has him backing off. "Need a little more time, got it. Although I've got some great weapons I could show you." Again with the look. "Okay, okay."

He slides off the bed to prop his back up against it and crosses his ankles. I narrow my eyes at his lax position, considering I'm as tense as it gets.

"Are you ready? This is a good one. Look," he says indicating his arm, "I've already got chill bumps. Get 'em every time I tell this story."

Oh joy.

"We had been staying in this small town right outside of Lexington, Kentucky, Ravenna I think it was. My sister had got a call about a girl haunting the woods there and luring in spectators the people in the area were tired of dealing with. Number one rule when chindi hunting: never, and I mean *never*, let emotions get the better of you. Guess what I did?"

"You forgot rule number one."

"Bingo. A chindi can mess with your emotions, play with them like strings on a guitar. She was captivating enough with her beauty, but the sadness in her eyes… it took my breath away."

Seeing where this is going, and feeling relaxed enough to want my own answers, I continue for him. "You became her friend. She turned on you. Almost killed you. But somehow you managed to deal with it, and voila, no more ghost or whatever."

He crosses his arms over his chest, with a displeased smirk. "Typical story, huh? Too mundane? Well, let me tell you when you're there, it doesn't feel too mundane, I assure you."

"I never said—"

"And it wasn't like I said 'Oh, shit' and saved myself. If it hadn't been for my sister noticing my messed-up attitude, I'd been chindi meat."

"I get it! Crazy, killer ghost hunting not the least bit boring, at all. Defensive much?"

"I am when it comes to my talents," he says, as normal as someone who cooks pies for a living.

But we're not talking about pies here, we're talking about ghost killing. Freaking ghosts!

At that thought I begin to clam up again and staring down at my drawings helps on a zero level. I can feel Cooper's eyes on me, waiting me out to see if I'm ready to share the truth with him, or ready to embrace what is about to begin. One thing I'm sure he doesn't realize, is that if I tell him the truth and he confirms what we both already suspect, there's no way I'm walking away and leaving it all to him. This thing has taken my life away, and I'll be damned if I let someone else get it back for me.

"It was a normal night," I begin, my voice straining to be above a whisper. "Don't all moments that shatter us start without problems? Homecoming was over, but Bryce and I didn't want to call it a night. Like everyone else, the excitement of the game and then the dance was still flooding through our veins. We could have gone to any of the number of parties happening that night, but Bryce wanted to be alone. Just me and him. I'm the one who decided to go to the overlook. I'm sure you've heard stories about the overlook."

"A little bit. We're still new in town and asking a bunch of questions right off the bat raises suspicions... among other things. If you're wondering if I know about the lights, the answer is yes. And from what I've heard about them, it's my belief and my sister's, that they are orbs."

"Orbs?" I ask, having heard the term before, but not remembering its meaning.

"They're spiritual thumbprints, a representation of someone's life."

My muscles stiffen. My thoughts run wild. "There's more to it than that, isn't there?"

"Yeah," he drawls. "Normally, orbs fade after the spirit moves on."

Doesn't take a genius to get what he's saying. "So, all those mysterious lights in the hollow are lost spirits?"

"Or trapped. It happens. And if they're trapped, this thing you drew has something to do with it." He holds up the darkest of the drawings. "Tell me more about this."

"Right." Clearing my throat, I pick up where I left off.

"You want to walk down to the cabin?" Bryce asks, with mischief in his voice.

"God no! I hate even driving by that place. You know Amber said they heard a girl screaming there last weekend."

"Yeah, and she's a reliable source."

That's true. She does like to embellish a bit.

Not caring to talk about her, or anyone else for that matter, I lean in real close to Bryce and wait for him to close the distance. There is no hesitation on his part. God he's such a good kisser. He knows how to hold me. Treats me as if nothing else exists for him. I hope that I never take it for granted, or never leave him with doubts about how I feel. There truly is no better guy.

His fingers tighten around my neck and he pulls me closer, deepening the kiss. I think I could stay like this forever, safe and secure in his arms with no sense of anything but him. The world can kiss our—

Whoosh.

Fear attacks my gut as a cold breeze tickles my skin and I jerk back away from Bryce. "What was that?" I ask and run my hands over my skin. Uneasiness begins to overtake me, telling me something isn't right. It's the last day of August. A chill like this isn't even a thought until late October, early November.

"What was what?" Bryce asks, as he searches the darkness around us.

I start to tell him what I thought I heard but find no words to describe it. Not wanting to embarrass myself, I ignore the gut-gnawing unease and shrug it off.

"Nothing. Never mind."

"You sure?" he asks, concerned.

I nod and bring myself close to him. When our lips meet again, his arms encompassing me in safety, the unease starts to ebb. It's doesn't take seconds before I'm lost to his touch and forgetting about the—

Whoosh. Whoosh.

I jerk to my feet, knocking Bryce over in the process. "Don't tell me you didn't hear that. You had *to have heard it." My voice is rushed with panic. My whole body begins to shake as terror takes over.*

Bryce kneels up on his knees and wraps his arms around my waist. "I didn't hear anything, babe."

His touch does nothing this time to help ease my jitters. Every cell in my body is urging me to run. When my muscles tense, Bryce tightens his hold on me.

"Hey, hey it's okay. Come here."

He tries to pull me to him, but I refuse.

"I want to go," I say in a rush, looking wildly through the darkness, seeing nothing but shadows. Another chill spreads down my arms, causing me to shiver. I can barely hear over the rush of my heart pounding and my brain screaming at me to leave. "Please, Bryce. Let's go."

Hearing my desperation, he's quick to his feet and grabs my shoulders. His eyes search mine through the darkness, the three quarters moon only giving us enough light to see our outlines and a slight sheen to our skin. After a quick assessment, he nods.

"Let's go."

As I'm turning toward the car, something at the edge of the tree line, like a dim fog, catches my eye. I stop and try to focus on where it is. Another shadow moves to my left, this one darker, but when I turn, it's gone. What the hell?

"Are you okay?" Bryce asks and starts guiding me toward the truck.

I shake my head, confused, strung out, and ready to go.

Whoosh. Whoosh. Whoosh.

I scream and clutch at Bryce's side. Tears start to stream down my face. I know something is not right. Bryce turns, whispering he heard it this time.

"Stay close baby," he murmurs against my temple. I can hear the concern in his voice, even if he doesn't want me to. I can also feel the slight twitch in his hand as he takes mine.

Regret starts to seep in and mix with the fear. Why did I have to insist we park so far away?

Whoosh.

Another flash catches my eye but when I swivel around, again I see nothing. Flashes of movement around us keep me distracted, as if the shadows are dancing when no one is looking directly at them.

"Jo, look," Bryce says and turns toward the overlook. Past the rocks and pillars, the mysterious lights have come alive. Along the treetops, bright lights hover right above the leaves, reflecting off the creek winding through the valley.

As if drawn to get a closer look, Bryce lets go of my hand and walks toward the cliff. I stay rooted in place, frozen with fear. A tear rolls down my face and through the haze, something moves to my right. Fear for myself becomes an afterthought as a dark shape envelops Bryce. As if in a bad dream, I reach out, screaming for Bryce to run, and when I reach him, some invisible force throws me from him, tearing us away from each other.

My eyes flutter open sometime later. Dust fills my nostrils. Dirt seems to have made its way in every orifice in my body, the crunch between my teeth proof. Frantic, I look around for Bryce. His frightened eyes are the last thing I remember before blacking out. He had been standing by the wall.

I fight through wave after wave of dizziness as I stumble to my feet and toward the rocks. My lips begin to chatter and for the first time since I came to, I notice I'm freezing. It doesn't deter me. I have to find Bryce. My legs try to give out on me more than once and my hand makes contact with the smooth, cold surface of the rock wall. I lean on it for support.

"Bryce!" I scream, frantic and ready to leave. More so now than before. The uneasiness I felt before isn't as strong, but the memory is an impression I will never forget.

"Bryce!"

I keep screaming his name, praying he answers me. I continue to keep one hand on the wall for support, even though the top of the rough-cut rock ends at around three feet, so I have to stoop to lean against it.

I'm almost to the end, unsure whether I dare walk closer to the cliff, when I touch something wet and sticky. I close my eyes, praying with everything I have left in me that it's nothing bad, and bring my hand closer to my face. But as soon as I open my eyes, a scream rips from my chest and I collapse. My sobs and screams of Bryce's name echo through the valley as I wipe his blood from my hand.

"The rest, as we say, is history."

When I finish, Cooper stares at me for a few moments, then lets out a small whistle.

"Damn. I need to take you on the road with me so you can tell my stories." He rubs his hand across the back of his neck, and for the first time in a long time, I wish someone would do that to me. I have been tense for so long, and the thought of someone rubbing it all away seems almost unimaginably pleasant.

"What happened after that?" he asks.

"I sat there, against the rocks, staring off into the darkness as the lights danced around the valley. When morning came, I found a trail of blood that led from where I was sitting to the cliffs edge. I crawled, knowing what I was going to find, until I reached a point where I could glance over the ledge."

The memory of Bryce laying in a twisted mess causes my stomach to lurch and I jump to my feet, needing to move.

"I wasn't sure before, but I am almost positive now. I think we are dealing with a nukpana."

"A what?"

"It means evil spirit, and it's quite the interesting story, let me tell you. If you ever decide to trust me, maybe you can come over to my house one day and I'll tell you everything you want to know. About what I do, my heritage."

He smiles, and I swear the tips of his ears turn red. *Is he blushing?*

He just baited the hook. Of course, I'm intrigued now. How could I not be? Not knowing what to say, I look away and begin scanning the titles of books on my overstuffed shelf. I want to say sure, when? Question is, are we really at that stage in this weird interaction.

"Anyway," Cooper says, jumping to his feet and clapping his hands. "I really need to get going. I told my sister I would be home by ten and when I don't show up on time, she goes out looking for me, guns a-blazing. Literally."

"Okay," I reply, wringing my hands and feeling awkward. "I still have a lot of questions."

"I know, and I'll be here to answer them for you. Why don't you come over to my house for dinner tomorrow?"

The look on my face must say it all. *No freaking way.*

"Or I could come back over here," he suggests.

That would be better, at least for me. Tyler's mug pops into mind. He's off tomorrow. Maybe Cooper coming over isn't such a good idea. If Tyler even heard a hint of what we were talking about, all would not be well. I'd rather miss that pony show.

"On second thought, I guess I can come over to your place. It'd save a lot of hassle with my brother," I explain. If he only knew Tyler, he wouldn't have even suggested it.

"Okay. Sounds like a date. I mean, or... whatever you want to call it."

Reminding him the front is easier, he open my bedroom door. Before it closes, I call out to stop him. My hands are a sweaty mess. "If this thing is real," I start, my mind still refusing to be completely receptive, "does that mean Bryce's death isn't my fault?"

Cooper comes back into the room and stops inches from me. Hooking his finger under my chin, he raises my face so he can meet my eyes.

"You've known all along it wasn't your fault, but when it seems there's no one else to blame, and grief becomes so unbearable you can't breathe, can't cope, sometimes it's easier to lay blame where there is none. Whether it be directed toward yourself or at others. Much like Kirk does with you." In an intimate move I'm not prepared for, Cooper cups my face. "I promise you, Jo. We will get to the bottom of this and there will be closure. You have to trust me."

I nod, unable to find the words to express my gratitude.

We exchange goodbyes and once I hear the front door close, I collapse on my bed, arms spread wide. I have no clue what to make of the little bit Cooper told me tonight. Grasping at the idea that there are real ghost... chindi... whatever... hunters out there is unimaginable. Yet apparently there was a hunter sitting right here in my room, identifying said ghost through my drawings.

Rolling over onto my side, I reach over and turn off my lamp and allow the strands of white Christmas lights around my headboard to dominate the night. But no matter how much light I have in my usual dark room, it does nothing to keep the ghosts from my past—and present—at bay.

Chapter Seven

Act normal, keep the truth to yourself, and don't be defensive.

I read what must be Cooper's twentieth text and roll my eyes. He's been texting me all morning and giving me 'advice' on how to talk to the police. Keep your answers short and platonic. Act upset. Don't mention anything about ghosts or weird sounds. Blah. Blah. Blah. Like I'm going to go all crazy and start spouting incoherent things about ghosts. This town doesn't need any more ammo to use against me.

"Jo, you coming?" Tyler yells from down the hall.

I stretch and take a deep breath. I know he's in there, sitting at the kitchen table A cup of hot coffee gripped in his hand, as if he's a welcome guest. *Yeah, this is going to go well.*

I walk past the mirror in the hallway and pause long enough to run my fingers through my hair and rub away yesterdays smeared mascara. As expected, Officer Tucker is sitting at the dining table, mug in hand. His eyes sharpen as I walk around the counter and pour myself a cup of juice. My eyes stay locked on his, challenging, until the brim of my glass obscures the view.

"Ryleigh," Tucker says, his idea of a warm greeting.

"Tucker," I reply and set my glass down with a clank. "And we both know it's Jo." I remind him, although I shouldn't have to. If we are going to be informal with first names, the least he could do is use the name I go by. Although my full name is Ryleigh Jo, when mom and dad brought me home from the hospital Tyler refused to believe I was a girl and would only call me Jo. Needless to say, the name stuck with everyone in town, even when I started growing hair and eventually boobs.

"Why don't you have a seat?" he suggests.

Not feeling any need to get all cozy with the chief, I sit at the opposite side of the table so we can enjoy a nice stare down. Tyler sits in the side chair next to Tucker, creating a barrier between us.

The next fifteen minutes pass with typical police questioning. Can you describe what happened? Was there drinking? Other witnesses said this, can you concur? *Ms. Vanguard, do you think I'm an ass? Why yes, yes, I do.* I smile to myself, imaging his reaction to my brutal honesty.

"May I ask what's so funny, Ms. Vanguard?"

Your face. "Nothing."

He gives me a good stare down, to which I smile in return. "If you could focus, I've only got a few more questions and then we will be finished."

Thank you, god.

"Your statements thus far match that of the others, which leads me to believe this may have been an accident."

Nice drop of 'may have been' there Chief Tucker, now comes the 'but' part.

"However, there is one matter that I need to clear up. Why were you at that party Jo when it was made clear by memorial organizers you were not to attend?"

Memorial organizers, seriously?

"You know I have every right not to answer this very personal question, or any question you've asked me so far, right? So why don't you tell me why you feel you need to know this?"

"It's a simple question," he say, challenging me.

"She has a point, Chief Tucker," Tyler says, speaking for the first time. "And as her legal guardian I have the right to ask how it pertains to the investigation."

Tucker rests his elbows on the table, his loose aging skin wrinkling against the hard-wooden surface. "Let's drop the pretenses here, Tyler. You know I think highly of you and your family, we all do. But when it comes to this girl right here," he says, pointing a finger in my direction, "the questions and skepticism begin to build. First there was what happened last year, and now she's at the same place, and another person dies, it seems a little—"

"That's enough!" I yell, knocking over my chair as I jump to my feet. "I am so sick of every prick in this town, yes you included, blaming me for what happened last year! I'm also tired of hearing the word 'accident', which I'm sure you will call what happened Friday night too. Here's a thought *Chief*, how about you start thinking outside of your small pea brain head for once?"

I storm out of the house, ignoring Tyler's plea as I go. I don't make it a block before I get a text from him to please be careful. He might not understand how I'm feeling, but he knows that I need space to cool off and think. Right now, my emotions are all over the place. Angry. Hurt. Sad. Mainly, scared and confused.

I'm pissed because I'm tired of all the watchful eyes and skeptical glances. If it wasn't for Tyler, I'd leave this hellhole of a town wearing a Kiss My Ass shirt. But he's sacrificed too much for me to just walk away. I'd be in double the misery I am now.

I'm hurt because of everyone's inability to see how much pain I'm in. How can they not understand or see how much I'm hurting right along with them?

I've felt this way for a long time, thought I was almost past it, but in light of recent events, I'm learning that was a sad padded lie. It's all resurfacing and building an inferno of pain inside of me. But it's not all just pain. Fear and determination are beginning to build walls around the sadness. I may be the only one willing to figure out the truth behind Bryce and Kaylie's deaths. So it's no surprise that after hours of walking I find myself on the street that leads to Cooper's house.

My phone vibrates in my pocket, maybe a sign from the universe that I need to turn around and forget this whole thing.

I'm sorry I can't be there for you. My dad has me in lock down. For how long is anyone's guess. He's pretty pissed and upset. I love you.

Before I can reply, my phone beeps with another text from Millie.

Cooper called me last night and said you were handling things pretty well. I'm glad to hear that. Jo, I know how you dislike all things new and fun right now but give him a chance. He's not all that bad and I know you could use someone to talk to right now. At least until I'm out of jail.

Or maybe it's a sign I'm on the right track, I think. I text her back with a quick 'we will see' and then put my phone on silent. I'm about to step into unknown territory and jumping like a scared cat every time my phone beeps is not a part of the badass front I want to present.

My knuckles sting as I knock on the door, my force a little harder than intended. *Thanks nerves. Let's go for breaking my hand next time.*

The door is yanked open and on the other side stands an older female version of Cooper. All snarky greetings I had planned vanish as I stare at her fuming face.

"Let me guess, you're her," she snaps.

I cross my arms over my chest. The universal step one warning to back off. "There's a broad spectrum of 'hers' in the world. You may want to narrow it down for me."

Narrowing her eyes, she returns the warning with her arms crossing over her chest. "Yep. You're the one." She gives me a quick once over. "I always wondered what pretty face would break my brother. Looks like I was wrong on his standards."

If I'm going to have to deal with her to get answers from Cooper, screw it. Cooper can come to me, and Tyler can think whatever he wants. I start heading back, but as I reach the bottom step, I'm grabbed by the elbow.

"You're going to have to find yourself some backbone if you plan on stepping over the threshold, because on the other side, there's no room for weakness of any kind."

Unlike Cooper's dark green eyes, hers are brown, and hold a challenge. "What are you? Strong or weak?"

I don't need time to think about it. I also don't feel the need to reply. Shouldering past her, I walk inside the house, take in the surroundings, then walk into the living room to sit down on the couch. A small entryway, with a set of wooden stairs leading to the second floor, separates the living room and dining room. I can see a hint of a vintage kitchen from where I am sitting.

Cooper's sister comes inside and shuts the door, a smile on her face. "Good choice."

"What's a good choice?" Cooper's voice travels down the stairs, his footsteps heavy as he bounds down the steps. When he sees me, he almost misses the bottom step. "Jo," he says, surprised. "You're early."

Confused, I look at the clock to see it's noon and remember I was supposed to come over for dinner, not lunch.

Feeling awkward, I stand. "Sorry. I didn't realize what time it was when I left my house. It's been a real crappy morning. I can come back later." I make for the door, but Cooper rushes to stop me. His hand fans out across my abdomen as he blocks my path, causing a fire to spread through my stomach.

"Please stay," he whispers. "It gives me more time to show you some things," he finishes a little louder and steps back.

"Are you sure?" I ask, noticing the breathy way my voice sounds. Anger and embarrassment wash through me. Knowing Cooper heard it and thinking I'm betraying Bryce makes it easy for me to bounce back to my standoffish, snarky self. I cross my arms over my chest in a gesture of how I now feel. Or at least how I want to portray my feelings.

"I'm sure," he replies and turns to his sister. "This is Jada. She's tough but understanding. Whatever choice she had you make, it was for a good reason." He doesn't ask any more about it, which I respect.

"She did well... so far," Jada says. "We will see how she does after she's heard your story. Either way, she's your problem now. I've got to run. I'm supposed to meet a fellow hunter in Lewisville, probably won't be back until tomorrow." Jada slings her duffle bag over her shoulder and gives her brother a hard look. "Be good and stay out of the woods until I get back. Got it?"

"Yes, ma'am." He gives her a boy scouts salute as she walks out the door. "She can be such a pain, but she's the best. Just don't piss her off."

"Yeah, charming," I mumble and begin looking around the house.

Pictures of a happy family litter the mantel above the TV that sits inside a fireplace hearth. *Nice use of the space. May have to steal the idea and talk Tyler into doing something like this. Lord knows we never build a fire.* I pick up the picture on the end, its silver frame glinting in the light.

"Your parents skip out on you too?" I ask, staring down at the nice-looking family, a picture that closely resembles the one that sat on our mantel—until I smashed it to bits.

"I wish. I think that would be a better thing than what we're going through." There's a slight drop in his shoulders as he walks toward me and takes the photo. "This isn't exactly the dream lifestyle, especially when your kids get old enough to understand, and start hunting on their own. It took a toll on my mom."

"Oh my god, I am *so* sorry. I didn't mean… or know…" *Well this is uncomfortable.* I've got to start realizing that not all parents are like mine and that tragedy also strikes those who really love their children. Here I am talking smack about his deceased parents, who he quite obviously misses.

"Whoa… don't go freaking out on me yet," he says with a nice smile, a smile I'm starting to have a real like and hate relationship with. "My parents aren't dead. My mom's ill. The doctor who is watching over her said she had a psychotic break or something. It happened not long after I started going out on my own. My father is staying with her and refuses to leave her side until she's better. Until then, me and Jada are taking care of things."

Things. Is that what we're calling them now? "Cooper, I shouldn't have…. I'm sorry. My own parents skipped out on me late last year and in my mind—"

"You automatically jump to the worst conclusion when it comes to parents," he says, chuckling. "I get it. I'd probably do the same thing if it was me."

"Thanks," I say and drop my head to look at my intertwined fingers in front of me, still embarrassed. Man, no wonder I've been so confused here lately. This guy has put me on an emotional rollercoaster ride, one I haven't experienced in a long time, and one I don't like. It seems I can go from elated, embarrassed, angry, and back to embarrassed in four comments flat.

"All right, it's time for a little show and tell." Cooper places the picture back on the mantel and then jerks his thumb over his shoulder. "First, I've got to change. Jada had me working out all morning and I stink something fierce."

I smile as he jogs around the corner and then belittle myself for doing so. Why couldn't the person I need answers and possible help from, be a girl? No, the universe had to send me a guy. And not just any guy. Oh no, it had to be a cute guy with a fun personality, someone who can make me crack a smile for a change. Although this is a good thing, it also makes me feel horrible. I shouldn't be laughing and feeling relaxed around Cooper, not when I'm still mourning for Bryce and trying to find answers. What would he think?

Flashes of Bryce's concerned face the other night at the party assault my brain, but I'm quick to shake them. That is a whole new bottle of psychiatric pills I don't want to pop right now.

"Hey, Jo!" Cooper's voice booms down the hallway that goes past the stairs. "Come here."

My stomach knots and a sudden wave of nausea hits. Is he asking me into his bedroom? *Deep breath, Jo. What are you, twelve? Grow up, get over yourself, and get your big girl butt in there.*

I may need that trip to the therapist after all.

Like a moron, I continue to stand there and debate with myself. Cooper sticks his head around the corner, brows knit with confusion. "You okay?"

"I'm not sure. I'll let you know once the argument's over."

Confusion really sets in then, but I'll give him credit, he is quick to catch on. "If you're uncomfortable being here alone with me, we can go somewhere else."

Seriously? He has to be a gentleman too?

Feeling as if defending myself will make me look like an even bigger pansy, I hold my head high and walk past him and down the hall. When I walk into his room, I have to wrinkle my nose against the foul smell. I thought my room was bad, but it doesn't hold a candle to this one. A mixture of clothes, food, and what I presume is trash litter the floor, bed, and small sofa. The only light in the room is a small bedside lamp. And is that... lord I hope that's melted chocolate and not sh—

"Yo, Jo. Over here."

I swivel around to find Cooper standing in the doorway to a room across the hall.

"That's Jada's room. And be glad she's not here. She doesn't like people in her space."

"I don't see how she can stand being in her own space, let alone other people."

Cooper laughs as I walk past him and into a much neater version of the pepperoni and trash terror I just came from.

"I agree. She's not much of a housekeeper, that's for sure. She's always too busy meeting other chasers or working a lead. I can usually bet on finding her on the couch nine times out of ten."

A large curtain—I say curtain but it looks more like several white bed sheets—hang from metal hooks that run along a wire, completely covering one wall. I sit down on the small sofa across the room from it, figuring whatever

Cooper is wanting to show me lies behind it. It's out of place compared to the other poster-covered walls.

Without any dramatic 'here it is, the moment you've been waiting for,' Cooper walks over to the sheet and pulls it back.

"Welcome to my office."

If I wasn't so taken aback by what I was looking at, I'd come back with a witty comment about the poor floor plan or sucky lighting, but right now, my mind is focused on the wall. A huge piece of corkboard has been fastened to the plaster, covering every inch of it. Pinned in place is an enlarged map of the town and surrounding mountains, with circles and lines leading to smaller pictures of places and people pinned around the map. One picture in particular catches my eye.

I rush across the room to get a closer look. "What is this?" I demand and turn my accusing eyes on Cooper, while my finger rests on a picture of me.

"It's not what you think. I'm not some stalker creep, promise. Let me explain everything to you, and then, if you still have questions you can ask. Deal?" The hope in his eyes, and the pleading for me to trust him, still almost doesn't work. I don't like the idea of my picture hanging in someone's room—his room—on display to stare at whenever.

"This better be good."

Relief floods Cooper's face.

After we are both comfortable, him on the bed and me on the sofa with a soda, Cooper begins his story. "Many moons ago, there was a disturbance in the air surrounding a Navajo tribe. This caused—"

"Cooper," I interrupt, already not liking where this is going. "I don't need a bedtime story."

"Fair enough," he agrees. "I guess I was getting a little carried away. It's how I was slowly introduced to our lifestyle growing up and this is the first time I've ever shared my secret with anyone besides a chaser. Sorry about that."

"It's okay," I say, laughing. "Tell me about you, the chasers. And how about why my picture is on your wall"

Clearing his throat, Cooper tries again. "A chaser is what we call people like me. We're you're basic ghost hunters, but without the flashing lights and infrared technology."

"I still can't wrap my head around it," I mutter. "I mean, why is there a need for chasers? Ghosts can't harm us, can they?" This, I'm learning, is what really scares me. The fact that ghosts are real doesn't surprise me—I've always been kind of a believer in that area anyway. But it's the realization that there may be something out there, something most can't see, that is able to kill.

"Depends on the spirit. Most ghosts, I'm going to say eighty-eight percent, are harmless. Sometimes, it's harder for some to let go versus others. It's the nukpana you want to beware of."

Here is the point where my nightmares are going to become a reality. But I'm in it one way or the other. "I've heard you use that name before. What is it?"

"It's an evil spirit. The name was given by the Navajos after they encountered that disturbance I was so politely trying to explain to you in my 'bedtime story'. It was an evil spirit that had maintained dominance in the valley they had settled in. They had to get rid of the spirit to protect their people."

"And there's been other spirits like that since?" I ask.

Cooper laughs, a full gut-twisting laugh that leaves water in his eyes.

"Um, I didn't think it was all that funny," I say.

"If you were a chaser, you'd see the humor in it. Believe me. To answer your question, yes, there have been *many* nukpana's since then." Cooper wipes his eyes and gets serious. "There's no way to be completely rid of them. If there were, we would have already done it by now."

Cooper has a vague expression as he focuses his attention on the floor. I let him have a moment to deal with whatever he is thinking or feeling before asking any more questions.

"So this," I say, pointing at the wall across the room, "goes along with all this how."

"This is my research," he says and gets up to go stand by his pride and joy. "Jada always wants to put it in her room, but you've seen it. No way am I spending hours in *there* trying to put clues together." He shivers and makes a disgusted face. "Anyway, this is what I've got so far. It's not much now, but it's a start."

"So you're like a ghost detective."

His smile broadens. "Sure am, with some badass benefits."

Standing, I go over to stand opposite of him. "So you're saying I'm a clue."

"Yes," he admits.

"How?" I ask.

"In the beginning it was because of the accident last year. But I'm starting to wonder if there's more to you than I first thought." His green eyes observe me with an intensity I want to run from, but also want to live up to the challenge.

"What makes you think that?"

"Because you've seen it, the nukpana. You *can* see it. Most can't. I'm more than positive now that is what we are dealing with. Another chaser informed us about this chindi. Jada didn't want any part in it, mostly because with only one death reported in the last two years, it didn't seem too pressing for us. I was the one who insisted we come here. And after digging around some, and seeing what happened the other night at the party, I'm convinced the hollow is haunted by one hell of a spirit. Maybe the most powerful one I've ever seen or heard about."

"How are nukpanas created?" I ask.

"They feed off other spirits."

Not what I was expecting. I was thinking by time and experience, not spirit murder. How twisted is that? "How do they feed off other spirits?"

"You know how humans eat food to be sustained? Well, a spirit can feed off a weaker spirit's energy, which not only sustains them, but also gives them more strength, so to say."

"Why?" I ask, disgusted, and not understanding why a spirit, something that is already dead and that could move on, would want to do this.

"It's evil, Jo. It exists in all forms of life and death."

Doesn't that make you want to have babies?

"Sorry," Cooper says and makes as if he's going to give me a hug.

I step back, holding out a hand. "For what?"

"You looked sad." He runs his hands through his hair, frustrated. "This is not how I pictured this going, at all."

"What did you expect, Cooper? That I'd be jumping for joy and hugging your neck for being so honest with me? I mean, I'm glad you are, because I need to know the truth, but it's a little overwhelming for us ordinary folks."

I crack my knuckles, a nervous habit I have when I don't have a pencil in my hand, and start pacing his bedroom. There's not much space between the furniture, but I make do to try and walk off my restlessness.

Time to get down to business. "How do you kill these things... the nupkina or whatever?"

"Nukpana," he corrects, and walks out his bedroom door. "Follow me."

I follow him back through the house and up the stairs. Excitement ripples through me at the idea of seeing some sort of weapons room. I've been around plenty of guns and knives, but this will be different. These are ghost fighting weapons, they have to be badass. Imagining something from Men in Black, I'm disappointed when Cooper opens the door leading into the attic.

"Herbs, vials, and crap," I grumble. "Where are the massive weapons and spirit fighting spears?" *Yeah, say that five times real fast.*

"So impatient," Cooper says, mocking, and goes to pick up a tube filled with powder. "You know, these herbs and vials and crap are important."

"Yes, because crap always sounds necessary."

With a smirk on his lips, Cooper shakes his head with amusement. Setting down the tube, he walks over and shuts the door. Behind it on the wall is a yellow pushbutton.

"Wait, wait, wait," I stammer. "Is that a secret button? Can I push it?"

"Oh, no!" Cooper declares. "Chasers only." With a satisfied smirk, he pushes the button.

And just like that, trumpets sound and fireworks boom in my head as row upon row of swords and other types of weapons are revealed. *That's what I'm talking about!*

"This here is my family's pride and joy." Cooper holds up a stone knife with twine wrapped around the hilt.

"How old is that?"

"Don't know the exact year, but it was the first knife ever used on a chindi. As you can tell, it's very old."

I reach out to take it from him, kind of excited to hold something so sacred, but Cooper jumps back as if I'm a poisonous snake ready to strike.

"I don't think so," he says, his mischievous grin growing. "You can't just waltz up in here and touch anything you want. You have to earn it, and this," he says, holding the knife out with pride, "is the king ding-a-ling. To touch this, you must surpass the master."

"You're an idiot," I note, and with fast reflexes reach out with my finger to run it along the blade before he can pull it out of reach.

"Ha. Still not the same as holding it." To ensure I quit trying to grab his precious stone knife, Cooper locks it back inside a glass case. He double checks the lock before turning back to me. "What do you think?"

What do I think? Good question. "I'm not sure," I reply and start touring the room. "What am I supposed to think Cooper? Before Friday night, I thought the world was simple, very simple. Life and death. Happy and sad. But then you open this door, a very scary door, and everything changed. Maybe you can tell me what I'm supposed to accept, because I have no idea."

He digs his hands deep into his pockets and blows a burst of air between his lips. "I guess Jada was right. I thought you might be able to process all this and find closure, but maybe that was a rash decision."

I swivel around. "Are you calling me weak?"

Cooper throws his hands up and shakes his head. "That's not what I meant. Jada told me that people who pass age ten are hard to convince that anything outside of their everyday lives is possible. I always thought that was crap, maybe because I don't like feeling like a freak all the time and wish there were a few more believers around me, but maybe it's not."

Makes sense. "I don't think you're completely wrong, but it is a lot to take in and accept as real. In fact, it may not ever feel real for me until it's over. Two things I can tell you though. One, if you're being serious, I want to help. I don't want to become some chaser or anything, but I do want to know the truth and stop whatever is going on."

"You should, which is why I wanted to tell you. Unlike what Jada said, I didn't tell you because you have a pretty face. You are pretty, but I've seen hundreds of pretty girls and never once thought about telling them my heritage. You though... you are carrying the weight of Bryce's death and I think that's because you are being haunted by the nukpana. You must have seen something, maybe even seen him, that night at the overlook."

Great! Nothing makes a gal feel better than hearing she's being haunted by some evil spirit.

"What's two?" he asks.

I snap back to attention, and try forgetting all thoughts of evil spirits floating around me. "I don't want rumor of this getting around. People already think I'm crazy enough."

Cooper looks at me like I'm crazy. "Did you hear a word I said about not telling anyone my story until I met you? Or did you miss that part... a couple of times?"

I blush. "Sorry. I did hear you, still a little overwhelmed and want to make everything clear."

"I understand."

Feeling a little better about this, I smile. This could be a new start to truly putting what happened last year to rest.

"Where do we start?"

Chapter Eight

"Baby, you have to run!" Bryce grasps my shoulders hard, his tear-filled eyes searching mine.

"I can't. I—"

Something rushes past us and I search the darkness to see what it is, but find nothing. Then, as if appearing out of thin air, red eyes framed by a light mist rushes us.

"Run!"

~

Fingers snap in front of my face.

"You okay?" Tyler asks, eyes filled with concern.

"Yeah, why?" I ask, and go to take a bite of my cereal, only to gag when I taste bitter, soggy blueberry muffin rather than my favorite cereal.

"Oh, I don't know, most people don't stir their orange juice in with their muffins while looking off into the void when nothing is wrong." He pushes a new plate of muffins and bananas across the bar. "Now talk to me."

Yeah, like I'm going to jump off this bridge so easily. "It's really nothing. I dread going to school today is all. Not only is it going to be awkward, but after what happened at the overlook, I'm sure I'll catch more love than usual."

Tyler is the next one to stare off into the void. He recovers faster than I do though. "You want to stay home today?"

"Thanks but I think we both know it's best if I go." Last year after Bryce's funeral I refused to go to school for weeks. The counselor eventually called and threatened suspension and staying back a year if I didn't come back.

Let's just say I didn't get greeted with flowers and hugs when I finally did return.

"Okay, but if at any time you feel like you need to come home don't hesitate. I'll deal with Ms. Sassafras."

Ah, Mrs. Holt, how we love her rude, sassy butt. She's particularly nice and loving to me.

"Will do." Grabbing a muffin off the plate and picking up my bag, I walk out the door and give Tyler a blueberry salute before taking a bite and shutting the door. Millie pulls up, right on time.

The gloom and doom of the day sets in heavy as I get in the Jeep and have to sit under the scrutiny of Millie's sad face. "You ready?" she asks? No need to clarify what I need to be ready for.

"Let's go."

Once at school, we don't make it ten feet from the Jeep before we're ambushed.

"Where you been hiding all weekend, mole?"

"And another one bites the dust."

"Watch it, killer walking."

I steal myself, only for a moment, and then turn on Kirk and his goons. "Nice. Real nice. Too bad you're not smart enough to come up with some new material. Maybe you should try googling insults for dumbasses. Maybe there's an educational video with pictures for those who don't get the jokes at first."

I turn and start for the building. Of course, I know it's not going to be that easy.

"Think you're so smart don't you, Jo. Too bad it won't do you any good where you're going to end up."

"I'll save you a seat and we can find out," I reply over my shoulder.

When silence follows, I think they've thrown in the towel for now when I'm grabbed by the elbow and spun around.

"Don't walk away from me." Kirk gets right in my face, his features too much for me to handle this close and I want to scream at him to get away. Instead, I resort to slapping him, classier that way.

"Don't get in my face," I snap.

My handprint on his cheek disappears as his face turns a deeper red. I know what's going to come next but I don't shy away from it. I will not back down from him, not now. But before he can draw his fist back, Cooper steps in between us and shoves Kirk back.

"Where I come from, any guy who hits a girl deserves nothing but the best beat down in return. You prepared for that?"

Kirks jaw flexes, his fists tight at his side. "You don't know what you're doing, man."

"Actually, I do," Cooper replies. "And from where I was standing, she was doing you no harm."

Kirk chuckles, a mirthless sound. "You're going to regret this moment the day she's trying to kill you."

"You need to back off with that shit. We were all there Friday night. I know, as well as you do, that she could not have pushed or done anything to Kaylie. You were closer to her than Jo."

Kirk shoves Cooper. "You better watch what you're implying," he warns.

"Got a better explanation?" Cooper says with a sneer. "Jo have supernatural powers or something I don't know anything about?"

Kirk looks at Cooper as if he's speaking a foreign language.

"As fun as this has been," I say, growing tired of the banter, "the bell rang five minutes ago. Kirk, if you have a problem with me, feel free to find me any time."

He skirts around us with his friends in tow, and mumbles something about my time coming. This might sound scary to some, but considering I've heard that threat for over a year now, I'm thinking my time is well off in the future. That's if he ever man's up, of course.

After they're out of ear-shot, I turn on Cooper. "What was that?" I ask, defensive.

"What?" he asks, brows knit with confusion.

"I don't need you standing up for me." I push past Millie, hating the small bit of pleasure I feel. It's been a long time since anyone besides Millie or Tyler has stood up for me, and I appreciate it, though I'm not about to let Cooper know it. Seems like every day this boy is digging his way deeper under my skin, he doesn't need encouragement.

Millie and Cooper let me go without complaint, following behind. I do hear their mumbled conversation. He wants to know what my deal is, to which Millie says she doesn't know but figures it has to do with me being uncomfortable with what happened Friday night. Little does she know I've dealt with what happened, thanks to Cooper, who is the only other person besides his sister who knows what is really going on, and who plans on putting a stop to it.

Avoiding Kirk the rest of the day proves to be impossible, but instead of intelligent remarks and names as I pass, as usual, he gives me calculating glances, almost as if he can sense I'm hiding something. If he only knew.

Avoiding Millie and Cooper is just as hard. They're around every corner I make, thanks to knowing my schedule and my usual stops. Each time I pass them, I ignore their pleas to stop and talk, not out of hatred or anger, but because I'm afraid. I'm afraid that Millie will see through my lies when she begins to sense my secret—that there are changes I feel coming. I'm afraid of the truth that will be revealed the more Cooper and I dig into the town's history. Will we be believed?

But mostly, I'm afraid of Cooper and how he makes me feel. Not a day passes, sometimes not even an hour, when I don't think about Bryce. I loved him with every ounce of my being. He made me laugh, cry, and could help ease my fears and sadness with a simple smile. On the first day of kindergarten we became friends, and stuck by each other when teams were chosen for tag or dodge ball. During the summers our mothers would arrange play dates at the park because we missed each other. As the school years passed that friendship turned into 'do you like me check yes or no' notes that always had the answer yes by them. I don't know how many times a week Bryce would ask me that, mostly when I would call him a name during lunch and act as if he was the most disgusting thing on the planet. We had our share of fights and disagreements, but in the end, we would always talk them out, and make one another smile.

A part of me feels like I am betraying Bryce, or replacing him if I get too close to Cooper. Another part of me says I can't live the rest of my life alone, but it's too soon, even if it is friendship. There's no denying that Cooper is a nice guy, with the perks of cuteness, so any friendship formed may lead to other feelings that go beyond that line.

Lighten up Jo. You've only talked with the guy a few times. No need to have a complete loathing episode.

I chuckle at myself, knowing I'm being silly. I'm sure once we get started on the fact-digging we will be so wrapped up in the puzzle we won't even notice one another. Right?

As I'm rounding the corner of the gym and head for the parking lot, I'm grabbed from behind. Startled, I scream and turn swinging. Lucky for Kirk, he catches my hand before it makes contact with his face.

"What the hell, Jo?" he asks, as if we are the best of friends.

Yanking my arm out of his grip, I step back and look around to find we are alone. Ms. Wilshire deemed it necessary to make me stay after class to clean the marker board and write 'I will learn to respect my elders' one hundred times after popping off about her lack of reality. *That'll teach me I'm sure.* Now here I am, sizing up Kirk, alone, thanks to the delay.

"Like I have to explain myself to you. I'm not the one lurking around in the shadows."

He crosses his arms over his chest, his stance wide, like he's trying to be intimidating.

Please.

"Let's call a truce for now, okay? I need to talk to you."

Call a truce? Sure, I'm going to fall for that. "Oh, that sounds great. Why don't we go get some ice cream?"

"I'm being serious Jo," he snaps.

A truck drives by, and he's quick to grab my arm to drag me behind the gym.

"So this truce, doesn't cover speaking to me in public."

Kirk snorts. "You're still a freak, and being civil with—"

No need to hear the rest of the crap vomiting out of his mouth. Obviously he didn't get his own truce memo. I'm out of here.

"Jo, wait."

Still walking.

Kirk runs around me, hands stretched out to stop me. "Okay, okay. I'm sorry. I really do want to talk to you."

I cross my arms over my chest and cock an eyebrow. "You've got one minute."

I'm not sure what this talk is going to be about, but never would I have thought I would see Kirk get nervous talking to me about anything. Before he decided to make my life a living hell, we used to be friends, and could talk about a lot of things. He's always been an easygoing guy and never have I seen him have trouble speaking to anyone, until now.

He rubs the back of his neck, seeming to search for words. "Now that you're listening to me I don't know what to say."

"That's a first," I remark and sigh. I can't believe I'm fixing to say this. "It's still me, Kirk. The girl you used to be able to tell anything to. Quit beating around the bush and get to the point."

"It's not that simple," he hisses.

"Uh… Yes it is. You open your mouth and start forming words. Simple."

His jaw flexes several times, lips tight, as he looks across the parking lot. "Did you see anything… unusual Friday night?"

If I was asked to guess what he wanted to talk to me about, I could have made a million tries and still not come to what I think—maybe even hope—he is hinting at. If Kirk saw something strange that night, maybe it's possible I can convince him it was the same thing that took Bryce from us. I will myself not to get too excited though. This is Kirk I'm talking to, and him thinking outside the spectrum of reality is a big jump.

"What do you mean by unusual? A lot of crazy, unusual things happen at parties." *Some things I'd rather never see in my lifetime.*

He shakes his head. *Uh-oh, I know what that means. It's time for denial.*

"This is stupid. It has to be if I've resorted to talking to you."

"Yes, me, the crazy girl who might actually believe you."

Knowing him and our past relationship, he's about to walk away or continue to drag this unpleasant conversation on into infinity. Time to take a chance. Unzipping my backpack, I pull out my sketchpad and turn to my latest drawing. After talking with Cooper last night, sleep was not going to come easy. Not only because of the nightmares, but also because of the monster haunting my thoughts. So instead, I drew that beast, in several different shades, his image imprinted in my mind.

"You mean this." I hold up the drawing and watch his eyes go wide. He steps back, shaken, and I'm sure he's about to ask me a ton of questions. It's obvious that this is what he was referring to. I'm surprised, though, when he turns and walks away.

"Kirk," I call out, confused as to why he's running away.

"I can't.... Just forget it, freak."

Okay, resorting to calling me a freak when it's clear he saw the same thing is low, and really pisses me off. "Sure thing, panty waist."

Why even approach me if all he was going to do is bail? I had been naive to think for one minute that he might actually treat me like a human being. And as stupid as it was, I wanted him to. Sure, I've hated him for treating me so bad, and blaming me for his brother's death. But through the hate, I've missed him—missed my friend—no matter how many times I've told myself I didn't. He didn't realize it, but I needed him more than anyone else this last year.

I make my way across the steaming hot asphalt, having declined a ride from Millie after she told me I would have to wait until after her homecoming meeting. As I'm exiting the parking lot, still upset, I glimpse over to Kirk's truck to see him sitting there, a blank stare on his face. His shoulders are lax, his jaw tight. Whatever he's thinking about I hope it brings him to his senses.

I arrive home to find that Tyler isn't there, and a note is waiting for me.

Hey sis, I got called into work for a few hours. I'll be home around ten. We need to talk.

P.S. There's a postcard on your bed. Don't trash it before reading it.

I don't know what disturbs me more, the 'we need to talk' bit or the warning about the postcard. There's only one person that comes to mind who would send me a postcard, and if it's from him, Tyler can consider that puppy burned.

Not liking the pressure I suddenly feel, I drop my bag and head back out the door. It's only when I reach Sumner's pond that I wish I had brought my backpack. With no paper or pencil with me, I keep walking and place the textures and colors in mind to draw later. Maybe with a little more peaceful sketching tonight I may be able to sleep better. A girl can hope anyway.

It isn't until I'm standing in front of Cooper's house that I realize I need to chase some of the fear that's been building up in me over night out of my head. And who better than the chaser himself?

Right before my knuckles rack against the wood, I pause. Maybe this is a bad idea. As I stand there second-guessing myself, once again the door opens and there stands Jada.

"Can I help you?" she asks, with one perfectly manicured brow arched.

No turning back now. "Do you wait at the door to creep out your neighbors all day or something?"

Her answer is a raised eyebrow.

"Is Cooper home?"

"No," she snaps.

Deciding I'd rather talk to a rock than her, I turn to leave.

"Wait," she calls out. "Jo, is it?"

I pause and wonder if I'm hearing things. Her snippy tone has changed to a more welcoming one, and when I look over my shoulder, I see her face has softened.

"Why don't you come inside? Cooper should be back shortly."

I weigh my options, and decide getting to know Jada may not be such a bad thing, even if she does turn out to be the snob she's appeared to be so far. If I'm going to be hanging around to help Cooper, I might as well get to know her good and bad sides, that's if she even has a good side.

I make myself comfortable on the couch as Jada walks into the kitchen. My head rests against the plush cushion and once again I feel lost without my bag. I don't think I can handle Miss Hospitality's silence for too long, so if Cooper doesn't show up in the next thirty minutes, I'm out of here.

"You thirsty?"

Startled, I jerk my head up to see Jada placing a tray on the coffee table. There's an assortment of snacks and a pitcher of lemonade nicely placed on the silver platter.

"So this is your game, huh? Poison me so I don't rat you guys out?"

Jada laughs, amusement clear on her face, though the laugh is a bit discomforting. "If I wanted to get rid of you, I have more efficient ways of doing it than poisoning you."

Way to make a guest feel welcome.

"So what's your deal? One minute you look like a Rottweiler ready to attack me, the next you're all 'welcome to my home,' and now we are at death threats. You suffer from some hormonal imbalance or something?"

"No," she clips, offended, but then her features relax. "I'm protective of my brother. He's all I have left."

"That's not true," I say and instantly wish I could take my words back. It's not my place to get into her family business.

Jada's eyes narrows and she shakes her head. "I guess he's bared all to you. While it's true my parents are still alive, they're not here for us. It's only me and Cooper."

"Yeah, but at least you know they still care about you." Unlike my own parents. I turn my head, trying to hide the anger from my face. This is not a conversation I want to have with a girl who was threatening my life only moments ago, even if she was half joking.

Jada seems to take the hint. "So what all has he told you?"

I shrug. "The basics. What you hunt, and why. How spirits can become evil and how you kill them."

"Did he also happen to mention that it's dangerous?"

What does she think I am, clueless? "I kind of picked that up on my own."

"Did you?" she speculates. "You picked up on how a nukpana can get into your mind, twist your thoughts, and make you do things you don't want to do? You guessed that without a clean kill, the evil spirit can come back, stronger, kill you, and take your soul to feed off of?"

Wow, she's making this whole fear thing so much better. I'm glad I made the walk here for relief. "I get it, okay? It's dangerous, but the way I see it, I'm already in trouble. My life here is over. Everyone thinks I murdered my boyfriend last year, when in all reality it appears as if some crazy, soul-sucking spirit did it. And then, as if *that* didn't shatter my world, I've been haunted by the spirit ever since and thought it was some twisted interpretation of my guilt and grief."

Jada sits back and crosses her arms, her eyes calculating as she looks at me. "Cooper told me about your drawings, said it's why he had to tell you. But do you want to know what I find funny?" She doesn't give me time to answer. "This isn't the first time we've encountered someone who is being haunted by a spirit. And yes, you are being haunted. You spotted the demon in its form and it wants you for himself. That's what nukpanas do. They make an… imprint… so to speak in your mind, so you don't forget them. They want you to uncover who they are so you have to come back to them."

Thunder booms outside, causing me to jump and my heart to race. I glance out the window to see the thunderheads rolling in. I try to relax, telling myself Jada is trying to work me up on purpose, but it does little good. Nor does the loud booms of thunder that are pulling on my nerve strings.

"It's okay to be afraid, Jo. It's what keeps us alive. But falling to that fear is what will get you killed."

Nice. Real nice. I'm so glad I came here. No amount of drawing Sumner's pond tonight will help relax me now.

"If you're going to help my brother like he says you want to, it's best you remember that. And also, to listen to what we teach you. It may be the only thing that saves your life. Because if we don't kill this nukpana, it sounds to me like it will kill you."

"Are you saying it was after me the other night?"

Jada shrugs. "I believe so. Cooper didn't want to tell you, but I think you should know. That incident last year, with your boyfriend? I have no doubt you weren't meant to survive."

This keeps getting better. Guilt begins to gnaw at my chest, choking me until I feel like I can't breathe. "If I had died, would that have saved Bryce?"

She wastes no time in answering. "No. It wanted both of you, but something must have happened to stop it."

Speaking Bryce's name and talking about the danger I might be in brings the images of him warning me to run to mind. Tears begin to build so everything becomes blurry. I look down to hide it and blink them away as I twist my hands in my lap.

"Can spirits that have been killed by the nukpana—" My voice breaks and I clear my throat before continuing. "Are they trapped?"

I hold my breath, waiting for the answer I don't want to hear.

"Yes. And the only way they can be freed is to kill the spirit feeding off them."

The front door slams and in walks Cooper with a stack of papers in his arms. The smile on his face falls when he sees me sitting on the couch with tears threatening to spill over. Hearing Jada's raw honesty spurs my need to end this. Embrace the fear, use it, but don't become a victim of it. I'll keep it in mind.

I stand to my feet and take some of the papers from Cooper. "Let's get started."

Chapter Nine

Hours have passed since Cooper and I set up our research center on the kitchen table. We've read through hundreds of news stories and still have forty more years of stories to go. I've learned more about my small town in one night than I have in the last seventeen years, and some of it is a bit too telling. For instance, Mrs. Gardner, soon to be Ms. I'm sure, was seen tossing Mr. Gardner's belongs out on their front lawn. Not sure how this was news worthy, but it sure caused a stir in the gossip column on June 22, 1976.

Jada brings us some more tea as Cooper continues to tell us about his encounter with Ms. Stella, the town's librarian. When he scrunches up his nose and points his finger, I burst out laughing, picturing Ms. Stella's flustered face.

"Narrow your eyes a bit more," I say between gasps and clutch at my side. Cooper does as I say before losing control and joining in on the joke. Poor Ms. Stella, I don't know that she will ever find a man that appreciates turned-up noses and strict manners the way she does.

"I thought I was going to have to sedu—"

A loud banging at the front door interrupts him and all humor he held on his face vanishes as he looks over at Jada.

"Were you expecting someone else?" she whispers.

He shakes his head and eases out of his chair when another set of loud knocks shakes the door. Cooper and Jada both start to go for weapons they keep on top of the cabinet in the foyer when Tyler's voice booms through the wooden door.

"Jo!"

My eyes go wide and I look at the stack of papers in front of me. Sure, the copied news headings look innocent enough, but in light of recent events and my sour attitude, it wouldn't take Tyler two seconds to realize something was up. It's not like I've taken an interest in the latest news before, or any year before that.

As Tyler continues to beat on the door and yell warnings that someone better open the door before he knocks it down, I hurry to gather my stack of unread stories and shove them into a backpack Jada hands me.

"Here," Cooper whispers, and hands me half of the stories we found that mentioned an accident at the overlook. "Take these and read through them again. Highlight anything you think might be useful."

Shoving them in the bag with the other now wrinkled papers, I hang the bag carelessly on the back of the chair and take a deep breath. Time to get defensive and act like nothing is going on. As much as I wish I could tell Tyler, and even though he's said he's open to what I've been telling him, I need to wait until I know he will listen—*really* listen—and believe me. Otherwise, he may swing the other way and decide to put me in an asylum or something.

I interrupt Tyler's parade of assaults on the door and narrow my eyes at him. "What are you doing here?"

Anger storms his face, while disbelief widens his eyes. "What am *I* doing here? What the hell are *you* doing here? I've been looking for you all afternoon, Jo. If you hadn't left this damn thing behind, again," he says, shoving my phone at me, "I wouldn't be here."

Ignoring all the missed calls and messages from both him and Millie, I shove the phone in my back pocket and cross my arms. "Yeah. What's the big deal?"

"What's the big deal?" he snaps. Pulling at his hair, he does a full circle and then throws his hands out in frustration. "God, you don't get it, do you?" He takes a shaky breath, one I know is from concern and anger. "Just get in the damn truck."

Jada pulls the door open further, and steps up beside me. "You going to be okay with him?" she asks, her eyes narrowing on Tyler.

As much as I appreciate the concern, I really wish she hadn't asked that, and the fury on Tyler's face is why.

"Who are you?" he demands.

"I'm Jada," she answers, head held high. "Cooper's sister."

Adding to the fun, Cooper chooses that moment to step up beside me. He's not as confident as his sister and I don't know if it's a show he's trying to put on for Tyler, or true terror from facing my brother again.

"I'm sorry, once again. We were just hanging out and lost track of time."

"I knew you would be trouble from the moment you poked your head through Jo's broken window."

He has no idea.

"Which by the way, you still need to pay for."

"Yes, sir."

I go into the dining room and grab the backpack Jada lent me, and storm out the door. Cooper says he'll see me around as I pass, and I detect a bit of disappointment in his voice. I'm guessing an angry brother wasn't part of his 'how I imagined it' plan either. Understanding the loneliness he's probably felt his whole life, I turn back around and promise to call him later. Tyler starts the truck and jerks it into gear before peeling away from the curb. The sound of the engine roaring and the gears changing is the only noise that carries us home.

Before Tyler comes to a complete stop in the driveway, I'm out of the truck and running for my room. I hide the backpack under my bed, my main intent on getting in the house, and fling myself on the bed. As expected, Tyler bursts through my door.

"Are you kidding me? I'm the only one who has a right to be mad right now, so don't even pull this hissy fit crap with me. Do you have any idea how worried I've been today?"

"I don't understand you," I remark and get to my feet. There are so many questions colliding in my life right now, at least I can take care of this one head on. "You say you want me to move on, to be happy again. But then when I try, when I take that brave step to go talk to someone, you get pissed."

"I don't know him, Jo, and neither do you. Going to his house without telling anyone is dangerous."

"Who do we really know until we've crossed that line? No one. But for once, in a long time, I felt... free. Free from my guilt and self-hatred. Free from the pain I feel every damn day. But it took me crossing that line, Tyler, to find that freedom."

I step back, taking a breath, and absorb what I just said out loud. Since the moment Tyler came knocking on Cooper's door, this whole attitude was supposed to be a deflection to keep him from suspecting something else. This honesty and raw emotion I'm spewing out, has passed right by an outraged sister pissed at her brother and smacked into an emotional wall. One I didn't want to confront. Yet, here I am, confessing it all out loud to my brother.

Tyler looks lost for words. *Make that two of us, buddy.*

When he finally does speak, I can still hear a struggle in his voice.

"Let me make this clear. I am glad you have found someone who can make you feel that way, make you laugh again. It's what I've been praying for. But Jo, these past few days have been scary as hell for me. Seeing you Saturday, laid up in here, tormenting yourself again, I thought I had lost you all over again. And I get why you went off on dick face yesterday morning, you had every right to, and I don't blame you, but then you were gone and I had no clue where you were. So imagine me, sitting here and calling Millie over and over, having to turn to said dick face to keep an eye out for you, while images of you sobbing under the covers, of you screaming in your sleep, of your eyes filled with pain, kept running through my head. As much as I tried not to, I kept thinking the worst. I know I told you I would be all 'judgment free' and I am trying, but when you pull a stunt like this, the worst always comes to mind. And for good reason."

Inhaling deep and closing his eyes, he whispers, "I went up there today, just to check."

My stomach knots as a warm flush spreads through my body, causing my heart to speed up a few beats. Four months, two days, and eight hours after Bryce's death, after mom and dad had said they had enough, after countless nightmares and drawings I didn't understand, I felt drawn to visit the place that centered around the beginning of my downfall. I stood on the edge of the cliff, on the far side of the safety wall, and stared out over the vastness of the hollow. The creek sparkled down below as the moon's reflection danced on its surface. That night, the mysterious lights floated above the tree lines, vanishing and reappearing feet away in the blink of an eye.

I knew that with one step I could be with Bryce again. I could be free of the pain, the guilt, and the anger. No longer would I have to listen to my mom crying to my dad about my attitude, or how lost I was. Tyler could stop hovering over his little sister and move on. I would be mourned by some, but not many.

No matter how hard I tried to convince myself of this, that it would all be over, I couldn't take that step. I didn't want to. A part of me felt ashamed for not being able to do it, for not being able to let those I loved go and to move on, no longer to worry about me. I knew then that even when I walked away from the cliff, I still wouldn't be able to move on myself, I would still be hung up on what happened. But I had to continue with my life.

It was a battle I waged for hours before those bright headlights shined across the mountain and blinded me. Tyler had stepped out of the truck, fear and panic on his face as he ran toward me, yelling my name. He thought the worst of me, seeing me like that, thinking I was about to end it all. He didn't know how long I had been standing there, or the determination I had within me not to let go, not yet. I didn't bother to ease his mind either as he pulled me toward his shaking body and into the truck. I had let him think whatever he wanted to as I sat numb beside him.

"I wasn't going to do it," I whisper and collapse on the bed. "I know that's what you thought, and I'm sorry I let you think that, but I couldn't do it. I went up there that night to get away, to be in the place where I last saw Bryce and to think. Not that it did any good. It seemed to only make things worse."

Tyler sits down beside me and wraps his arm around my shoulders. "I was so scared that night, seeing you like that. I still get scared, which is why I'm so pissed now."

"I swear to you, Tyler. I'll never do that to you. I've told you that."

He nods, but I'm still unsure if he believes me. He hugs me tight and whispers he loves me, to which I reply the same, something I haven't done in a long time. He leaves with a promise to talk more tomorrow. When the door clicks shut, I make a silent promise to him to do better, to be the sister he needs. He deserves it, and one day, when I have proof, I'll tell him the truth. Then, together, we can start to rebuild our lives the way they once were. At least, I hope we can.

As I'm scooting up to the top of the bed, my hand lands on something smooth and glossy that gives under my fingers. *The postcard.* With a frustrated huff, I get comfortable and read it.

I miss you, baby girl. Hope to see you soon.

Dad

It's no surprise to me the postcard is from my father and not my mother. He was always the parental figure around here. And as much as I try not to think about it, I do miss him and his 'chin up, kiddo' advice. I don't know whatever possessed him to follow mom and walk out of our lives, maybe she had something to do with it, but I wish he hadn't.

I'm pulled from my thoughts when my right butt cheek begins to vibrate and I jump. Pulling my phone from my pocket, I see that it's yet another text from Millie.

Where in the hell are you??????????

Ten questions marks, this is getting serious.

Hey! I'm home now. I've been at Cooper's. In the doghouse with big bro. See you in the morning?

While she's typing her reply, I change and turn all the lights off but my dark red acrylic vase lamp. The exotic, dark feel I was going for when redoing my room over the summer has been the only change I've liked about myself.

With Cooper? All afternoon?

This is followed by a dozen smiley faces.

I want full details in the morning. I'll be there at 7:15 so we have plenty of time to talk.

I smile and can imagine her squealing in excitement.

And don't worry about big bro, he loves you.

I know.

I type, followed by.

I love you too.

That will shock her, even more so than the news about Cooper I'm sure. I can't remember the last time I told anyone besides Tyler I loved them. But it's time to break that pattern. One never knows when a spirit-sucking fiend will come steal your soul, after all.

After getting a love you back text from Millie, I open up the main screen to see that I've missed several calls not only from Millie and Tyler, but also from Kirk. Well there's something that hasn't happened in a while. Opening my text screen, I see that I also missed five texts from him.

Can we talk?

This is Kirk, in case you lost my number.

Don't be a bitch Jo. I need to talk to you.

So this is how it's going to be.

Fine. Whatever. Freak.

I clench my jaw, wishing he was here in person so I could give him a piece of my mind. Resorting to the only option I have, considering I don't want to freak my brother out again by leaving to go confront Kirk, I punch at the screen.

For one, I know who this is. The jerk who has been nothing but an ass to me.

For two, don't try to plead with me then call me a bitch.

For three, why should it be any other way?

I toss the phone aside after I hit send, not expecting a reply. After adjusting the light on my lamp so it's brighter, I pull the backpack out from under the bed, then separate the read stories from the unread stories. I start to skim over the headlines again in the read pile.

Every two to three years there has been an accident at or near the overlook. How could town officials not see this before? Or have they not said anything for fear of sounding crazy? Sounds reasonable. I know I'm not ready to go screaming through the streets waving my cuckoo flag just yet.

Cooper gave me the copies from 1952 to 1990. I don't know if that was intentional or not, but I'm grateful. Solving the mystery and finding out what happened to Bryce is why I'm doing this, but having to read the story from that night might put me in a hole I don't want to fall back into.

After highlighting the dates, location, and names of all the ones I've read, I start in on the ones dated in the 1950s. I read late into the night, highlighting what seems important, even as my eyes grow heavy. When I'm about to call it quits, my phone rings, scaring me back awake. Kirk's name flashes across the screen.

"What?" I groan into the phone.

"Because I want it to be another way," he replies in way of answer, confusing my muddled, sleep-deprived brain.

"What?" I ask again, confused.

"You asked me why it should be any other way after ignoring my texts, and I'm saying I don't like it this way. I want it to be another way."

A scene from Carrie, covered in pig's blood, flashes through my mind. "Nice try, Kirk, real nice, but I'm not that stupid." I pick up the papers scattered across my bed and begin to place them in neat piles.

"Jo," he says my name with desperation. "Please. I know you know something and I can't deal with this anymore alone. Something is...."

He continues but I'm unable to focus on what he's saying while looking down at a name I recognize. Jesse Ford, brother to victim Jessica Ford. I didn't know Mr. Ford had a sister.

"Jo!" Kirk yells, grabbing my attention.

"Yeah, that's great. Listen, I've gotta go. Meet me tomorrow at lunch under the oaks." I hang up and call Cooper.

"Hello?" he mumbles, sleep heavy in his voice.

"Cooper, it's me, Jo."

He chuckles. "Kind of got that when your name flashed across my screen. What's going on? You okay?" he asks, more alert now.

Hearing his concern and how excited I am to talk to him makes my anxiety spike and causes my stomach to tumble. "I'm fine. Did you get any more reading done tonight?"

"A little bit. Why?"

"I think I'm starting to see a pattern connected to the overlook, at least in the years you gave me. I found something else. Jessica Ford, died in 1953. She was survived by her brother Jesse Ford, and parents Lila and James Ford."

"Okay," he drawls, not understanding the importance.

"I know Jesse Ford. In fact, I believe he's family somewhere along the line. I think we should go see him and hear what he has to say." It's a long shot, last I heard Jesse Ford lived down by the branch and was a harsh old man, but I think it's worth a try.

"That's great, Jo. You want to go tomorrow?"

No. I want to go right now, but considering it's one in the morning, I guess tomorrow will have to do.

"After school?"

I want to go first thing in the morning, but being a better person for my brother and friend to Millie does not include skipping out on them, again.

"Sure. Goodnight, Jo."

I smile, hating myself for doing it but unable not to. "Goodnight, Cooper."

After hanging up and stuffing the papers back in the bag, I get up to hide the backpack under the bed. Unable to hide it out of sight, I reach under the bed to see what's in the way. The soft feel of something plush grazes the tip of my fingers. I reach in farther, already knowing what it is. After pulling out the familiar teddy bear holding a picture of me and Bryce, I push the bag back to the wall and stand up.

Sitting at the edge of my bed and holding the teddy bear in a tight grip, I stare down at the picture. I never used to be the type of person who thought everything was a sign, that finding something, having the same dream, or sensing the same feelings at a certain place meant anything. Now that theory has changed. How could it not?

So what does this mean?

Be happy, Jo.

Or....

You're starting to forget me, Jo.

Feeling conflicted and unable to sleep, I grab my sketchpad and do the only sure thing I know to do. I draw.

Chapter Ten

"Spill it," Millie demands before I can get the Jeep door shut.

"There's not much to tell," I reply and look back toward the house. Tyler stands in the doorway, coffee mug in hand, a scowl still on his face. He kept his promise to talk this morning, and what a talk it was. I wish I could say we only disagreed on a few things and that it all ended with smiles and hugs. But that would be a big, fat lie. Truth is, we yelled, a lot. His demand that I come home straight after school didn't sit well with me, and not because I wanted to defy him, but because Cooper and I had made plans to go talk to Mr. Ford. Could I tell Tyler that, though? No. That would lead to a whole new line of questioning. Instead, I pulled the defensive teenage crap about not being a child and that it would be nice to have a little trust thrown my way.

I sigh, hating this day already and prepare myself for Millie's curiosity. What I wouldn't do to be able to crawl back into bed.

"Okay," she drawls, "tell me what not much there is to tell."

"I don't know. We talked. He asked me about the area, I told him there wasn't much to tell." Stories we read off copied newspapers from our area told a different story, but there's no need to share that bit of information with her. "I asked him about where he's from. Turns out, they travel a lot, so he had a lot of interesting stories. Then

Tyler came pounding on the door around ten and took me home. There's your spill," I sum up with a smile.

"You kill me," she says and shakes her head. "Did you meet his sister? Is she nice?"

"Oh yeah, nice and sassy. She and Tyler would really hit it off." I mean it as a joke, but Ms. Matchmaker's eyes light up.

"Did you introduce them? Tyler could really use some down time," she knocks her elbow into mine, "if you know what I mean."

"Um, yuck. And yes, they met. Eyes glaring and full of attitude as they stared one another down."

"That makes for some sexy tension."

"Instead of playing matchmaker for everyone else, maybe you should focus on yourself. Sounds like you need a little romance." When her cheeks redden, flags go flying. "Wait. Are you seeing someone?" I accuse.

Silence.

"Millie?"

She bites on her lip, trying to force the smile that's trying to form to stay put. "Not really."

"Let me give you a reality check here, Sweetie. Not really means yes. Who is he?"

I know Millie like I know myself and her worrying her lip now doesn't mean she's trying to hide a smile, but contemplating honesty to save someone's feelings. Great.

"It's Kirk," she blurts out, and then glances over at me as she puts the Jeep into first gear and kills the engine.

I stare straight, wondering if I heard her right and wishing I was wrong. *Kirk? Really, him?*

"I'm sorry, Jo," she says, taking my silence as anger and wanting to explain.

I hold up my hand. "Stop."

I can't freaking believe this! Why? Why does it have to be him? There are seven billion people on this planet and she picked him. *Him!* How can she do this to me? He's the biggest ass I know, especially when it comes to me. Anger and hurt pours through my veins and I want to yell at Millie for making such a lousy choice.

But then I check myself, with flashes of the old Kirk flashing through my mind. Why not him? When he's not being a jerk to me, he's a pretty good guy. I should know, I've seen him vulnerable and at his worst. I've seen who he really is when he isn't putting on a show for everyone else. Once upon a time we were good friends. He was a guy I could turn to when I needed to talk, without worry of gossip or judgment. Sure, he has some problems but who doesn't?

"He came over a lot this summer and we started talking," she rushes to explain. "I should have told you sooner, but—"

"You thought I would be mad at you," I say and glance at her. "I don't know what to think. I'm surprised."

My door opens and there stands Kirk, all dark circles and bloodshot eyes. He glances at Millie, his features softening. "Hi, Millie."

"Hey."

The affection he held for her is gone when he looks back at me. "I need to talk to you. Now," he commands and I start to pop-off that I'm not some dog, but stop myself.

How am I supposed to handle him now? Can I still be rude and witty while he's making the moves on my best friend, who is apparently smitten by him? I miss the non-confusing days. I knew where I stood and where he stood, all snark and no fake smiles. I'm already starting to miss the good ole days.

"Here," Millie says and hands me her keys. "You guys can use my Jeep to talk. I'll vouch for you if you're late. Lock her up when you're done."

She leaves before I can argue and Kirk walks around to get in. There's always a plus side to everything I guess, and in this case, if I go ahead and get this over with maybe I can take a nap during lunch.

"What's on your mind, Rowan?"

"Let's cut the crap, Vanguard. I know you saw something Friday night, I saw it in your eyes. I admit, at first I played it off as your crazy nonsense. But now…." he trails off, leaving me to guess the rest of what he's thinking—like that's simple anymore. In any case, I'm not going to make it easy for him. He has to say it.

"I've told you before, you're going to have to be more specific."

Frustrated, Kirk reaches across to my floorboard and yanks out my sketchpad from my open bag before I can grab it back, and flips it open in mid-air.

"This! What is this?" he demands.

I take back my sketchpad and fight the urge to slap him across the face. What is it with everyone thinking they can grab my personal stuff? Geez!

"I don't know, okay? It's something I've seen a couple of times and that has haunted me for over a year."

His face pales. "A year?"

"Yes," I snap, "a year." I fight back building tears and lower my voice. "I saw it the night Bryce died."

His heavy breathing sounds through the cab. "Do you know what it is?"

I start to answer him, but pause. "Why are you asking me? Did you see it?"

He stares straight ahead and grips the steering wheel. "Friday night," his voice breaks and he clears his throat, then wets his lips and tries again. "Friday night, when I let go of your arm and turned to see what happened, I saw something." He shakes his head. "I can't explain it. I saw it, but when I looked directly at where I thought it was, nothing was there. Then I rushed to the cliff, saw Kaylie lying at the bottom, and I swear I saw it again. After the cops and paramedics showed up, I told myself I was seeing things, that it was from the panic, but when I got home—"

"You kept seeing it," I interject.

He glances at me, eyes shadowed with fear. "Yeah. I haven't slept since Friday night."

"Not because you're having nightmares about it but because you feel as if it's lurking in your room, watching you."

He swallows hard, as sweat begins to build on his forehead. "How did you know?"

"Hello?" I all but shout and point to my sketchpad. "What did you think, I dreamed this thing up to attack you? I've seen it too, moron."

He opens his mouth, no doubt to ask what it is, again, but I cut him off. "It's called a nukpana. It's an evil spirit that must absorb other spirits for power."

"What does it want?"

"I don't know."

"Where did it come from?"

"I don't know."

"How does it—"

"*I don't know*!" I rub at my temples, urging the headache forming to go away. "This is new to me too. I didn't know anything about it until Cooper—"

"Cooper," he says, harshly. "I knew there was something fishy about that guy."

If you only knew.

"He's not fishy, he's here to help, Kirk, so don't go all crazy on him. It's... kind of his job." I was hoping to keep Cooper out of this, but of course, I had to go spout off his name in my frustration. I tell Kirk as little as I can about Cooper, but enough to keep him from riding me for more information. Once I'm finished, I make him promise not to say anything to anyone and in return, I would keep him updated.

"And whatever you do, don't tell Millie."

"Why?" he asks, like it's the most ridiculous request in the world.

"The fewer people who know about this, the better. Plus, I don't want her to worry about us. Do you know how crazy it would sound if we told her we were seeing a spirit that was killing people for their souls? And trust me, if you throw me under the bus, I'll get back up, take the wheel, and run you over."

He nods, understanding on his face. "I won't say anything." He goes to get out of the Jeep, but I grab his arm.

"One more thing," I say, with warning. "Whatever you have going on with Millie better not be some ploy for your ego. You got me?"

He flings off my arm. "Don't you worry about that," he says, but not in a way that makes me believe he doesn't care about her. I can see it in his eyes and in the way he talks about her. Whatever they have shared over the summer, and continue to share, has affected them both in the same way.

I let Kirk go on ahead of me, not caring if I get a tardy slip or not. I need a moment to mentally brace myself for the long day ahead.

~

Millie honks as she passes me on Main Street, right before I cross onto Oak to head home. Cooper lags behind me, phone to his ear and a drink in the other hand. I'm a few paces ahead of him but can still hear the argument he is having with his sister, plain as day. Apparently, he didn't tell her of our plans and she's pissed he didn't include her. I'm not complaining.

I've come to the conclusion that lying to myself anymore is futile. No matter the guilt I feel, I am glad I have Cooper by my side to go with me today, and also glad that his sister isn't there to impose. He isn't as open with me about his life as he is when she is around. And, as hard as it for me to admit to myself, I am rather enjoying this friendship we have building. Not a whole lot, but a little. Okay, maybe I am still lying to myself.

Relief floods through me when we get to my house and I find Tyler isn't home. Cooper follows me inside, but I have no plans to stick around. I dump my school bag on the counter, tell him I'll be right back, and head up to my room to grab the bag from underneath my bed.

Before rushing back downstairs, I remember to grab my phone from my school backpack, not needing another fiasco like yesterday, and head toward the garage door. I turn to lock up behind me, but see that Cooper didn't follow. Where is he?

Poking my head back through the door, I find him standing in front of the refrigerator and looking at the pictures hung by magnets on its surface. Embarrassed, I curse myself for not taking down the one of me stark naked beside Tyler in a small blow up pool when we were little.

"Hey," I say, and hope he doesn't hear the hitch in my voice. "We've gotta go. Tyler could be home any minute and I'd rather not deal with him right now."

After taking one last look at the photos, he turns and walks into the garage. I lock up before getting in the car and send Tyler a quick text that I'll be gone for the afternoon. He's quick to reply before I can put my phone down, asking me where I'm going, but I hit ignore and put the phone in the console.

"Where are your pets?"

That's an odd question. "I don't have any pets."

"Huh," he grunts.

I'm waiting for a follow up explanation, but when he doesn't give one I ask.

"I don't know." His cheeks redden and he looks down at his hands. "It's stupid, just forget it."

"I think I've had my fair share of embarrassing stupid moments, the least you could do is give me one." I smile.

"You know that I've traveled my whole life, never getting a chance to claim roots anywhere. I've always wondered what that's like, being able to say this is my home, where I grew up. Growing up, I had plenty of imaginary friends."

We both laugh.

"But I also had an imaginary lifestyle. I imagined a house with pictures hanging everywhere, artwork from school pinned to the fridge, and a dog digging through the trash. I guess that's my idea for every ordinary family: a house, dogs and cats. No packing boxes taking up the garage, ready to be used for the next move."

"Why would you think that's stupid? Sounds perfectly normal to me."

"That's the thing. It's not normal. For some maybe, but not for everyone. I mean, look at you. You've lived here your whole life, but you don't have any pets, no art work on the fridge. Instead, there's pictures of you playing naked in a pool, and last years' calendar. I'm not saying that's bad, but that we all have a sense of what's normal, when really nothing is normal."

"I don't know whether I should agree with you, or take offense for not being normal." I elbow him and smile, letting him know I'm only teasing. "I do get what you're saying. I used to think I lived a normal life, that how I lived was how everyone lived. Then reality hit and I realized there is no such thing."

My arm is resting on the console between us, my hand dangling off the end only inches away from Cooper's resting on his leg. I swallow, suddenly feeling too close to him. As if he can sense my unease, he reaches up with his hand and clasps mine. *Not helping, dude.*

"I'm glad we got that call." He smiles, his intense eyes staring at me as I try and focus on the road. "It's been a long time since I've had friend." *Friend, or someone you wish was more than a friend?*

As the pavement turns to dirt, I have to downshift and am thankful for the excuse to let go of his hand. Maybe it would have been better if Jada had come with us. Then we wouldn't have this awkward tension between us. Or am I the only one feeling that way? Swallowing hard, I try and shake it off.

Mr. Ford's old, rusty mailbox comes into view and I slow down to inspect his driveway. As I feared, it's rutted and littered with potholes. No way am I driving my beauty down that. A little dust never hurt anything, but losing my muffler might. I pull over to the side of the road as far as I can without getting in the ditch, and kill the engine.

Cooper looks out his window. "Are you kidding me?"

"What?" I ask, and grab my phone from the console.

"How do you expect me to get out?"

"Carefully," I answer.

Huffing, he gets out and tries to hang onto the door to keep from sliding off into the standing water in the ditch. And fails. I laugh and watch as he gives up and trudges up to the front of the car.

"Don't worry, mud is in right now."

He tries kicking off some of the muck. "I'm surprised living in an area like this you would chose such a classy car."

"It's a classic, kind of hard to refuse."

A dog barks off in the distance, one that doesn't sound too nice, or small. Cautiously, we walk up the driveway and listen closely. I pray that the thing is on a leash in the back somewhere.

Mr. Ford's house comes into view as we get past the last row of pine trees and blackberry bushes. As feared, sitting on the faded porch, hackles standing, teeth bared, stands the dog. I stop, and throw out my arm for Cooper to do the same. No leash, not good.

"Better be prepared to run," I warn.

The front door of the faded brown house opens and out walks Mr. Ford, a cane supporting his weight.

"Don't worry about Booger. He's harmless, never bit a person a day of his life." He sits down with a huff in a rocker that has seen better days. "What can I do for you?" he asks. "You're not some salespeople are you? I don't buy any of that catalog crap."

When we don't answer and the dog continues to growl, Mr. Ford scolds the dog. "Now settle down, Booger. We can't hear anything for all that racket you're making."

The dog whines and settles down to rest his head on his front paws. Able to breathe again, I continue on up the driveway and answer his questions. "Hi, Mr. Ford, we—"

"Now, I'll have none of that crap 'Mister Ford' bull. I may be old, but I'm not formal. Call me Jesse."

I smile, liking him already. "Well, Jesse, we aren't here to sell you anything, but we were wondering if we could possibly ask you some questions."

"About Jessica," Cooper adds.

The warm welcome on his face is replaced by a scowl. "This have anything to do with that young girl getting killed the other night?"

"Yes, sir," I answer. Please, don't turn us away.

Rocking back and forth a few times, Jesse's face loosens a bit and he gestures to the other chairs on the porch. "Have yourself a seat."

We both oblige but I make sure to give Booger a wide berth to be safe. The worn wood creaks under our weight, but surprisingly holds up.

Jesse looks over the rim of his glasses, curious yet skeptical. "What do you want to know?"

Where to start? I don't even know. Do we come out and ask him about the evil spirit, or tread lightly? I should have discussed this more in depth with Cooper on the way up here rather than talk about our fantasy thoughts on life.

"Can you tell us how she died?" Cooper asks, jumping in to save me from my spiraling thoughts.

"She fell off the cliff," Jesse answers in a harsh tone. "It was in the papers."

"But papers sometimes don't tell us the whole story," I say, finding my voice and getting my ducks in a row.

"That is a very honest statement, young lady. Are you here for some school paper or something?"

"No," I answer and rush to explain why we are here. "I'm sure living on the same road that leads up to the overlook, you hear and see a lot of things, so maybe you'll remember this time last year when Bryce Rowan fell from the cliff."

He nods. "I do."

"I was there with him that night. It was just the two of us. But we... weren't alone, not really."

"Ah," he says and begins rocking again. "So you've seen it."

Relief blossoms through me and I look over to Cooper, seeing the same expression on his face. Maybe we are not as alone in this as we thought we were.

"Before I tell you Jessica's story, let me enlighten you about something. The mind is a tricky foe. This world is full of things we cannot see, and not because the world refuses to show us, but because our human minds refuse to see them. It closes us off and doesn't allow us to see all the things around us, not until we make it see. There are some, a few spiritually chosen, that can witness what others cannot. You," he says and points at us, "are a part of the chosen. As am I."

The way he says it, the pure belief, makes it sound like something special. But is it really? Or is it a curse? I guess it could be both. A curse to see but a blessing to help protect against.

Mr. Ford looks out across the yard in a faraway stare.

"It was a cool summer night, rare for July. Jessica and I had been fishing down at the forge, you know the spot I'm sure."

I nod, although he doesn't see it.

"We caught several fish that day, more than usual and I had refused to leave our sweet spot until I could no longer see my line in the water. Jessica had been furious and said mama and papa would be just as mad. I didn't care, I had a basket of fresh fish as my reward."

He smiles, no doubt from the memory. When he continues, that blank stare returns.

"We were loading up our gear in the wagon—we still used a horse and buggy in them days when we were staying close to home. Dad didn't think it was necessary to waste gas when a horse was still good enough."

I wonder what that would have been like, living in a time when it wasn't so strange to see someone traveling by horse and buggy. Now it's viewed as a photo opportunity.

"After loading up all our gear, I had walked down to the creek's edge to wash my hands when the horse got spooked. I figured it was some rodent that had got him all in a tizzy, but during his fit he broke a clip that latched him to the wagon. Jessica continued to complain as I tried fixing it. Not an easy task in the dark. When she saw that I didn't bother none about her tantrum, she started walking circles around the horse and buggy, kicking at the dirt as she did."

Sounds like a typical sister.

"I'd almost finished rigging the horse back up, when all of a sudden she stopped and screamed my name. I rushed to her side, swearing that if this was some prank that I was going to pull her hair out. Jessica never did like being out at night in the woods, so I figured it was her imagination. But when I reached her side and saw the fear in her eyes, I knew she wasn't playing. She kept yelling at me, telling me there was something standing by a tree next to the water." He shakes his head. "I looked, but never saw anything and scolded her for being so childish. I went back to the horse and he started his fussing again, making it harder for me to rig the clip back to the buggy. Jessica followed me, begging me to listen. But I didn't.

"Once the wagon was finally secure again, we loaded up and headed back up the mountain. Jessica was quiet, which was unlike her. She always had something to say about something."

The affection he holds at the memory of his sister is enduring, as is his tone for her. Every mention of her name holds love, while remembering her personality brings a smile to his face. It's something I often feel myself about Tyler, even when I'm mad at him.

Jesse struggles to continue and I start to tell him it's okay if he can't, we understand, but he clears his throat and continues.

"We had reached the top of the mountain, to the overlook, and you could see the will o' the wisps dancing amongst the trees, even from the road. Jessica begged me not to stop, but I didn't listen. The view was a treat I never got tired of observing.

"Back then the rock wall wasn't there like it is now, so I pulled the horse up not too far from the edge and told her to stay put. She continued to plead with me, even as I got off the buggy and told her to stay quiet, that everything was fine. And it was, until the winds picked up. And then came that sound."

"Like something whirling around you," I remark, all too familiar with the sound he's trying to describe.

"Yes, that. The horse got spooked again and bucked, breaking that damn clip again. The wagon tipped to the side, the side Jessica was sitting on. She screamed and got out of the wagon when I told her to. I was worried the stupid horse would go barreling off the mountain, as wild as he was acting. I steadied Jessica by my side and made sure she was okay. When she said she was, I went to try and calm the horse. Then the noise came again.

"Jessica's hysterical cries filled the valley as she pointed toward the tree line to the right of the overlook. This time I caught a glimpse of a dark shadow moving through the thickets, but the horse bucked again and I had to turn my attention back to him. So much was happening," he shakes his head and stops his rocking to lean on his cane.

"I was chosen that night to see, see more than most folks do, of what the world holds." He lowers his head, his voice dropping. "But it wasn't until Jessica fell over the cliff's edge, and I saw her body twisted at the bottom, that my mind decided it was time to reveal the truth to me. I saw it there, by her side as I looked over the edge. Its form was human, but its body was made of mist. The head was deformed, but I will never forget those red eyes as they looked up, glistening with satisfaction."

His chest rises as he breathes deep and then puffs out his cheeks as he exhales. "It was a sight that haunts me to this day. I tried to tell my parents, and the authorities, but no one believed me. They called it shock," he says in a sour tone.

"Have you been back up there, to the cliff?" Cooper asks.

"Nope," he grunts. "Inherited this place after my folks passed, but never have I set foot past my property. I know what lurks in these woods. The monster, and the idiots who believe that monster is some kind of god."

"Ah, shit," Cooper says and stands as he laces his fingers behind his head.

"What am I missing?" I ask, not understanding what Jesse's last comment means, or Cooper's outburst.

Jesse raises an eyebrow and gestures for Cooper to explain. Dropping his arms to pinch the bridge of his nose and blow out a breath, he looks down at me.

"Sometimes we run into... covens."

"Covens?" I say it as a question but not because I don't know what it is, but because there are no such things around here.

"Yes, covens. There are a lot of them out there, most not associated with the nukpana, but every now and then we encounter those that worship evil spirits."

"Had a feeling about you, son. You're one of those... ghost hunters or whatever." Jesse dismisses the technical name with a wave of his hand.

"You know about us?" Cooper asks, surprised.

"Boy, you don't live as long as I do and not hear a thing or two. You should talk to Mason Edwards. He lives on the other side of the ford, just on the other side of the mountain."

Wait. I'm still hung up on this whole coven thing. Screw who knows about chasers.

"Let's stay on topic, boys. Shall we?"

All I get from Cooper is a nod, although I can tell he is still reeling from finding out Jesse knows what he is. Jesse however gives a low whistle.

"It's been quite some time since I've heard a woman be so commanding. It was one thing I loved about my dear Emily. Whenever she wanted me to take off my—"

"Whoa," I yell. No matter how nice and laid back I find Jesse, no part of me wants to hear whatever it was he was fixing to say. "How about you keep that to yourself, that'd be great."

Cooper finds my awkwardness funny and shoves against my shoulder with his hand. "Oh, come on, Jo. Let the old man relive a little past love."

"Maybe some other time," I snarl and narrow my eyes at him, which only causes him to laugh harder. I can feel my cheeks blazing.

"No, no. The girl is right. No need to fill you two young doves on the action this house has seen. And boy were there some times."

"Jesse!" I warn.

"Right," he says and clears his throat. "The coven. Ah, they've been around for a while. I heard it started back in the early nineteen hundreds when a family kicked their middle daughter out of the house for trying to seduce a minister." Jesse rubs a hand over his eyes. He looks tired. "Listen, I'm feeling a mite worn out. I don't get many visitors comin' up here, and... it's been quite a spell since I talked about Jessica, and what happened. Do as I say, go see Mason. He can tell you more about the coven."

We thank Mr. Ford and promise to visit him again, to which he promises to share more details about his love for his wife next time around. *There's some inspiration to hurry back.*

It's not until we are almost to Cooper's house that he breaks the silence.

"You know that Mason guy Jesse was talking about?"

"I've heard of him, but never met him."

"You feel up for another meet and greet?" he asks and grabs for the door handle when the car comes to a stop.

"Sure, but not tomorrow. I need to spend some quality time with my brother. I've kind of put him through the wringer lately."

"I get that."

Speaking of siblings, Jada comes out of the house, arms crossed and a scowl on her face.

"Guess it's time for me to face the drama," Cooper remarks and gets out of the car.

"Yeah, good luck with that."

He waves goodbye as he heads up the driveway. As I'm heading home, a smile spreads across my face as I think about the success of the day. I also realize how happier I've been and pray that the others can see the change I'm starting to feel.

It isn't until I'm pulling in my driveway to see angry eyes following my car, that I know the change hasn't been seen yet.

Chapter Eleven

Wide eyed, I stare up at the ceiling and ignore the flashing numbers on my clock telling me how late it is. Tyler hadn't been as mad as I anticipated when I arrived home, but Millie was. She was sitting on my front porch as I pulled into the driveway, and I could tell she was upset. My first conclusion had been that it was about Kirk, but I was wrong. It was about me.

Turns out Kirk can't keep a secret. I will give him a little credit, he didn't tell her everything. In fact, he didn't tell her anything except that something was going on and that he couldn't tell her or else I would cut his balls off. And at this point, the chance of it happening has increased.

For over an hour, Millie chewed my ass out about how she thought we were friends, best friends, but that friends like that don't lie to one another. I kept trying to tell her I was doing it to protect her and that I was her friend, that I was sorry. In the end, I caved and told her everything. But by that point, she thought I was making things up, told me that wasn't funny and how she couldn't believe I would stoop so low as to conjure up some stupid story to try and pacify her.

I roll over onto my side, exhausted but unable to hush my thoughts. What was I going to do about Millie? Should I go beat in Kirk's head now or wait until morning? How could there be a coven right here, in our small population fifteen hundred town, and no one know nothing about it? Or did the police know about it but kept it quiet so as to not freak everyone out?

My phone buzzes on my nightstand, the light blinding me as I try and make out the name. Cooper.

Hey, you awake?

I bite my lip and contemplate answering him. Why not? It's not like I'm going to fall asleep anytime soon.

Yes. Too much on my mind.

Same here.

I stare at the screen and begin to stress about what to reply. I hate texts like this when you know the other person is expecting some kind of response, yet you have no idea what to say. Tapping at the keys, I'm about to go for a normal 'what's on your mind' reply when the screen beeps.

Can you meet me?

Instinctively, I look toward the door. Can I meet him? Tyler came home early from work, told me he was exhausted, and considering he has to be at the mill bright and early, I'm sure he's asleep.

Sure. Where?

You tell me. You know this town better than I do.

Thinking for a moment, I choose a place that is close to the same distance for both of us.

At the town square. Twenty minutes?

I get a smiley face in return and jump up from the bed to change. After sliding on my Chucks and taking a quick peek in the mirror, I turn to the window close to the oak tree and curse when I remember I had to tape the whole thing up after it got broken. Freaking Cooper and his lack of stealthy coordination. My stomach tightens when I realize I'm going to have to go downstairs to leave. I almost go to text Cooper I'm canceling, but with a hushed 'screw it,' I open my bedroom door.

In the last seventeen years, I don't think it has ever taken me this long to reach the front door, ever. And that includes those pesky toddler years. Every step I take, I pause and hold my breath to listen for movement from Tyler's room. When satisfied I've not been detected, I take another step. Once my hand finally hits the cold metal of the door knob, I'm out the door and running down the street with a sigh of relief. Next task at hand, getting back in.

The August humidity is still thick in the air. The street lights cast shadows along the sidewalks and I quicken my steps, unnerved and second thinking my decision again. *Really, Jo, sneaking out at night while being haunted by an evil spirit. Smart, real smart.*

Cooper is standing by one of several three pronged lamp posts that line the square, his fingers laced behind his head as he sways from side to side.

"Sure you're not tired?" I ask in greeting.

"I'm sure. You know tomorrow is going to suck, right?"

I chuckle. "Quit your bellyaching, and come on."

He follows without question, even when we reach the courthouse/police station and I knock aside the No Trespassing sign to get to the fire escape. I peer around the building to double check we haven't been spotted. It isn't until the old rusty metal ladder protests under my weight that he speaks up.

"Are you sure this is safe?"

I roll my eyes and keep climbing. "Safe? What can be classified as safe? Everything we do in life has a risk. Just getting out of bed each morning can be dangerous. It's not a matter to what is safe, Cooper, it's a matter of what are you going to allow to hold you back." I look down at him over my shoulder and smile. "You going to let some squeaking metal hold you back?"

Rising to the challenge I just dished, he starts to climb.

After hoisting myself over the top ledge, with Cooper falling right in step behind me, my breath is stolen by so many emotions.

"I can't believe they're still here," I whisper, walking over to the lawn chairs sitting on the other side of the roof. My feet get soaked from the small puddles that have formed on the flat roof. I run my hand along the torn cloth, remembering all the stolen nights spent up here with my friends.

"Are you sure it's okay for me to be here?" Cooper asks, digging his hands deeper into his pockets and scrunching up his shoulders.

At first I think he means because of the sign to keep out, and I start to give him crap for being so straight lined, until I see his perplexed face. His quiet tone has nothing to do with getting in trouble and everything to do with the affection of memories he sees in my eyes.

"It's fine. I promise." I gesture toward the lawn chairs. "Come have a seat and enjoy the illegal view."

He's hesitant at first, but then conceded and comes to join me. We both take long, relaxing sighs as we sit back and enjoy the moment of peace.

"I haven't been up here in a long time," I whisper and look out across to the square, the street lamps shining bright against the darkness of the mountains in the distance.

"It's beautiful," Cooper remarks. "Did you spend a lot of time here with Bryce?"

"Him. Kirk. Millie. Whoever needed a small reprieve in the middle of the night." I start laughing, thinking back to the one time we got caught. "Kirk—he's always been the loudest one of the bunch—had tagged along with Bryce one night. Bryce and I had just started dating, and he was pissed he had to bring his brother along with him. Me and Millie beat them here and had already made ourselves comfortable, with a beer already open, when we heard Kirk's scream. Seconds later something crashed into the dumpster with a loud bang and we rushed to see what the hell was going on."

I laugh again, causing tears to form and soak my lashes. "There was Kirk," I gasp between giggles, "hanging upside down, face all red. One of the rungs bolts had given under his weight about halfway up and caused him to slip. He's lucky his pants leg snagged the rusty metal instead of him falling on his head. I swear every dog in the neighborhood started barking and, of course, being on top of the police station didn't give him a chance to free himself before two cops barged out the back and caught him red-handed."

"Did you get in trouble?"

I wave my hand in the air. "We all got a warning, and the cops made a show of taking us all home and discussing the matter with our parents. No amount of hard scowls and chores deterred us from returning the next Friday night." I shrug. "When you live in a small town like this, you can't lose the few things you enjoy because a few people frown at you."

"Wow," he says and splays his hand on his chest. "That was deep."

I smile over at him. "Think I should submit it to Hallmark or something?"

He winces. "I'm not sure it's greeting card worthy."

I chuckle. I have to admit, I'm enjoying his company. A star twinkles and then dims, catching my eye as it continues the process over again. I stare up at it and feel a blissful peace settle over me. This, I've missed. That is until Cooper's pinky lightly brushes against mine and I flinch. Our chairs are close, but not that close. Did he do it on purpose?

Not wanting to dive into that thought pool, I look over at him and smirk. "So, tell me Mr. Chaser. What is the scariest thing that's ever happened to you?"

"What, you haven't had enough ghost stories for one day?"

Kind of, but it's one of the reasons I'm here, and it's all I know about him. "Then tell me something about you, something no one knows."

He shifts in his chair, obviously uncomfortable with my suggestion.

"There's not much to tell. All I've ever known, or had time for, is hunting nukpanas. When I'm not researching an area and chasing a lead, I'm listening to my sister tell me about what she's heard other chasers are up to." He shrugs. "I'm pretty lame."

"That can't be true," I prompt. "There must be something. Everyone has something they enjoy outside of what they have to do: sports, reading, watching trashy TV shows."

"Jada runs the remote when she has time, and personally, I could care less about the crap she watches. You would be surprised at the girl crap she watches. You've seen her cargo and combat boots style, not to mention the messy room. Discovering a girl like that sits around watching HDTV and Project Runway may sound ridiculous, but she does, a lot."

Thinking about it a minute, and remembering our conversation about our fantasized idea of a normal family life, something occurs to me about Jada. "Maybe that's the life she's always dreamed about. Like when you think about a nice house, with a picket fence and barking dog running through the grass. Makes sense to me."

Cooper looks thoughtful. "I guess, but if it is, she's doing a horrible job making it a reality. Like I said, you've seen her room."

I laugh, remembering the mess. "All right, enough about Jada. I want to hear about Cooper."

The tips of his ears turn red, a reaction I'm learning happens when he gets embarrassed. "I'm telling you, there's nothing."

I cross my arms, lean forward, and give him a hard look. "I don't believe that."

Looking up at the stars, he huffs. "I like to write."

Hmm, my interest has been piqued. "Stories or a journal?"

"Stories."

Before I can ask what kind, he continues.

"Most of them are about what we do, experiences we've had, but with a lot of…" he trails off, his cheeks taking on a blush this time.

This has to good. "With a lot of what?" I push, eager to hear his answer.

He covers his face. "I cannot believe I'm about to say this," he says, his voice mumbled by his hands. "Romance."

I sit up further, surprised. Why, I don't know. He's expressed his loneliness and dreams of a family away from the life he lives. So why not mix a bit of romance with the reality of his life? Makes sense, although I'm still a little surprised to hear it coming from him. Each day that I get to know him, I'm starting to see him more and more as a smart, strong headed guy. Someone who is brave enough to face the demons of the world but comfortable enough to sit back and eat pizza and tell jokes. Hearing about his dream life the other day had given me a glimpse of his soft side, but never did I think that softness went this deep.

"We talking boy meets girl and they kiss a few times, or we talking hard-core romance with some steam?"

After seeing that I'm not going to laugh my ass off at him, and that I'm intrigued helps him to relax. "Most are in the middle, but there are some with a little steam."

He shrugs again. "Living on the go has not only stolen any kind of normal life I've dreamt of having, but also normal teenage sexual angst. It might make me sound weak or lame, but I use words to live a life I can only dream of."

He doesn't say it, never has, but I can hear the rest of what he leaves out as if he said it aloud. He's lonely. I think about what I know of him and his family, the moving, the secret life and not being able to tell anyone. A life like that leaves no room for making friends, let alone romance or relationships. Jada probably feels the same way, which is why she is so protective of her brother. Like she said, he's all she has.

And while I've had a romantic relationship and many friends throughout my life, a place to call home, this last year has been a lonely one. I can't imagine how it must feel to have lived your whole life this way.

Whether it's the sadness I feel or the slight understanding of how he feels, I know there's one thing we have in common. Which is why when I reach over and take his hand in mine, intertwining our fingers, I don't feel shame or guilt. The gesture isn't because I feel sorry for him, it's because at this moment, and in many moments in the past, we've both felt alone. Now, here we are together, friends, who can confide in one another about things others don't understand or know about.

A smile tugs on Cooper's lips as he looks at our hands and then over at me. He squeezes his hand tighter around mine and settles back into his chair, no longer embarrassed about his confession. There's no reason to be embarrassed. He's human, with dreams and desires just like everyone else.

We sit under the night sky, quiet and enjoying each other's presence, until the clock on the square hits five. The faint light of morning starts to shine on the horizon, a light hue of blue that will soon give way to a bright and beautiful morning.

When we part and head for home, there's an unspoken gratefulness in Cooper's tone, as well in mine. It's nice to have someone to lean on when it all becomes too much, someone who's not going to look at you as if you are crazy and give lecture after lecture because they think they know the truth.

Tyler's truck isn't in the driveway when I get home and I know he's left for the day. It isn't until I get to my room and see the angry scrawl of his handwriting on a piece of paper lying on my pillow that all the peace I felt evaporates.

I'm going to kick your ass when I get home, and you better be here!

Oh, I'll be here all right. And when Tyler's done with his outburst, it's going to be my turn.

I pick up my phone and send a quick text to both Cooper and Millie explaining that I won't be at school today. Before crashing into oblivion, I send Cooper another text to meet me here with the rest of the newspapers at noon. If Tyler wants the truth, by god he's going to get the truth.

Chapter Twelve

"Are you sure this is a good idea?" Cooper asks again while popping the lid on the highlighter off and then on again. I reach over and take it from him, unable to take the annoying click any longer.

"It'll be fine." At least, I hope it will be.

The sound of the clock ticking on the wall jolts my nerves with every passing minute as I arrange and then rearrange the stories spread across the table.

It wasn't until 1949 that the town published its first newspaper, *The Dover Times.* The first murder published happened a day after they started publishing. What happened before that is anyone's guess.

Cooper scans over the first few publications again, and then after a few minutes, growls with frustration. "None of these stories give us a clue as to who we are dealing with, or why."

"What are you talking about?" I ask, not sure what he's getting at. We've highlighted all the deaths and can trace the pattern back for sixty years. How is that frustrating? It's proof that these are not mere accidents.

"It's not all about the deaths," he snaps, but when he sees my shocked expression, his face softens. "I'm sorry. I didn't mean how it sounded. The deaths do matter. I hate that they happened, of course. But I need to know more, Jo. Who this is. Why the spirit is so bent on vengeance. How the person died. Those are important facts. Facts we don't have."

"I didn't know it was important," I admit. Not once have I wondered those things. All I've cared about is stopping it. "Why does the how and why matter? Shouldn't stopping it be what we focus on, not its history?"

Cooper sits back and takes a drink of his coke, his face tight with a frown. "It might sound simple, find it, kill it. But it's not. Finding out how he or she died is an important part of figuring out how to kill it."

Before he can explain further, the sound of Tyler's truck pulling into the driveway alerts me. I look at Cooper with dread. "It's show time."

He looks a little sick, but resigned.

When Tyler walks into the house and sees us sitting at the table, several sheets of paper in front of us, he sighs and walks over to the counter and tosses his keys down. He doesn't say anything as he walks into the kitchen, or while he pours himself some tea, or while he leans on the stove and takes a drink. He acts as if we aren't even in the room, which does little to ease my nerves. He's mad, real mad.

Tyler slams his glass down on the counter when he's finished, and I flinch. Pissed doesn't even begin to describe him right now, and to be frank, it's scary and something I never like being prey to. Bracing his hands on the counter, he finally looks at us. "What's this about?"

So much for a great opening speech, that sucker done tucked its tail and is hiding in the deepest part of my brain, sucking its thumb.

"You wanted to talk," I say, and in one breath, one sentence, I'm able to find my dignity again and face off with him. "Isn't that what you wanted?"

"I said *we* need to talk, Jo. And you know I meant me and you only. What's *he* doing here?"

"Cooper is here because I asked him to be here. You want to talk, and so do I, though I expect what I have to say, you're not going to like." *Or believe, for that matter.* The more backup I have in this explanation, the better.

And right on time, there's a knock on the back door. I smile at Cooper as I stand and go to open the door. Jada's usual annoyed expression greets me, her arms crossed, but I smile anyway.

"Jada. How nice to see you."

"Shut up." Brushing past me, she joins Cooper at the table. When she starts to grab for one of the paper stacks, he slaps her hand.

"What," Tyler says, his voice full of warning. "is going on?"

"Have a seat," I instruct, as the back door opens again and in walks Millie and Kirk. *Okay, the gang is all here.* Seeing that Kirk is in the lead, I narrow my eyes at him. "You ever heard of knocking?"

"I never had to before," he says with a sneer.

"Oh jeez," I say and tap my chin. "I wonder what has made me change my mind about you being invited over."

"Moving on," Cooper says, giving me a pointed look.

He's right. We're not here to fight and bicker. We have more important things to deal with. Things that endanger all of us. And before all that, I have to figure out how to explain it all to my skeptical brother.

As if a shot of adrenalin has been pumped into my veins, my hands begin to shake and my stomach twists when I start to speak. *Yeah, like now is the time to start freaking out. Right when he's sitting in front of you. Smart, Jo!*

"There's a ghost haunting the overlook and killing innocent people every couple of years," I blurt out in one quick sentence.

Thank god, I can still breathe. I was sure with every word I said, I was going to pass out. Looking at the expressions on Millie and Tyler's face, though, kind of makes me wish I had passed out. I didn't get a lot of buy-in.

"Cooper," Jada hisses, obviously not happy that we are spilling their secret to more outsiders.

Cooper whispers they can talk about it later.

"I'm going home." Millie tries jerking her hand out of Kirk's, but he keeps a tight hold on hers and stays rooted in place.

"You need to listen, Millie," he says.

But it's not Millie I'm worried about, although I would like for her to believe me. It's why I invited her over here. I'm tired of all the secrets and am ready to get whoever will believe me on board. As much as I would love to have Millie by my side during this, it's Tyler who I'm waiting for an answer from. As soon as the explanation was out of my mouth, he hung his head and shook it. Despite the talk we had about the thing in my sketchbook, and his new profound outlook, it's obvious he doesn't believe me. He probably thinks this is my next step in losing all sanity.

He's slow to pick up his head, deliberate I think, and then zeroes in on Cooper. "You," he shouts, getting to his feet and grabbing the front of Cooper's shirt. "All this bullshit started when you started poking around. I'm going—"

"Take your hands off him, is what you're going to do or you'll have a size nine wedged in tight." Jada sits calm at the table, but I can tell, and know, she could be up and across the table in seconds.

She doesn't need to defend Cooper, though. As soon as Jada's finished talking, he grabs Tyler's hands, turning them up and out so that Tyler loses his grip on his shirt, then pushes him back as he stands.

"How ironic that you lay blame on me, when I'm the only who listens to Jo. Maybe if you had listened to her a year ago," he says through clenched teeth, stabbing his index finger into Tyler's chest, "she might have been able to heal by now."

"Tyler, please," I beg, "just listen. I have proof, look." I gesture to the papers. "We've also talked to Jesse Ford and about what happened to his sister in 1953. I promise all of you, we are not making any of this up." I pick up one of the stacks. "Please, look at these. I've highlighted the dates, locations, and names. Every single one of these you see here," I say, and point to all the papers on the table, "are deaths at the overlook that were considered accidents."

I walk up to Tyler, getting close and forcing him to look me in the eyes. "But it doesn't make sense. There's no way there could be that many accidents in one location."

"That's why they put up the rock wall. It's not—" Tyler starts, but I shake off his attempt at an explanation and interrupt.

"The wall hasn't stopped anything! The only thing capable of stopping it is them." I point to Jada and Cooper, who hold their heads high.

Tyler's eyes flick to Cooper and then do a small roam over Jada, a little too long. She appraises him in return and I swear when his gaze reaches her face, she smirks and raises a challenging eyebrow. What kind of challenge, I'm not sure, but I'd rather not find out. Cooper gives me his own appraisal and smiles, wagging his eyebrows in suggestion. *Please boy, you wish.*

"That just sealed the deal right there, let me tell you." He shakes his head. "I'm going to leave, and when I come back, I don't want anyone here but you, Jo. Understand?"

"You don't want to believe me?" I grab my backpack and yank my keys off the wall hook. "Fine." I storm out into the garage, hoping he follows. If he won't believe me, maybe he will believe Mason Edwards.

As I knew he would, Cooper follows me. After starting the engine, I pause long enough to see Millie scream something at Kirk before she runs out the back door, with him chasing after her. Jada leans over to whisper something in Tyler's ear before he runs toward the open garage door, with her following close behind. Seeing his keys in hand, I slam the car into reverse and dump the clutch.

"Angry?" Cooper asks.

"Nope," I answer and shift into first gear. "Determined." As I accelerate, I look back in my rearview mirror and am pleased to see Tyler's truck speeding down the driveway behind us, with Jada riding shotgun.

He follows along, lights flashing and horn blaring every so often for me to pull over, which I ignore. We make it past Jesse Ford's place when a sudden sick feeling overtakes my whole body. As we get closer to the overlook, the feeling gets worse.

"You okay?"

Must look like I feel. "I'm fine," I lie, then reconsider. "I think I'm going to be sick," I tell him, and start to pull over.

"Jo, no!" Cooper warns and it pulls me to attention.

Alarm makes the nausea worse when I realize where I was about to stop. The overlook. The headlights dart over the rock wall as Cooper grabs the wheel to keep us on the main road.

"It could be a trick." He runs his hands over my forehead, wiping at the sweat. "I'm right here with you, Jo."

Cooper continues to talk to me, telling me bits and pieces of his childhood. I don't understand the words. The only thing that registers with my mind is the sense of reassurance that he's still with me, that we are going to be okay.

When we reach the bottom of the mountain, I feel like I'm being pulled back into myself and away from the numbing fear I was captured in. After parking the Mustang, I get out and stumble to the creek to rinse my face. The cool water is nice against my clammy skin.

Cooper helps me to my feet and braces his arms around me so that we are chest to chest. He brushes the hair sticking to my face away and dips his head so I look at him.

"Hey, it's okay. You're okay."

"What happened? Was that the nukpana messing with me or something?" I ask, my muscles trembling from the tension that held me captive.

"First panic attack?"

"What?" I ask, breathless. "No. I mean, I've had a few before but nothing like that."

I don't know how long he's been doing it, but I notice his hand is running up and down my back, right along my spine, and I want to shiver all over again. This time for a different reason.

"There's different stages to fear and panic. What you just experienced is the worst stage you can reach before your body completely shuts down on itself."

How nice. "I felt like my heart was going to explode."

"The surest sign of all." He lays his hand on my chest. "But you survived and are back to normal."

Dust goes flying when Tyler pulls in behind us. "What's going on?" he asks, as he and Jada get out of the truck.

"Nothing," I explain and hurry back toward the car. "Just wanted to make sure you were keeping up."

Cooper rushes to my side before I can get my door open. "How about I drive?"

"Yeah... I don't think so." *Let some guy I've never seen drive before get behind the wheel of my prized Mustang? I think not.* It still bothers me to drive it, with memories assaulting me every so often, but to see someone else drive it would only make things worse.

The rest of the drive is uneventful. Dusk is starting to fall, causing the woods to appear a bit creepy. They used to not be, I never even thought twice about being afraid in the woods, but now... let's say creepy has taken on a whole new meaning. The simple word isn't anywhere near big enough to describe it. I'm thankful I'm not alone and have not only Cooper with me, but Tyler and Jada following close behind. Without that, I know for a fact I wouldn't be up here again. Not knowing what I know now.

"We're getting close," I whisper, more to myself than to Cooper. The road dips down toward the ford, just on the other side of where Mason lives. A dark shadow in the water catches my eye and I slam on the brakes as the tires reach the waters' edge. Tyler jerks to a stop to avoid hitting me.

I look back to see him stick his head out the window. "What's the matter?"

I shake my head, not sure myself, and get out of the car. "There's something in the water."

"I don't see anything," Tyler and Cooper both say.

It's close to dark, but there's still plenty of light left for me to see that something is under the water.

"It's right there." I point to the darker spot in the water. *Or maybe I am going crazy.*

"I see it," Jada pipes in. Thank god.

Tyler rubs the back of his head. "I don't see anything, and if your whole plan was to get me up here so you could spook me, lame try."

I roll my eyes. "You're so full of yourself. You should try taking a dump."

The water is chilly, even in late August after months of blaring heat, thanks to the natural springs that feed into the creeks and keeping them cool.

The water is only calf-deep toward the middle, which is why they named this place Phillip's ford. Philip was the man who first owned the land Mason now owns. No matter how dry all the others creeks are during the summer, this stream here stays steady. And when it floods, it doesn't take long for the excess to run off and for the levels to return to normal.

"What is it?" Tyler calls out when I pause.

I shrug. "I can't see anything. It's too dark." I take another step, needing a closer look, but when I do, my foot slips into a hole and I fall chest deep into the water. As I struggle for purchase with my feet, my hands flail, then grab onto something furry and stiff. Two pair of hands grab me by the arms and I'm hauled out in one fast tug. Cooper stands on one side, making sure I'm okay, while Tyler stands on the other and peers down into the depression.

"There's something in there," I say, breathless.

After hesitating for a second, Tyler reaches down and pulls. I scream and step back as he drags out the carcass of a black boar with a noose around its neck. Jada is still standing by the water's edge, but when she sees the boar, she begins to speak in hushed whispers. A prayer?

"What happened to it?" I ask, still stepping back but unable to take my eyes off of it. A noose is wrapped around the poor thing's throat, the rope so tight it's started ripping at its skin. All the boar's teeth are gone, as are its eyes, and when Tyler flips it over, there's a huge hole in its chest.

"Did someone take its heart?"

Neither Tyler nor Cooper answer me as they both stare wide-eyed down at the drenched, black boar.

"Yes," Jada whispers and pulls a big ass knife out from underneath her pants leg.

What the hell?

"They use them for their dumbass rituals. How long, Cooper?"

"Not long," he replies.

"Since...?" I prompt.

"Since they killed it," Cooper answers.

A gunshot rings through the air, killing all the questions and curiosity I had. Standing on the other side of the ford, barrel aimed at Tyler—the closest target—stands Mason Edwards. He pumps the shotgun, a warning to let us know it's ready and he's willing.

"I don't want no explanation or stories. Get back in your cars and go back to where you came from."

"This is a county road. It's public access," Tyler exclaims.

I flinch, whether because of the gunshot or the flying bark doesn't really matter. He's done his job of scaring me, and from the look of everyone else they feel the same. Mr. Edwards pulls two more shells from his blue flannel shirt pocket. For a man living this deep in the woods and totting a gun, he doesn't appear the crazed lunatic one might expect. Still, he's looking plenty dangerous right now.

"I won't warn you again."

"We just want to talk to you about the coven. Jesse Ford said—"

As if possessed, a blank stare comes across Mason's face, and his grip loosens on his gun. I blurted the bold explanation out hoping to get this reaction, and for him to know we aren't just kids fooling around up here. But when something rustles the leaves on the ground his hard expression returns.

"I won't be telling ya again. I promise, I'll fill ya full of lead."

I want to scream at him to quit waving his gun around, especially when he gestures toward the boar with it, aiming in both Cooper and Tyler's direction in the process. But being the smart girl I can sometimes be, and considering the situation, I keep my mouth shut.

"You think that boar there committed suicide after pulling its teeth and eyes out? It'd be best if you got on out of here. Don't want to end up the same way, I'm sure."

It's clear we're not going to get any answers out of him. I'll have to tell Mr. Ford about our pleasant encounter with his friend, and hope he will tell us what Mason refused to. Before I get into the car, Mason calls out.

"You'd be smart to stay in town. No need to be wandering in the woods at night, unless you're foolish."

I pull out behind Tyler and follow him up to the first ridge, where he pulls over and we all get out.

"What was that guy's deal?" Jada looks through the trees and down toward the bottom, as if she can still see Mr. Edwards and his gun.

"I don't know," Tyler replies, rubbing at the back of his neck. "I don't know much about him. I don't think anyone does. I've never seen or heard about him lashing out like that before, though."

Jada pulls out a small handgun from behind her back, checking the clip and putting the safety back on. "He may want to go back to a less confrontational way of life before he pisses someone off who can put a few holes in him before he can even think of putting his finger on the trigger."

My eyes widen, surprised, but not from her harsh warning. How many more weapons is she sporting, and where? Her black tank top with gray cargo pants look slim and sexy, and nowhere near lethal.

"You got a problem?" she asks, and takes a step toward me. I guess you could say I was staring a little too hard.

Tyler steps in between us. "That's my fault. Our parents raised us to believe cavewomen didn't exist anymore, so you can understand why she's confused. After the other day, I should have told her the truth."

Tyler is serious, real serious, challenging even. However, Cooper has lost it, laughing silently, leaning against the truck, his hand covering his mouth as his eyes water.

"Dude, you have got to tell me when you're going to diss Jada like that so I can record it. I've never seen anyone with the balls to stand up to her."

She steps closer to Tyler, their chests almost touching. "And for good reason."

Am I the only sane one here?

I step between Jada and Tyler. "I would suggest you two just whip them out and measure, but considering you lack one," I say, eyeing Jada, "how about we move on to the bigger problem at hand?"

I turn to my brother. "Tyler?"

There's no need to emphasize my questioning tone. He knows.

"A noose around a boars' neck and an old man waving a gun still isn't enough to convince me."

Figures.

"But, I will stick around and give you the benefit of a doubt."

"Why?"

"A couple of reasons," he says and looks from Cooper to Jada and then back again. "When you mentioned the coven, I saw the look on Mason's face. And Jesse is a respectable man." He wraps his arms around me and pulls me to him. "But the main reason is because you're my sister, and after my hot headed butt had time to cool off I realized what an ass I was being. I've stuck by you this far, might as well see where this crazy train goes."

"Funny," I say and push away from him.

"Plus, I have a promise to keep," he admits, referring back to his 'non-judgmental' promise. I smile, glad that he remembered.

After Jada suggests we go back to their house, we get back in the vehicles. The Mustang's engine roars to life, the rumble giving life to nature's silence, but not dissolving the unease. A deep, gut wrenching feeling as if we are being watched takes over, and I look out into the darkening forest. The last rays of the day are all that's left from the already setting sun, which isn't enough to help see what's hidden under the blanket of darkness that has set on the forest floor.

"Jo, you okay?" The concern in Cooper's voice takes me back to earlier, when he kept me from losing all control as I drove us through the mountainside. Maybe I shouldn't drive this time around after all. I'm all for protecting my car and keeping unpleasant memories at bay, but barreling off the side of a mountain isn't the way to accomplish it.

"You want to drive?"

His eyes widen. "Are you serious?"

I get out of the car, showing how serious I am. Cooper struggles out of the passenger side, eager. When he starts to walk past me, I grab his arm.

"There's one thing I need to know. You have driven before, right?"

Offended, he shakes his head and gets behind the wheel. I close my eyes, take a deep breath, and hurriedly force it out. It may sound stupid to some, but this is a big step for me. This car is not just any car to me, it's a part of my family history, a memory of what I used to have and a way to continue to remember. This car was part of some of the most important moments in my life. When I was five and grandpa took me for my first ride in it…, when he drove over to tell us grandma passed away…, the day he gave it to me..., and when I lost my virginity in the backseat, as Bryce held me tight in his arms.

Tyler pulls out onto the road, his truck lights flaring to life as he takes the hairpin bend in the road up ahead. Cooper glances at me, only for a second, and winks before dumping the clutch and stomping the gas as he shifts from first to second. Gravel kicks up as we drift around the bend, the stretch of road Tyler had been so careful to take at a safe speed.

I grab at my chest, sure that I've left my heart back there on the side of the road. "Stop!" I yell, whether from fear or anger, who knows or cares. No way in hell am I letting him drive my car like this! Looks like I'm screwed either way when it comes to the panic department.

Cooper slows down and smiles. "Sorry. I couldn't resist."

"Pull over now!" I insist.

"Jo, I promise I won't do it again. My ego is grounded, I won't let it out to play for a week." When he sees my doubt, he grabs my hand. "I promise, Jo."

The lights on the dash reflect on his face and allow me to see his intense expression. All the worry I had about my car vanishes and I nod, trusting him. *What the hell, Jo? Are you insane?* I ask myself, wondering where the girl went who would have clocked him one for being so reckless. Confused, I turn to stare out the window.

The feeling of being watched returns. Only the faintest of outlines are visible now, with the only shadings being dark against faint light. I keep my eyes on the passing blurs of trees, sure that eyes—or a lot of eyes—are watching us. As we go around another curve, a deer crosses the road and Cooper slams on the brakes. I say a silent thank you god, thankful we missed the deer, for its sake and my car's.

It's easy to distinguish something walking on four legs versus two, tall versus short, long, pointed ears versus something that has ears you can't see. So when I see the shadow of something running on two legs toward us, no other visible features under the cloak of night, I scream for Cooper to gas it. It's clear that is no deer.

Without question, he does as asked, leaving behind dust in the red glow of the taillights. And also what I'm sure is a person, standing in the middle of the road, watching us disappear.

Chapter Thirteen

Dry. It's the only thought I can comprehend as I get to my feet, my mouth feeling like I've sucked on cotton all night. *Need water.* I laugh at myself as I run my hand over my face and quietly walk down the hall. What am I, a zombie or something? *Thirsty. Me need water.* Maybe Tyler was wrong. Maybe cavewomen still do exist, but only when we're in our hazy, sleep-deprived state.

After getting a bottle of water out of the fridge, I shut it and lean back on it for support. After getting a long drag and feeling satisfied, I put the empty bottle on the counter. A scream rips through me when the breakfast nooks light comes on, revealing Tyler sitting and looking at me.

"You jerk." I mean for it to come out in a more heated tone, but I fail, my throat now sore from screaming. I grab another bottle of water as he laughs, and join him at the table. "You scared the crap out of me," I tell him, and slap him on the arm.

Seeing that he's in the same clothes he wore earlier gives away that he hasn't been to bed yet. I glance at the clock to see that it's 3:15 in the morning.

"What are you still doing up? And sitting in the dark?"

"I heard you coming and shut the lights off." He shrugs. "Didn't want to miss the opportunity."

"To what, give me a heart attack?"

"Yeah." He smiles, but only for a moment. "I couldn't sleep. I've been reading over these." He gestures toward the pile of copied newspapers.

I had noticed them again when I first sat down but didn't think anything about it, since they've been sitting here since early this morning.

"You know it's not like me to jump on the conspiracy theory bandwagon."

I do know that. He's always thought little of what people say is the truth, and always relied on facts. Never has he speculated about anything outside of what he's read or been told. No, what if's or maybe's. It's what made growing up with him so fun. I was always the one speculating and getting into heated debates with him for hours, which always ended with both of us rolling our eyes at each other, followed by some name calling, before we walked away.

"But I think you're on to something. If it wasn't for these," he says and picks up one of the stacks, "I doubt I would be admitting it. But I looked over all the stuff you highlighted. This is pretty odd for such a small town, and especially since it keeps happening in the same area." He rubs his hands over his face, and I hear the scrape of his two-day-old stubble brushing against his skin. His eyes are heavy and bloodshot from lack of sleep.

"So you believe me?" I'm shocked to hear him finally admit it. I thought it was going to take a lot more to convince him.

"I'm not sure I'm fully on board with you yet, you know the ghost stuff, but there is something going on that's for sure."

I'm stunned, amazed at what I'm hearing. Not because Tyler is small minded and I've achieved some amazing hurdle, but because he's here with me now, understanding on some level that this isn't all coincidence. That means the most to me.

"You know you don't have all the facts, right?" Before I can explain that I know that, he continues, "The first newspaper was published in," he snaps his fingers, as if that will help him remember, "the late 1800's I think. It ceased publication before the 1900's. I don't remember the exact years. The next paper published wasn't until 1926, but its funding was cut and there was no choice but to suspend publication in 1930."

"That's a random fact to know off the top of your head," I remark.

"I had to do a history paper in high school. I chose to do it on the founding council and had to do some digging through the libraries archives."

I pick up the oldest date of the papers: June 8, 1949. "That's a pretty large gap," I mumble.

"Meaning we don't know how far back this goes."

"Or why," I add, thinking about what Cooper said. "Tyler, we need to know why this thing started killing people at the overlook. Cooper said it was important in figuring out how they kill it, but also..." I take a deep breath, centering myself. "I need to know."

Tyler grabs my hand. "We'll figure it out." He doesn't promise, but I can hear it in his firm tone. "I'll go to the county library today while you're at school, see if they have any records of the original papers."

"What about work?" Tyler hardly ever misses work. Come to think of it, I don't think he's ever missed a day.

He shrugs. "It won't hurt for me to take a few sick days."

"If you think it's okay," I say and stand. "Oh and if the county library doesn't have any records of the earlier papers, check with the Dover library again. Cooper might not have thought to look past the current newspapers publication."

After that, I urge Tyler to bed before crawling back into mine. Sleep comes easy, knowing I have him on my side now, and I'm surprised by my blaring alarm clock in what feels like only minutes later. Ugh! After going through the five grief stages of 'get your butt out of bed', I get dressed as quietly as I can so as not to wake Tyler, grab some pop tarts, and head out the door.

Not feeling like driving today, I start walking. I know better than to expect Millie to be outside. I haven't seen or heard a word from her or Kirk since yesterday afternoon. I don't blame her. If she was to walk up to me today in school, slap me in the face, and walked away calling me a freak, I still wouldn't blame her. After all the crap I've put her through, she's probably thinking this is another stage, another layer, to my self-destruction.

I do miss her, though. Miss her yelling at me, and urging me to smile, which she normally succeeded at doing by telling some lame joke or tidbit of gossip. It felt weird having Cooper to talk to now, a guy I had hated over a week ago, but who is the only person at school who will talk to me. A week ago, that person had been Millie. If she wasn't so mad at me, she'd be proud. She may still be happy for me, but in a sour way.

It's for the best she's not here. As much faith as I have in her, I don't know that she could handle this. She has too kind of a spirit to be tarnished by the evil we are uprooting.

"Hey Vanguard, want a lift?"

I was so deep in my thoughts, I didn't even hear the Jeep pull up. I turn to find Kirk and Millie pulled over next to me. Kirk holds the door open for me. I'm surprised to see the hopeful smile on her face, and get in, thankful for the chance to get to talk to her. Kirk shuts the door, bows, and turns to go. "Ladies," he says, waving at us.

Okay, weird. "Are you not coming?" I ask.

He turns back to us. "I thinkest thouest protestest too much. Me havest to get to schoolest."

I'm killing Mr. Miles for thinking a Shakespearean semester was a great idea. So will Mrs. Holt once she has a school full of students trying to back talk with too many 'ests and not enough brains.

"You're horrible at that, ya know." I yell out the window.

"Jealous!" he proclaims, hand over his heart.

"Not in this lifetime or any other."

Millie pulls away from the curb.

"Whatever, Freak!" he hollers.

I flip him the bird, to which he replies in kind. Rearranging my backpack in my lap, I say, "This should be an interesting semester."

Millie laughs and turns on Water Street. The opposite of the direction we need to be going.

"Where are you headed?"

"I have to pick up donuts for the State something or another board that is visiting campus today." We pull up in front of the market and she kills the Jeep. I think she's about to get out when she turns toward me instead of the door. "I'm sorry I ran out on you yesterday," she rushes.

"Don't even sweat it. I would have done the same I'm sure." I try reassuring her but it doesn't work.

"No, you wouldn't. You're strong, Jo. So much stronger than you give yourself credit for. I've seen you face down situations you didn't want to deal with, with your head high, shoulders strong, and determination in your eyes. I've never seen you back away from anything. Except," she pauses, tears filling her eyes, "yourself."

You know those lovely moments when you're put on the spot and know what's being said about you is the truth, yet you don't know what to say or how to act. Yeah, those moments, I hate with a passion. Who likes admitting their faults and talking about their weaknesses? I know I sure as hell don't.

"Okay, I agree, but can we not talk about me right now? I want to know if you believe what I was trying to tell you guys before you rushed out of the house like your ass was on fire."

She sets back and stares out the windshield. "Kirk talked to me about it. He told me what he knew. Jo, I'm going to be honest with you, I don't know that I can believe what you guys are suggesting."

"Is it a religious reason or sanity reason?" I ask, knowing her faith is a big part of what makes Millie, well, Millie.

"I think both, but mainly the sanity. I don't know all the mysteries of the world. Who does? But I do know that if you need me, I'm there. And if you prove me wrong, you get to say told you so for the rest of our lives and never will I doubt you again."

"I wouldn't say never."

After helping Millie deliver the donuts, I'm dismissed to class without even an invitation to enjoy one of the delicious glazed delights. *Figures.* The rest of the morning goes by in a blur. I feel like I'm sitting still, while my mind zones in on a million questions that have nothing to do with what the teachers are rambling on about.

Those questions are intensified when I notice Cooper isn't here today. Where is he? I check my phone, but see no messages from him. I send him a quick text, asking if everything is okay. Between obsessively checking my screen and wondering what Tyler, and now Cooper, are up to, I'm going crazy.

It isn't until Mr. Bradly sends me to the office for sassing, that I decide I've had enough for one day. I need to go home. Mrs. Holt scowls when she sees me walk into the office. *Oh, just wait. You'll have a permanent dent between your eyes before the year is out.*

"Ms. Vanguard, what a surprise." Her voice laced with sarcasm.

"Why, yes, yes it is," I reply, with as much sarcasm, if not more, and the biggest fake smile I can muster.

Shaking off the pretenses, she sighs. "Tell me what happened so we can get on with our day."

"Nothing much. Mr. Bradly asked me a question, I wasn't paying attention, so I said 'why don't you tell me, then we both can know', to which he sent me to the office."

"Ms. Vanguard, that mouth of yours is going to get you in a lot of trouble."

Is that supposed to be slam? Didn't feel like one.

"You've got three days of lunch detention."

"Yeah," I drawl. "About that. I'm going home right now and I don't know when I'll be back, but we can start my punishment when I return."

"Do you have a note?" she asks, full of authority.

Ugh!

"Nope," I answer, adding a pop to the p for emphases.

"Then I'm afraid you cannot leave school grounds. You know the policy, all enrolled students must have legal guardians or those requested by the guardians' permission by note, email, or in person before you leave school property."

God, she sounds like she's reciting the handbook word for word.

"I know that, but I'm still leaving."

Mrs. Holt gets to her feet. "Ms. Vanguard, if you leave this office without your brother's permission, you will—"

"Be in big trouble with my legal guardian, yeah, I get it." I wave her off and turn to exit the door. "His number is in my file if you need to call him," I say over my shoulder before the door clicks shut and I head for the parking lot.

It being the first day of September has made no difference to the blistering sun. It's still glaring, still hot, and way too damn humid. By the time I make it home, a heavy line of sweat causes my shirt to stick to my back, while my hair sticks to my face. Tyler's truck isn't in the driveway so I assume he's at the library. I look down to check my phone again to see if Cooper has called or texted, and almost knock over a plant sitting in front of the door. That's odd. Anyone who knows me and Tyler knows that we can't take care of plants. Proof is the flower pot hanging from the porchs roof with dead brown leaves hanging over the side.

The plant on the porch is green and luscious, with the buds of yellow flowers about to bloom. A yellow rose bush, maybe? Clipped to the pot is a note.

Don't come looking for death.
It will find you one day, on its own, on its own terms.
If you stay away, it won't take you until you're old and ready to go.

Death threats? Charming.

Chapter Fourteen

Doesn't yellow mean friendship?

I send the message and put the rose bush as far away from the house as possible. I may be overreacting and if so, no reason to kill the poor thing yet.

Yes, but what kind of friend would leave you a note like that? Millie sends back.

That's what I was wondering.

Maybe Mrs. Holt sent it express after I walked out of her office.

Honey, express is fast but not that fast.

True, but she could have sent them before I was sent to the office. The old buzzard never has liked me.

I still can't believe you stormed out of her office like that.

I didn't storm. I reply, a little defensive. *I glided. There's a difference.*

Not in her book.

Can you really say 'her book'? I think 'her sentence' fits better.

?

Her theory to life is summed up in one sentence. Be a bitch, act like a bitch. Her sentence.

Weirdo

Maybe. But you love me anyway.

She sends me a smiley face and I toss the phone aside on my bed and pace around my room, wondering where Tyler and Cooper are. I've texted and called both of them only to get nothing in return from either one of them. I wonder if my brother drives himself this insane when he doesn't hear from me or if I'm worse than he is.

I go to check out the window again to see if Tyler is pulling in the driveway, you know, because I may not be able to hear his big block V8. (Insert eye roll) Seeing that the grey pavement still holds no vehicle, I pick up my phone for the hundredth time and call him.

"Hey this is Tyler, leave me a message."

"I hate you. Seriously, call me."

I hang up and then proceed to call Cooper, and when it goes to voicemail, I leave the same message. Why are they not answering?

It isn't until almost three o'clock when Tyler shows up, with Jada riding shotgun. Unexpected doesn't even begin to describe my surprise. It's clear they hit it off better last night than I thought they had.

As I head downstairs, I begin to contemplate a relationship between Jada and Tyler. Lord knows it would do him some good to have someone to smile about and talk to regarding his life problems. I know he doesn't talk to his friends much about it, he's too proud. But with someone he really cares about, he may begin to open up.

The problem is, I'm not sure Jada is the right girl to do that with. Jada may have a humorous side, I don't know. But if she does, she keeps that sucker under lock and key.

Aside from that, there's the issue of her living arrangements. While talking to Cooper I discovered that this is the first time he's ever attended public school, and it was only so he could infiltrate the kids who were around Bryce. A part of me thinks there was more to it than that, as did the blush on the tips of his ears as he confessed to never going to school. They never stayed in one place long enough for him to enroll and Jada said it would raise suspicion if they moved so much. Homeschooling was the easier of choices, as were avoiding relationships.

It may not be my business to judge what's going on between the two of them, but it is my job to look after my brother. Then again, as much as it gags me to think of it, a fling may not be such a bad thing, for either one of them. I've had sex, know of the rush and happiness it can bring, and it's been a long time since I've seen my brother come home with a smile of satisfaction.

I get to the bottom of the stairs as the front door opens, and I shake away any thoughts of what might or might not be happening between Jada and Tyler. I think we have a little more to worry about than who is dipping their wick where.

"Where have you been?" I scold. "I've been calling and texting you for hours."

He holds up his phone. "It's dead. I forgot to charge it last night."

Walking into the kitchen, he sets a manila folder down on the counter and plugs in his phone. Jada comes in a few seconds later, and gives me her usual once over.

"Have you seen Cooper?" she asks.

I want to rip her face off. *Wait, why?* "No," I answer.

She walks off into the living room, leaving me alone with my brother. Good, that gives me time to interrogate.

"So, you and Jada," I prompt.

"Me and her, what?" he asks, an innocent look on his face.

"Oh, come on. You and Jada, as in you and Jada, or you and Jada, as in not you and Jada."

He rubs his hand over his freshly shaven face. *Cleaning up, are we?*

"Get to the point, Jo."

"You like her?" I ask, getting to the point as asked.

"Not now," he replies and points to the envelope. "Aren't you more interested in what we found?"

Hell, yes. As I open the envelope, he begins to clue me in on their findings.

"The county library had records from 1926 until 1930 that reported three deaths during that time. The librarian said that all records before that time had been lost in a fire."

I set down in the chair next to him. "Was there anything that might indicate who died, or why?"

"No," he says, his eyes drooping. "The first publication of the paper only highlighted the completion of the roadway, funding for a school, and the death of a boy who fell from the overlook."

My shoulders slump. My hopes for finding something in those records had been high. "So we're no closer to an answer than we were before, except for finding out that this started way before we had thought. How has no one noticed before?" It comes out as a question, but I'm not questioning it, not really. Jesse Ford knows. Mason Edward knows. I'm sure if we were to start asking, we would discover more who speculate, but who have never said anything. Why hasn't a proper investigation been done? It almost seems as if the town officials have been hiding this for almost a century. Why?

"I don't know, Jo. I'm beginning to wonder if—"

He's cut off by a knock at the front door. Jada rushes to answer it and in walks Cooper. She's quick to lay into him.

"Where have you been? You've been gone since early this morning."

"Don't worry about it. I'm here now, aren't I?" He brushes past her and goes to get a bottle of water out of the fridge.

Whoa. This is so not like him. He's been ignoring both of us all day and now has an attitude about it. I give him a questioning look which he ignores, and drains his water. If Jada and Tyler weren't in the room I would bug the crap out of him until he talked to me. Playing nice, I ignore my curiosity and turn back to Tyler.

"You're beginning to think what?"

He shakes his head like it was a stupid thought. "Nothing. I'm going to go try and talk to Mason again tomorrow. I would go tonight but I am beat." He gets up and goes to grab his partially charged phone. "Pizza?"

I nod, and while he's ordering I fill Cooper in on what Jada and Tyler found, which amounts to little more than zero.

"Is it really necessary to find out who this spirit is and how they died? Why can't you get rid of it and figure it out later?"

Clearly my question annoys him because he gets up from the table and walks to the door. "I gotta go."

"Are you serious?" I exclaim. My answer is the door slamming shut.

I turn to Jada. "What's his deal?"

"You." She cocks her hip to the side, crosses her arms, and narrows her eyes in on me. "Ever since he met you, he's been acting different."

Sure. Blame me. "Then why is he ignoring you?"

"Because last night after you left we had a fight. He had this dumb love struck grin on his face and I brought him back to reality."

"Which is?"

"You're not ready to move on, that you're still hung up on your ex and not willing to give him the time of day. More importantly, that when we finish this job we will be leaving again like we always do, heading out on the road to find our next case. It's what we do."

I jump up, outraged. "He doesn't have to live this life if he doesn't want to. He's a grown man."

"He is," she says and comes to stand inches from me. "But tell me that you are ready to give him what he wants. Tell me, no tell *him*, that he has a chance."

Cold bucket of reality over the head, anyone?

Tyler is off the phone now, and has clearly heard our conversation. He gives me a sympathetic look, which I don't like. He knows the truth, as well as everyone else, including me. I'm not ready. People who are ready don't feel guilt, don't live in the memories they cherish with someone else. They don't compare past and present, or wish the other person was still here. They allow themselves to move on, to accept what can't be changed, and try. The other person may never compare to how they felt about a past love, but they give them everything they can, with no shame.

I'm only starting to forgive myself and try to mend bridges between those I've put through so much. I can't do that while constructing a new bridge I'm not ready to cross, because if I do, it'll all come tumbling down to a pile of lies.

Finding no defense, I storm out of the house the same way Cooper did. Tyler rushes out after me and I stop.

"Where are you going?"

"For a walk." I look over my shoulder. "I'll be back. I promise. Save me some pizza."

I only make it as far as the park before the sweltering heat gets to me. As I push myself back and forth on the swing, I stare out across the park, dazed in a world of thought.

In the beginning, this was all about the nukpana and finding out why it was killing every few years so we could stop it. Now it's turned into a shit storm of problems. Millie getting mad at me and then trying to grasp the truth to help. Kirk playing nice so he can help. Tyler getting pissed until I told him the truth, then he relented and started to help. All of which leads them to give me questioning looks every so often, like 'are we doing this because we believe it or because we care about Jo?'

Then there's Cooper. He's the one who has been most helpful. The one who has listened when no one else could or would understand. The one who is only doing what he's done his whole life, his job, to stop this thing. Yet, he may be the one who gets hurt in the end. I don't want to do that to him. But what else can I do? Lie? Say that I feel the same way? No. That's not moral, nor is it the way I would want to be treated. I will not be the type of person who lies and gives false hope to someone to spare their feelings, because in the end, it only makes things worse.

When Millie pulls into the park and comes to join me on the swings, I'm not surprised.

"Figured I would find you here."

"Yeah, after looking in a few other key places first I'm sure."

"Thank god we don't live a big town. Tell me what's wrong, Buttercup."

I let my thoughts spew out of my mouth, everything, even down to Tyler and Jada.

"How did all the attention go from ghosts to all this crap?" I ask, still at a loss.

She looks thoughtful for a minute before she answers. "Because we're human, and filled with all these icky emotions that can screw up even the most important of tasks."

"Amen to that."

"What's your plan?"

It isn't until later when I'm sitting alone in my room that the answer comes to me, and I text the last person in the world I thought I would be asking for help.

Meet me at 11:00 at the end of my street. Drive your truck.

I have no worries that Kirk will be able to sneak away. Since Bryce's death, his dad has become a walking zombie, working long shifts, drinking beer until he can't function, then passing out in his recliner. His mom is on so many depression pills she's barely able to get out of bed every morning. I hated hearing the details when Tyler had told me, but I didn't expect anything less. I know the loss of loving someone I care about with my whole heart, but never can I imagine the pain of losing a child.

OK.

Guilt churns my stomach and chest as I sneak past Tyler's room, where I can hear him snoring away. It hits again when I receive a text message from Cooper saying we need to talk. I know he should be the one going with me tonight, but after learning what I did today, I'm thinking the less time we spend together, the better.

I reach the end of my street to find Kirk already waiting for me.

"Where to?" he asks, as I climb up into the truck.

"The overlook."

He hesitates, not that I blame him. When I'm sure he's about to try and talk me out of it, he puts the truck in gear and drives out of the city limits.

~

My plan isn't to die tonight, not in the least bit. But as I'm walking through the woods, sticks and leaves crunching under my tennis shoes, I have to wonder if I'm going to make it out of here alive. The panic I felt the night before is nothing compared to what I felt when Kirk pulled over on the side of the road near the overlook. I was sure that the highest level of panic had consumed me and I was doomed to succumb to my own fears.

It was Kirk who pulled me back this time. The friend I had before Bryce's death was there, rubbing my back and making sure I was okay. It must have scared him because before we parted ways, which was a stupid idea, he apologized for everything he had done to me. His voice had cracked when he admitted to how lost he felt without Bryce, how I was a daily reminder of his brother, and that he hated me for it. It wasn't that he ever thought I killed Bryce, he said, it was that I never let him heal from the loss of losing Bryce.

I understood that. I felt the same way when I looked at Kirk. Well, maybe not hatred but the sight of him brought back the pain. Pain I wanted to avoid but couldn't, no matter how hard I tried. After hugging and telling him we would work through it, we split up, him going south of the overlook while I went north. What we were looking for was anyone's guess.

I've never seen a coven in action before, or met anyone who was a part of a coven, that I know of anyway, so I have no clue what to keep an eye out for. A part of me keeps asking if they are even up here in the woods or do they congregate somewhere else? Do they live together all the time? Surely there isn't a need for a ritual every night. I don't know the answers, but I couldn't sit around anymore. Reading over the stories of those who had died up here made it that more depressing and there was a fire deep in my gut that needed action, that needed answers, but mostly needed it to stop. I didn't want to wake up one morning to learn of another death, to see another memorial, while we continue to pore over old records that tell us nothing.

Glancing at my phone's screen and seeing I've been out here for over an hour, I turn to double back toward the truck. I don't know why I thought coming out here, at night no less, would give me any answers, but it seemed reasonable. This is where it all started and where it continues to happen. My memory of figures dressed in black cloaks now has a name: it has to be the coven. The white mist apparition is the nukpana. But where are they now?

As I walk back, I think about all the ghost hunters I've watched on television and what they look for when hunting. One episode comes to mind, in which they discover skulls and bones, hanging from trees with thick, brown twine. Some skulls were even adorned with hair, cloth, feathers, teeth, and more. Whether that crap was true or not, I don't know, but considering I don't have anything else to go on, I'll give it a shot.

Shining my flashlight up into the trees, I keep an eye out for anything that looks suspicious. An owl hoots at me before flying off, not liking the invasion. Bird and squirrel nests are all I see, and by the time I reach the truck, I feel foolish. *Way to go, Jo. You've accomplished nothing but giving yourself a crick in the neck.*

Kirk and I had agreed to meet back in an hour, but he isn't at the truck when I return. Turning off my flashlight, I look in the direction he went and hope to see his light. Of course, I see nothing but darkness. Tired from the long walk, I go to open his tailgate, not wanting to sit in the stuffy cab without the AC running. It makes a loud screeching noise, due to the rust, before settling on its braces. A shiver wracks my body, but I ignore it, thinking it's the sound that jolted my nerves.

Turning so my butt is against the edge of the tailgate, I place my hands on the cool metal so I can pull myself up. My stomach tightens, not from using my muscles to heft myself up, but from the fear that spreads through my body as I look across the road. Tears brim my eyes as I look into the light red mist-like eyes of the nukpana. I try to scream, but my mind ceases to work as that all-consuming panic rushes through me again.

"Jo! Get in the truck! Now!"

My heart hammers and tears stream down my face as I look from the nukpana to Bryce. He's transparent but there once again, concerned and fearing for my life.

"Please, Jo," he begs. "Get in the truck."

From the corner of my eye I see the nukpana moving toward me. My mind and body get on board with one another again, and I jump from the tailgate and rush around the side of the truck. I jump inside, lock both doors, and hug my knees to my chest. *Is this really going to work?*

It's a ghost. They can move in and out of places, right? They're freaking transparent.

"It's okay."

I scream in surprise and slam my body against the door. I don't know if it's the hurt or regret on his face, but I respond and relax.

"I'm sorry," he whispers. "I'll go."

"No, wait. I need a minute," I say, breathless, trying hard to not hyperventilate.

He nods, understanding. It's not like I'm running into some old flame here on the street. This is Bryce, who died a year ago, taking my heart with him, sitting beside me. Not an easy thing to accept.

"Am I safe?"

He nods. "I won't hurt you."

"I... know that. I mean from him." I gesture toward the window and then make the mistake to look. Standing, floating, whatever, from the truck is the nukpana, the monster that has caused so much pain.

"Yes," Bryce answers. "He can't cross into anything that belongs to something living."

"But you can?" I question.

"My intentions are pure. His aren't. Living energy can feel that."

Interesting. And here I thought that only worked on vampires. There's a thought I've never considered. What else lurks in the world? *Focus, Jo.* Right.

Doing my best to ignore the monster peering inside, I turn back to Bryce. And let me tell you, that is a hard feat. I thought looking at the thing was hard, but turning my back and knowing it's standing right behind me is almost impossible. Seeing Bryce helps me manage.

Asking how he's been doesn't seem quite right, and I struggle with what to say. Thankfully, he does it for me.

"You look great."

"Thanks," I reply, and bite my tongue when I go for the 'so do you' instant response.

"Jo, it's okay. It's just me. I know I'm a ghost. I know I'm dead. Nothing you say is going to offend me." He pauses and looks to my hands digging into one another on my lap. "What hurts, though, is seeing you so sad. I hate it."

All my nervousness goes out the window, figuratively of course. No way am I opening that damn thing.

"How can I not be sad? You're not with me anymore."

"I know, baby, but listen. Every single person on this planet loses someone at one point or another. In order to survive, to honor their memory, you have to keep going, and live. I haven't seen you but twice since the accident last year, but that's all I need to see to know that you've put yourself through hell. And as harsh as this sounds, I would trade all the time we had together, give it up, just to know you lived a full happy life. I don't want to be the burden that keeps you from living, Jo."

Tears sting at my eyes and I have to fight to speak. "You are the best thing that has ever happened to me, how can I be happy that you're gone? Or live with the guilt, knowing it was my fault."

"It wasn't your fault, babe. It was that thing's. No, don't look at it. Look at me. It was his fault. How many times had we come up here before that night and nothing happened? It had nothing to do with you, sweetie. And anyone, I mean anyone, who says others wise don't know their ass from a hole in the wall."

I chuckle, loving that he can still make me laugh.

"Do you know what happened to it? Why he haunts this valley?"

"No," his passive voice tells me he's lying, as does his face.

"Bullshit," I challenge. "Please, tell me. I know people who can stop him and set you free."

"You mean that hunter?"

Oh, damn. "Bryce, it's not what you think." *Never in my life would I have thought I would be defending myself to a ghost.*

He smiles. "And what do I think?"

"Seriously, he's only a friend who was requested here to stop this thing. It's what Cooper and his sister, Jada, do. It's their job. Can you believe there's a job for that?"

"Don't deflect," he says, smiling. "Cooper, huh?"

I open my mouth, ready to defend myself again, but he waves me off.

"I'm messing with you. You're so cute when you get flustered." He loses all joking manner about him and looks out the window, pensive. "You swear that you will get help and not do anything on your own?"

"I swear."

"But see, how can I believe you when you came up here tonight?"

"I brought your brother!" As soon as I say it, I know it's a poor defense.

Bryce knows it too. "Yes, my poor clear-minded brother. He's so reliable. Tell me, where is he now?"

I close my eyes. "I don't know," I admit.

"And you expect me to—"

"Bryce, please," I plead.

"All right," he concedes, and I smile, excited to be getting some information. "His name was Walter T. Samuels."

A light flashes across the windshield and we both look to see Kirk coming toward the truck. We aren't the only ones who notices, either.

"You get his ass in this truck and get off the mountain. Do you hear me? Go to the hunters and free us, Jo. I love you." He makes likes he's going to kiss me, realizes he can't, and then disappears with determination set on his face. I catch a glimpse of Bryce ramming into the nukpana, now known as Walter.

Reaching over, I unlock the door and open it. "Hurry!" I scream. "Come on, Kirk. Hurry!"

The bobbing of the flashlight sways faster as he begins to run. When he reaches the truck, he jumps inside and starts it without question. I watch behind us as Kirk gasses the truck and we lurch forward. I pray I see Bryce again, but once the overlook disappears out of sight, I turn around a say a prayer for his safety.

"What happened?" Kirk asks, frantic.

"Walter T. Samuels is what happened. Now, we need to figure out why."

Chapter Fifteen

The first light of morning seeps into the room, and I stand and stretch my stiff muscles. After Kirk dropped me off, I came straight to my room and got to work, but no matter how many different ways I worded Walter's name along with the town's name in the search engine, nothing came up. Absolutely nothing!

Needing a break, I walk downstairs, decide against juice, and go for the coffee instead. Tyler walks down a few minutes later, still sporting his pajamas and bed head. I pour him a cup and add a spoon of sugar, knowing by the drowsiness on his face he needs it.

"Late night?" he asks as he takes a sip.

I'm sure I've got that whole deer in the headlights look right about now. "What makes you ask that?" I manage to keep my voice smooth, my expression passive.

Another sip. "You're still wearing the clothes you had on yesterday." He looks down at the paper. *Busted.*

"I called Kirk last night."

He snaps his head up. "Kirk?" he asks, like he heard me wrong. "The guy who lives right down the street and who you've been avoiding for the last year, Kirk?"

"That'd be him." I sit down at the table and take the sports section.

Wiping the dumbfounded look off his face, he takes another sip of his coffee. "Where did you guys go?"

Honesty? Lie? How should I choose? Seeing where the secrets got me last time, I go with the truth. "The overlook."

Tyler spews his mouthful of coffee all over me and the table. "You better not have said what I think you just said," he growls, wiping his mouth.

"What does it matter at this point? It's over and done with, and I've got work to do. By the way, do you have Jada's number?"

"What? No."

Liar. "Okay. I'll keep researching on my own and if I can't find anything I'll give Cooper a call later." I start to get up, but Tyler grabs my arm.

"What's going on, Jo?"

I bite my lip, worried he will think I'm lying. "You won't believe me."

He gestures to my chair. "Try me. I've stuck around this long, haven't I?"

Yes, he has, which is a lot more than I can say for those who should have—my parents.

Why do I keep doubting him? Looking at him and the care in his eyes as he waits to hear what I have to say makes me sad. Not because I think he won't trust me, but because I've held him back for so long, all because of our parents and because of the pain of loss I felt. In the back of my mind I still keep waiting, scared that I'll wake up one morning and there will be a note just like the one we found that morning we discovered our parents had bailed.

I grab his hand. "I'm sorry."

Talk about confusing the hell out of someone. Poor Tyler.

"For what?"

"For always holding you at arms-length and thinking the worst was going to happen. I've wasted so much time," I admit and hang my head.

"It may have taken you longer than others, and you need to understand you're still going to feel sadness, but this is your chance, Jo. This is your eyes being opened and your time to grab a hold of life and live."

Tears seep into his shirt as I hug him close. "I saw Bryce last night," I whisper.

He jerks back. "What?" His eyes wrinkle with concern. "Jo..." His quiet voice trails off.

"Tyler," I clip, stern. "Why would I—"

"I believe you," he rushes. "It's just... god, are you okay?"

"I'll admit, I was shocked, still am." I pause, remembering his encouragement and him making me promise I would get help to stop Walter. "He told me the nukpana's name. It's Walter T. Samuels"

Tyler forgets all about my encounter with Bryce and we focus on finding out what we can about Walter. The trouble I had before hits us head on again, and we both grow frustrated. We have a name now, but what good does it do if we can't find nothing out beyond that?

"Let's go to the county library again," I say. "If they don't have any information, maybe they can point us in the direction of someone who might. There has to be a record of his death somewhere."

I grab my backpack off the counter and start to follow Tyler out the door when his hand held radio beeps from its perch on the counter. He pinches the bridge of his nose and then looks from me to the radio. Growling, he hits the button to stop the beeping and listens to the dispatcher. When the warning is given of multiple injuries with entrapment, I set my bag back on the table and dig out my computer.

"It can wait. You go."

"Are you sure?" he asks, already clipping his radio to his belt.

"I'm positive. We can go when you get back."

After Tyler leaves, I keep searching, unable to think about anything else. I do searches on the town's history, leaving out Walter's name. I do searches on the county, on deaths at the overlook ranging back to the early 1800's. No matter what I look up, how I word it, or whose name I use, there is no record of Walter or his death that can be found on the Internet.

I'm walking up your driveway.

I jump to my feet, reading the text from Cooper again to make sure I read it right. I step to my left and then take two steps right, before doubling back to the left. *What's he doing here? Why didn't he call earlier? I think I'm going to be sick.* When he knocks on the front door, I almost run for my room. I could always lie and say I'm not home.

I know you're home. Open up.

Yeah, that's not creepy. Not at all.

Holding my breath, I open the door.

"It's about time," he says and brushes past me.

I slam the door, finding air easier to inhale through anger than awkwardness. "Pardon me."

"Look," he says, coming to a sudden stop, his back to me. "I know Jada said something to you and I have something to say too." He stands still, his muscles tight and his breathing hard. I'm not sure if I'm supposed to say anything or wait for him.

Seconds tick by and I'm unable to handle it anymore. I step forward and reach out, meaning to make sure he's okay. I'm not sure if it's the gesture and a misinterpretation of it or something else that causes Cooper to shy away from me, but it stings. It stings bad.

"I'm a grown man, Jo. I'm nineteen and since I was eight I have seen things that would send most screaming and running for cover. I don't need to be coddled by you or my sister. I know the truth and can handle it, got it?"

Testosterone, anyone?

"I understand that, but—" I start, but he interrupts me again.

"I don't want you worrying about what I'm thinking or how I wish things could be. Jada has pounded it in my head since the first time she caught me looking at a Playboy, that relationships don't work out for us."

"Why not?" I blurt.

He turns, finally, and looks at me with torn, sad eyes. "Why not what?"

"I don't understand how she can say that. I mean, your parents met and fell in love. Why can't the two of you?"

"It was by chance that my parents met."

This is wrong. Neither one of them should be going through life believing they are destined to be alone. That sucks. "Let me tell you something," I say, getting in his space. "You can try to convince yourself all you want, but we both know that is bullshit. If it wasn't, how have there been chasers ever since the first group formed back in the Navajo days?"

Cooper chuckles. "You do know that there are still Navajos living today."

I roll my eyes. "You know what I meant." I take another step. "You want to know what I believe? I believe that those chasers waited until they found that one. The one who they knew they could trust with this secret. Just like when you told me."

"That's different. I didn't tell you because—"

"I know, because I needed closure. It's still the same." I take another step and his back hits the counter. "You knew you could trust me with your secret."

"I need a friend, Jo." He blurts, his intense eyes searching mine. "I don't want to lose my friend. The past two days, all I can think about is losing you. You're the only person I've ever talked to outside of the hunting world." He cups my face. "I don't want to lose that, and I'm so scared that I'm going to."

My phone buzzes in my pocket and as much as I hate to, I pull away and check the screen. When Tyler is out on a call, I always wait and jump to answer his calls. Seeing his name, I push the green talk icon.

"Are you okay?" I ask, always nervous until I know he's safe.

"I'm fine, but it looks like I'm going to be a while. You may want to go to the library without me."

I glance up at Cooper. "That's fine. Keep me updated."

"I will. Be careful."

"You too."

I put the phone away and step back, giving us both some space. Cooper turns around and braces his hands on the counter and I can hear his sharp intake of air. I chew on my lip, debating what to do. Do I go back and wrap my arms around him, praying to god that he holds me like he did only seconds ago? Or do I move on, act like it never happened, that it never got that intense? I hate this.

"What's this?" he asks, turning and holding up the piece of paper with Walter's name on it.

"I completely forgot about that." How, I don't know, maybe because Cooper's intense eyes are making me question my logic to stay just friends?

I tell him all about what happened the night before with Kirk. When we get to the part about the nukpana, I swear if it was possible, his head would have exploded. Mad doesn't even begin to describe how pissed he is that I went without him. I knew that if I had found something it would come down to this, but not after the moment we just shared. *Nice timing, Jo.*

When I'm done, I smile at him, hoping me finding a small bit of information helps ease the anger he feels. Oh boy, how I was wrong.

"I can't believe you went up there, with *Kirk* no less. He was ready to kick your ass a few days ago. Were you trying to get yourself killed or something?"

"No," I growl and fist my hands. I let them fall to the table and look at him, exhausted. "I'm tired of lectures. You want to be my friend and come with me to the library to see what we can find out about Walter. *Or* do you want to go home alone and pout?"

Fifteen minutes later we pull into the county library's parking lot. Millie sends me a text asking where I am. After I reply, she texts back that she'll be there soon with snacks and coffees in hand. When she finally makes it, Cooper and I are no closer to learning anything than when we started.

"It's like he didn't even exist," I comment while flipping through 1881's town obituaries. This is the point we have resorted to, obituary scanning. There's this point, which I've already crossed, where the names become blurs and they all look the same. Deciding I need a break, I get up and let Millie take over.

"What's his name again?" she asks as she starts scanning.

"Walter T. Samuels." I close my eyes and worship the caffeinated goodness making its way down my esophagus.

Millie continues her search while I nod in and out of conciseness next to her. At one point, I remember my head being propped onto something. It isn't until someone nudges me and whatever was holding my head up falls to the floor that I peek through my lashes to see Kirk's mug peering at me. That is not a way I want to be woken up.

"Here," Kirk says, thrusting another coffee into my hand. "Drink up."

Sitting up, I look over the edge of my chair to see Cooper's flannel shirt lying on the floor. I pick it up and notice now he's only wearing a tight black t-shirt. I can't believe it happens, but I blush when he looks at me and smiles. *Good grief, I'm such a girl.*

"So," I prompt and take a sip of my coffee, almost choking on the first drink. What the hell did he put in this, liquid sugar or something? "Tell me you found something."

"Nothing, babe. You're right, he doesn't exist." Millie shrugs. "You want to go try and ask Ms. Stella. Maybe she's seen something we've missed."

What other choices do we have?

We pack up our stuff and head out. When I'm about to round the building for the side parking lot, my attention is halted.

"You won't find your answers in no library."

It's obvious the others don't hear the comment, but I do. I turn to find Mason Edwards, hand propped on his cane, eyes trained on the donut shop across the street.

Maybe I was hearing things. "Excuse me," I say and walk toward him. "Mr. Edwards. Hi, I'm—"

"Ryleigh Jo Vanguard, sister to Tyler Andrew Vanguard. Your parents left you in his care on April 28th of this year." He cocks and eyebrow, and glances at me. "Shall I keep going?"

"No," I snap. "I think you've made it quite clear you know who I am." It's a bit creepy he knows so much. "Now how about you tell me a little about yourself. You could start with why you were shooting at us."

Cooper, Millie, and Kirk have come back around the building, all masked with the same confused expression.

"First, I think I'll have some pie. It's a nice day for pie."

Unbelievable!

Mr. Edwards gets to his feet, leaning heavily on the cane. But I swear it's only for looks. He doesn't need that thing. I've seen him in action.

"Is that the same gun totting crazy man we ran into the other night?" Cooper asks.

"At the ford? Yes," I confirm.

The four of us follow him into the donut shop, wary, but weary. The smell of fresh pastries assaults my senses and my stomach growls in protest. When was the last time I ate something? Nudging the others, we all order a slice of pie and then go join Mr. Edwards.

He removes his hat and runs a hand over his semi-bald head. The few hairs that remain are short and grey. "It was 1864."

Got to love a story that begins like that. To say I'm excited is putting it mildly.

"The town was struggling due to the war, and because of the bushwhackers who took pleasure in burning whatever they wanted. It was a horrible time. Many couldn't afford to move or rebuild and they became desperate. My great-great-grandpa William C. Edwards was one of those people. The land I own now, down by the ford, is the land he owned then. But at one point in time, he almost lost it.

"Another one of those desperate men during that time was Walter T. Samuels. William and Walter worked side by side for years by offering up lumber services. William is the one who started the business, having plenty of land to be cleared, and hired Walter on after he was approached by him one day at the creek.

"One day, Walter heard about some silver mines that were said to be close to William's land. He shared the news with William and they made a deal to continue working, while also hunting for the silver. If they found it, they would split it."

Cooper slaps his forehead with his hand.

I point across the table, my voice stern. "Don't you dare ruin this story. I'll gut you." Cooper pales slightly as I gesture for Mason to continue.

"As I'm sure Cooper has already figured out, Walter found the silver years later. Him and William had gone out and had a weekend long celebration." Mason pauses to take a drink of his water. He swallows hard and narrows his eyes as he looks outside. "Everything was fine until Walter woke up one morning to find William hauling the silver out of the underground chamber he had discovered."

Mason shakes his head. "My great-great-grandfather William C. Edwards killed a man over money. There's a family legacy to be proud of."

"Wait," Millie says and looks to all of us. "That name sounds familiar."

"It should," Mason says. "William Edwards is known as one of the town's founding settlers. Little does anyone know that he built the town with blood-stained hands."

"So, Williams killed Walter for the money, and then gave a part of it to build Dover." Millie concludes.

"Yes," Mason says.

"So Walter wants revenge by what? Destroying the town?" I ask.

"Or taking control of it," Mason concludes.

I start to ask what he means by that, I mean Walter is a ghost for chrissakes, but the conversation continues before I get a chance.

"That's not all of it," Cooper adds. "I bet he's after that silver too."

Hell, now I don't know whether to stop Walter or sit back and root for him. Sure, what he's doing now and in the past is bad, but he was killed because of greed, he wasn't given a proper burial, and everything he had worked for was stolen from him. Yeah, I'd be up for a little revenge myself.

"How did he end up at the overlook if they argued near the ford?" I ask.

Mason rubs his head again, a nervous habit perhaps. "William tied him up, along with some of the silver, and loaded him up on a carriage. As William was heading to town to reveal his findings, he stopped at the overlook, saw an opportunity, and tossed Walter over the edge."

I look to the others, wondering what we do now that we know the truth. I want to ask Cooper but am afraid to say anything in front of Mason and the others.

"I've tried stopping him," Mason admits. "I first saw him when I was fifteen. I had been fishing with my dad when Walter revealed himself to us down by the ford. That's when my dad told me about what William had done, and how that's how we got all our family money. Three days later, my dad died at the overlook."

"Oh gosh, I'm so sorry," Millie says and lays her hand on his.

The rest of us chime in with our own sympathetic apologies. Not only has he been haunted by the taint on his family, but also by who he has lost to it.

"After that, I went looking for Walter. I had my shotgun ready too, but that coven, they're smart."

"What can you tell us about them?" I ask.

"They've changed leaders a few times over the years. Like I said, they keep themselves well hidden. That boar you found in the ford the other day, that was their handiwork. I don't know why, but their tactics to scare me off or commit suicide or whatever it is they've been trying to do over the years has intensified the past three years, and especially the last six months."

"When did William kill Walter?" I ask.

"May 25, 1864."

I write the date down and tuck it into my pocket. When Cooper gives me a questioning look, I shrug. "Just want to keep the facts straight."

Mason continues to tell us all he knows about the coven and the deaths that began in 1909, according to his family. The coven member don't live in the forest like I thought they might, but instead reside all throughout the county. They congregate in the hollow by the creek that splits it.

"Why does the coven need to help the spirit?" I ask.

"It's rare, but we run into cases like this from time to time. The nukpana will lure an unsuspected victim, I've told you about how they can twist your thoughts. He may have promised this person something, power even, in exchange for their help."

"But why? Can't they do things on their own?"

"Yes," he says, with his gaze transfixed on the glass in front of him. I wonder what he's thinking. He may be holding something back. Or it could just be hesitation. I didn't think about how awkward this may be for him, talking to so many outsiders about what he knows.

"The thing is," he continues, "the nukpana can use the energy given off of the living, as well as spirits, to sustain himself longer. Plus, they can do dirty work for him that is out of his range."

"What do you mean?" Kirk asks.

"A nukpana can only travel so far from where their body is left to rest."

Interesting. I wonder what kind of dirty work a ghost would need done? Ya know, besides luring in unsuspecting victims.

Mason tightens his fist on the table. "I think this town knows more than they let on, but won't admit it, which is why they rule all the incidents accidents."

"I've been thinking the same thing. But why do you say that?"

He looks straight at Millie. "Because the same families have run this town since it was rebuilt in 1864. Some of those names have changed, due to marriages, but the lineage is still there."

My eyes widen and I look at Millie as well. Her family has been a part of this town, not only as business owners but also council members since then.

"Oh my god," she whispers and covers her mouth. She's silent for a few minutes, eyes wide, and then suddenly leaps from her seat to leave.

"Millie, wait," I holler, as Kirk gets up to go after her. She rushes across the street and disappears around the side of the library, with Kirk closing in.

"I didn't mean to upset the girl," Mason says.

I continue to stare out the window, hoping to catch a glimpse of her. "She'll be fine," I mumble, hoping I'm right. Ready to hear the rest of what Mason has to say so I can go check on her, I turn my attention back to him. "Is there anything else you can tell us that you think might be useful?"

The question gives Mason room to tell us about the string of bad luck his family has endured over the last one hundred years, including losing his grandfather, his father, a sister, and a brother. After hearing it, I want to hug him and tell him he's so strong for continuing to hang on. But I don't, especially when he says it's one of the reasons he never had a family of his own. He says he didn't want his own children to suffer the blackened stain of their family name.

Cooper and I get up to leave and promise Mason that we will do everything we can to stop Walter. Before I'm out of reach, Mason grabs my hand, his frightened eyes looking into mine.

"I meant what I said. Don't go looking for death."

The warning sends a chill down my spine and I shiver. So he's the one who left me the roses. Creepy.

Cooper and I walk out of the pie shop and head back to my car, neither one of us saying anything. I start the engine and Cooper turns in his seat to face me.

"It's time you learned a thing or two about fighting a nukpana."

My nerves flop between excitement and fear as I pull out of the parking lot and head for Cooper's house.

Chapter Sixteen

Setting my bag down on the couch, I send a text to Tyler.

I'm at Cooper's. Feel free to come by.

After hitting send, I click on Millie's name to send her a text as well.

You okay?

Neither one of them reply and I put my phone in my pocket. I'm more eager to hear from Millie than Tyler. She was pretty shaken up when she left the café. Mason had only been stating what he believed, and he never said Millie's family name directly, but the implication was there. And that's all Millie needed to feel the weight of so many deaths on her shoulders. I pray that when all this is over we discover her family had nothing to do with what is going on, and that this was a secret only the Edwards family knew about.

"She'll be okay."

"That obvious, huh?"

Cooper comes to stand in front of me and brushes aside my hair, his eyes searching mine. "A little bit."

My body freezes, unsure of how to handle this situation. Perhaps being alone with Cooper isn't a good thing. He steps closer, our chests touching, and I have to look up at him. He breathes in deep and smiles. Why is he smiling? I'm not smiling. I'm about to freak out is what's about to happen.

"You ready?"

I raise my eyebrows, not knowing where he's going with that line of thought. "Ready for what?"

"To try and master the master." He chuckles and sprints away from me and up the stairs. "Although I doubt you'll succeed," he says over his shoulder as he reaches the top.

Determination sets in and I follow. "You are going to be pleasantly surprised, my man."

"Oh, so I'm your man now?"

The terror I'm sure crosses my face makes him laugh.

"I'm kidding." He continues to laugh, and when I narrow my eyes, he laughs harder, which causes him to snort. We both start laughing then, with several minutes passing before either one of us is able to get control over ourselves. I guess the giggles are like yawns, once they start, there's no stopping them, especially when you're being encouraged by someone else.

Cooper takes in a deep breath, squashing his chuckle and gets serious. "Jo, friends. I know that. And trust me, at this point in my life, I'd rather have you as a friend than nothing at all."

The attic door creaks open after he gives it a little shove. "After you."

I take advantage of him being a gentleman and rush around the door to hit the almighty button.

"Damn. I should have seen that coming," he remarks.

Shelves slide out from behind the walls, as lights flicker on to reveal the weapons. *Snazzy.*

"You like the upgrade?"

I fan myself. "Why it sure is lovely, Mr. Lewis. You did a fine job." I try drawling my voice out like I've heard the women from the south do in movies, but honestly, I think it comes out a little too squeaky.

Cooper's eyes light up and the tips of his ears redden. On any other given day, I've been good at hiding my feelings when his eyes roam over me. But today, I don't know why, but I can't. I bite down on my lip, nervous, and look away. This signals him to get back into action, and he clears his throat.

"Right. Let's start with some history on knives."

I screw up my face, confused as to why I need to know about knives. "They're pointy and can cut things. What else is there to know?"

"When killing a spirit, there's little more to it than that." He walks over and picks up the closest one. "This is a Scottish Dirk. It has a thirteen-inch blade that's an inch wide, and forged of steel. Most come with a rosewood finished hilt, which is good for handling, but it helps when we wrap it in twine."

"Why do you need to wrap it in twine?" I ask. If they're usually made with a rosewood hilt, it doesn't make sense to add to it.

Cooper's head slumps. "It's not the hilt that's the problem, it's that because the energy the twine is... I mean the rosewood can't be used to.... Dammit. I'm not doing a good job explaining this." He sighs. "Maybe I should get Jada."

"No," I say and place my hand on his arm. "You tell me."

His eyes soften from the anger he held toward himself, as I reveal my trust in him. Setting the dagger back down, he gestures for me to follow him over to the couch by the window.

"Remember what Jesse said about the mind playing tricks with us until it chooses to reveal the truth? That's pretty accurate. Delving a little deeper into that logic, one might begin to wonder how. How are there spirits? How can they feed off one another? How can you see auras?" He smiles. "We'll skip over all the hows—there's a lot of them—and get to the source. It's all based off of the elements around us. Some may refer to it as magic, but it's not. It's energy. The thing one has to learn once they understand this, is how to use that energy. It's all around us, in everything we do.

"Chasers have to learn how to use energy. Some have called us witches before, but we differ in many ways. Chasers don't worship nature or gods by holding rituals. We use the energy, and that's it. We know its properties and how to manipulate them. Think of us as supernatural scientists."

"Do Chasers have a beef with witches?"

"Not all. We actually have more respect for them than we do for those who don't believe or understand. Although, I will admit, there are a few witches who take things to extremes."

"Like the coven we are dealing with now?"

He weighs his answer. "Maybe. I'd have to meet them first."

I admire that. "I know this is off subject, but why did you need to know that stuff about Walter?"

He holds up his hand. "I'm getting to that. Now, I want you to be honest. What was the first thing you thought when you walked into this room for the first time?"

I think back and remember the letdown I felt when seeing nothing but herbs. I had wanted to see weapons, not plants. "I had expected more: weapons and armor and stuff."

"And that's the thing. Herbs. Fresh, unfiltered water. Sun light. Moon light. Trees. Air. They hold the properties of energy that we use. They are a part of our weapons. The vials of herbs over there," he says and gestures to the glass containers I had first seen when I came into the attic, "are not useful for energy. But, they can still be used for other things."

"Use lavender to relax."

"Exactly!" He gets excited, and I'm guessing it's from my ability to follow along. "The potted plants over there," he gestures to the row of plants on the opposite wall, "are for when we are preparing blades for combat."

Well, I was following along. "I don't get it. How can a plant help?"

He deflates a little and I hate knowing that I caused that. It's obvious that he has little faith in his ability to explain things to me, and my confusion isn't helping.

"Like I said, from its energy. Let me try explaining it this way. When a spirit first begins to form, it's because it draws off the energy around it. But it has to twist that energy in an unnatural form, making it impure, to take on its transparent state. When we use the energy, we keep it in its simplest form but so that each type of energy works in harmony. That's why it's important to understand each type of energy emitted from the things around us."

I rub circles over my temple. My head just might explode before all this is over. "I think I got it," I say, hesitantly. "Spirits twisting energy is bad. You using the elements like you're supposed to is good."

"Yes. What I was trying to explain earlier about the twine is all about energy. We forge our weapons in that energy and then wrap twine around the hilt to bind them together, so to speak. When we fight a nukpana, the whole good versus evil battle happens, but it's with the energies, not the beings."

This is some crazy, unbelievable stuff. "Do I have to learn all that to fight alongside you?"

"I'm hoping it doesn't come to that."

Is he talking about the energy stuff or me fighting with him? If he's thinking I'm not going with him to face Walter, he is sadly mistaken.

"But no, you don't have to learn any of that. Jada does it. She's better at it than I am. I mean, I'm capable, but I prefer her to do it."

Okay, so he was talking about me not fighting with him, then. He's got a surprise coming. "Energy enhanced twine wrapped around the hilt of a knife, got it."

Cooper continues to talk about the different kinds of knives and how they are used, what they are made of, and what makes it different from the others. I space out somewhere between trench knives and modern daggers, clearly not as fascinated with the sharp blades as he is. To me, they are all the same, and used for the same purpose.

My mind begins to wander, thinking about Walter and the man he was before. From the way Mason described, he didn't sound greedy. He was willing to share his findings with Williams and had never intended to keep them for himself. It's unfair his life turned out the way it did, and how it continues. I know it sounds stupid to feel sadness for a vengeful spirit who has taken so many lives, but I do. And here we are, talking about how to kill him again. Somehow, it doesn't seem right.

"You with me, Jo?" Cooper asks and comes to sit next to me after setting down the knife he was holding.

I rub my hand over my face, a sheepish smile forming on my lips. "Sorry. I kind of spaced there. What were you saying?"

"Don't worry about it," he waves off. "I don't even know why I'm telling you all this, you don't need to know about every bladed weapon there ever was." He gets to his feet. "Let's concentrate on the weapon we are going to be using."

He walks over and grips the black steel handle of a large, nasty looking weapon, a spark of admiration on his face. "This piece of cold steel is a beast."

I eye the long handle and sharp black metal dubiously, apprehension building in my gut. An axe? Does he expect me to use that? The thick solid steel handle is tapered, and leads from the hilt to the axe's base where the double-edged blades meet the handle. On one side the blade comes to a thick point, the tip a glinting silver instead of black. The other side is a basic axe blade, with the same silver design along the edges. Etched into the blade's head and down a portion of the handle are odd designs that intensify its beauty.

"Don't look so scared," he smirks.

"I'm not," I lie. Cooper raises an eyebrow, silently calling me out. I roll my eyes and hold out my hand. "I can handle it."

That entertains him and he steps toward me and places the cold metal in my hand. He lets go and the full weight of the axe settles and I strain under the sudden heaviness, crying out. Cooper must have been expecting this. As my fingers slip off the handle his hands are there, right underneath my own, and he catches the long blade.

I twirl my hand to pop my wrist. "That thing is heavier than it looks."

"Or you weren't as ready as you thought."

Deciding not to argue, or dig myself a deeper hole, I let it go and focus on what Cooper has to show me. For the next few hours Cooper shows me where to place my hands on the handle for maximum or minimum force. I never would have thought hand placement would mean much, but when it comes down to it, it means everything.

Once he's sure I have my hand placements down, he moves on to learning to move with the axe. Wielding an axe isn't easy, I learn. If you stand immobile, the axe's weight will drag you off kilter and can cause you to injure yourself. I'm amazed as I watch his muscles contract with every twist and turn his body makes. It's like he's dancing with death, but tight and in control.

Yeah, like you care about the damn axe.

I tell myself to shut up and pay attention, feeling silly that I've resorted to chastising myself. I know these lessons are important. I do. It's just that it has become a little harder to pay attention now that he's taken off his t-shirt to reveal a dark grey tank top underneath, his muscles in full view. And now, no matter how much I try to focus, I find myself biting my lip and watching him, but not for the reasons he wants me to.

"You want to give it a try?"

"Sure," I answer and stick out my hand. I try remembering all the things he showed me, but not much comes to mind except pre-losing his shirt stuff. I step forward, my hands firm, but Cooper places his hands over mine on the handle to stop me.

"Hang on a second," he says and walks over to the couch.

"What are you doing?"

"Getting my phone." He picks it up and places it in his pocket. "Just in case I need to call 911. I don't want to have to look for it."

"You're an ass," I retort but can't help laughing.

I surprise us both when I start swinging the blade and twisting my body with the weight, just as he taught me. His warning not to overdo the swing with too much of your own body weight behind it is one of the main points I remember him making, and I'm sure to do as he told me. It isn't until I'm confident and sure I've got this down that I make a mistake. A painful mistake.

My cocky side comes out when I turn to give Cooper crap for giving me crap and I roll the axe handle in my hand, spinning it from side to side. I'm not paying attention, and am more worried about showing off. The handle slips a fraction, my hands sweaty, and that's all it takes to tip the balance and I lose my grip on the sharp weapon. Cooper warned me over and over to always make sure the blades were pointed away from my body when not in use, but did I pay attention? No! The sharp point comes down hard on my calf and doesn't stop until it feels like it's taken off my whole leg.

I drop like I've been shot and stare at the wound. Shock. I'm in shock... I think.

Cooper chucks the axe aside, his voice filled with panic as he tries to portray a very in control person. "It's going to be okay, Jo. I've had way worse than this."

Silence. Wide eyes. Can hear my own breathing. Shock. I'm still in shock.

"This one time," Cooper continues and his words begin to make sense, "...it was way worse than this."

Click. Jo is back. I'm bleeding out and he's telling stories about some injury way back when? "Hey, duffus, I don't give a shit." The pain hits hard then, my right leg throbbing as blood wells from the wound. I feel a cold chill run through my chest and down my arms. Time for a little panic. "I'm dying here. My life's blood is draining out onto this ugly ass brown rug."

"Jo!" Cooper yells. "Look at me. Quit. Freaking. Out. It's not helping."

"Oh, I'm sorry. Are you the one bleeding to death?" My adrenaline spikes and I swear I'm going to pass out, from the anxiety or the pain I'm not sure.

Cooper shakes his head and mumbles something under his breath. I open my mouth to demand he tell me what he said, but change my attitude when he grabs for one of the knives.

"What are you doing?"

Without answering me, he cuts my jeans from the knee down and slips the torn fabric off my leg. Laughter is not what I'm expecting next. Complete horror, hold pressure to the wound while I call 911, those are the reactions I'm looking for, not amusement.

"You're lucky, that's for sure." He turns my leg so I can get a better look at the wound. "But I don't think you're going to bleed to death."

A hot flush fills my cheeks as I looks down at the small cut.

"You can thank this," he says, and holds up what remains of my pants leg. A metal button that was sewn in the seam about mid-calf appears to have stopped the tip from going any deeper than it did.

Cooper sits back and falls on his back, laughing deep from his gut. "Your face," he gasps, then starts laughing again.

I say nothing, feeling like an idiot, and go to retrieve the first aid kit I spotted above the mini-fridge by the door. When I come back to the couch, Cooper has gotten himself under control—a little—and offers to help.

"Thanks, but I got it," I snap. The anger isn't directed at him, but at myself. If I react this way when getting a minor cut during a training exercise, what am I going to do if something really bad happens when facing down demons? Cower on the ground and play dead? Ugh!

Cooper catches my tone and his eyes soften. "Hey, don't be embarrassed. It was a completely normal reaction. You didn't know how bad it was."

"It felt bad," I defend and dig through the kit.

Gently, he cups my calf and scoots closer to my leg. A shiver runs up my spine, through my chest, and to my abdomen. I have to fight to take a breath.

"A few butterfly stitches should do it." He looks up at me. "But I like girls with a few scars."

I'm going to be a complete wreck of crazy emotions before this is all over.

Cooper takes the first aid kit out of my hand. I approximate the gash is almost an inch, maybe an inch and a half long. It only takes two of the small bandages to pull the wound together. He then takes a bigger bandage to place over it. As he begins to wrap my leg with gauze, I grasp for something to talk about to distract me from his touch.

"I've been curious, why do you use blades instead of guns?"

"Hold this right here," he instructs and reaches for the medical tape. Once he has wound it around the bandage, he answers. "Remember what I told you about the twine and how it holds in the energy so we can pierce the soul? We haven't perfected that craft into bullets yet. Plus, it doesn't feel as badass." He smiles up at me and rips the tape from the roll.

"How does that feel?" he asks, his hands still gentle on my legs.

Which part? "Better. Thanks."

Figuring we've had enough for one day, we put away the weapons we have out and head back downstairs. I'm leading the way and checking my phone as I make my way down, but a movement below catches my eye. I glance up, figuring it's Jada, but come to a stop when I see Tyler, his hair ruffled and without a shirt. Cooper bumps into me and before he can utter a sound, I reach back and cover his mouth.

"I got it." Jada's voice travels down the hall seconds before she emerges, a shirt in hand. Tyler takes it and slips it on. *Well, well, well, it's about time.*

"I had a great time with you today," he says, pulling her to him. "And I meant what I said. I don't want you thinking about the future right now. Let's focus on the here and now, and worry about the then and later when the time comes." He kisses her forehead, and from this angle I can see her close her eyes and smile.

"I mocked Cooper so many times after he told Jo about what we do. But I am so glad he did." She looks up at him and nibbles his chin. "It's the best idea he's ever had."

Cooper huffs behind my hand and rolls his eyes.

They kiss and we stay quiet while I silently count to ten before continuing down the stairs, sure to make plenty of commotion, so as we don't get too much of an eyeful. The two pull away, Jada fidgeting with her shirt while Tyler runs his hands through his hair.

"Oh. Hey, Jo. I forgot you were still here."

Yeah, I bet.

"How did you even know I was here?"

"You texted me."

Oh, yeah, I forgot. That whole near death experience took a lot out of me.

"Jada told me Cooper was catching you up on some chaser stuff."

"He did. How long have you been here?" I ask, an innocent expression on my face.

He begins to stammer an answer, then notices my cut jeans and bandage. *Be it me who gives him a good reason not to answer.*

"What happened to your leg?"

I shrug. "Training incident. It's nothing major."

"One would have thought otherwise a few—" The air whooshes out of Cooper when my elbow meets his ribs.

"Like I said, nothing bad. It'll heal up in a couple of days."

Tyler and I say our goodbyes and leave. Before I pull out of the driveway I send Millie a quick text.

R u okay? I'm worried.

I don't expect a reply, but when I get one, I hit the brakes.

I'm fine. Overwhelmed. Sure u know the feeling.

Yea...Sux. Where r u?

I'm w/Kirk. Come by later?

I reply with a smiley face and pull out onto the street.

We stop at the diner on the way home, our conversation light until I inform him we spoke to Mason. He listens intently as I explain what really happened in the hollow. His face creases with disgust at the mention of the silver and how William killed Walter over greed. And like me, he doesn't know whether to cheer for the guy or take care of business.

I also notice the difference in his tone and how he seems… happier. I want to tease him about it, be the sister I should be and all. But I don't. I may one day, but today is not that day. He deserves whatever moments of happiness he can grasp.

After enjoying a piece of pie, we head home, with him following behind in his truck. I'm the first to see someone sitting on our front porch. It's only seven, but since daylight savings time isn't for a few weeks the days are still longer, even though the sun is beginning to set sooner. The dimming light doesn't allow me to make out who the woman is.

I park outside of the garage, not comfortable with boxing myself in. I wait until Tyler is parked and then together we walk up to the porch. I don't recognize the woman sitting in my grandfather's rocker but she smiles like she knows us.

"Hello, Jo, Tyler. It's nice to meet you."

"And you are?" I prompt.

"My name is Ester. Ester Samuels."

Chapter Seventeen

The teapot whistles, startling me and I jerk in my seat, as Tyler gets up to move it off the burner. I feel stupid for being so on edge but I guess lack of sleep and a day of blade training will do that to a person, not to mention my emotions playing with my nerves. And now, when the only thing on my mind was my warm bed and I was sure nothing could to stop me from trudging up the stairs to my room, here sits a woman named Ester Samuels.

"Are you okay?" the woman asks, questioning my wide, invasive stare I'm sure.

"Who... me?" I point to myself, as if the term me doesn't explain enough. "I'm fine... couldn't be better," I stutter, and groan to myself. *What's wrong with me?*

A knock on the door saves me from humiliating myself further. *It's about freaking time.* After hearing Ester was here to talk about an incident at the overlook in the 1970's, I had immediately called the gang and told them to get their butts in gear. I jump up to answer the door, while Tyler sets a fresh pitcher of tea and several glasses on the table. Millie, Cooper, Kirk, and Jada look at me expectantly when I swing the door open, to which I shrug and point toward the dining room.

After introductions are made, we all sit around the table to listen to what Ester has to say about why she's here. The only chair left is by Cooper. Our arms brush up against one another when I sit down and I swear I feel him tense. *Me too there, buddy.*

"I wasn't expecting such a crowd," she chuckles. Tyler starts to explain but she brushes him off. "I understand. It's nice to have friends that will stick by your side. It's refreshing to see."

It's the best thing in the world, I think and look to each person sitting around the table.

"Where do I start?" Ester mumbles to herself and laughs. "MaryAnn Sinclair, oh the stories I could tell you about her. She was wild and full of life, never had a dull day in her life. She was my cousin and dragged me everywhere with her. Of course, she never got in trouble when I always did, but I never quit following along with her."

The smile on her face fades into a frown, her eyes misting over with sadness. She wipes at her eyes and brushes her fingers through her wavy brown hair.

"She was only twelve when she died on July 11, 1972 up at the overlook. I should have done more that night, told her no, tattled on her, something, but I didn't. I followed her, as I always did, right out the window and up the mountain. The spirit came for us that night, and I know in the beginning, its intentions had been to take both of us. I was spared, although I didn't know why until I was older. My grandfather found me the next morning, shivering, and muttering things he didn't understand. Heck, I don't know that I understood what I was saying."

She pauses and lowers her voice.

"My grandfather took his life a few years later in that same cabin. He swore he could hear MaryAnn screaming, and kept saying it was his fault. I never understood how he could blame himself until later, when I moved out of town." She looks through the open window, the curtain fluttering from a small gust of wind, an empty stare. "It's a lonely feeling when you discover you're adopted," she whispers.

That's an odd statement to throw out there without reason.

"I couldn't even imagine," I say, not knowing what else to say.

"It's terrible. Well, I reckon things could have been worse. There's no telling what my life would have been like if I'd gotten stuck in the system. But still, I had so many questions, especially in my case."

What's that supposed to mean?

"Who adopted you?" Millie asks.

"Matthew and Crystal Reynolds. Know anything about their family history?"

Millie answers, "No," while the rest of us shake our heads.

"It's a long one," she chuckles, "so I'll stick to what's relevant to this story. Crystal Reynolds, formerly a Thompson," she glimpses at Millie, "was not my real mother, as it turns out. My real mother was Charlotte Bristol, great-great-granddaughter of Beatrice Jamison, Walter Samuels's fiancé."

Holy freaking crap. "Walter was engaged?" *Let's turn up the sad dial a little more.* "Did they have children?"

"Oh, no. It was a different time then. Child-boaring out of wedlock was rare. She married another man, Michael Hill, and gave birth to three children. One of them, her son, is your great times six or seven uncle. This I figured out after hearing you survived that night. I was curious to know if you were from Beatrice's bloodline or not and I wasn't surprised when I confirmed you are."

She may have not been surprised, but I am.

"What made you curious?" I ask, wanting to know more while an odd feeling churns in my stomach.

"I will get to that later," Ester remarks.

I allow my mind to wander for a moment, thinking what it would have been like if Walter and Beatrice had married. Would I still have been born? And if so, what would I have looked like? What would our family have been like?

"What happened to your mother?" Millie asks.

"Crystal or Charlotte?" she asks.

Millie is shy when she shrugs, her face full of remorse but curiosity. "Both."

"My real mother, Charlotte, died during child birth. I was her first child. I was also the last Beatrice would see born. She passed away a little over a year later, in 1961. She was almost 102."

"Holy cow, really?" I ask, eyes wide.

"No, Jo," Kirk chimes in, "she's lying. Beatrice is still alive and kicking."

I flip him my response, and rest my chin on my palm. Screw him and his sarcasm. Sorry if I'm the only one intrigued to hear about Beatrice, the woman who was engaged to Walter, and who lost him to greed and tragedy.

"Crystal and Matthew died a few years after MaryAnn passed away in a car accident. Her death tore the family apart. My grandparents would hardly speak to anyone after MaryAnn's incident. I heard Crystal whispering about my grandfather feeling remorse for what happened, and that it was killing him to know he was responsible. I didn't know what she meant about that until I figured out I was adopted and began my quest to unravel the truth. Never would I have imagined what I discovered."

I flick my eyes to Cooper, wondering if he heard the harsh undertone as well. A slight raise of his eyebrows tells me he did.

"What a quaint, small town this is," Ester remarks, her cool glance scanning each of us. "Full of lies, deceptions, and greed. Filled with the sins of the fathers'."

Not good! She's starting to talk crazy. That's never a good sign. In the movies, this is when the going gets bad. I glance at Cooper, who seems to be thinking the same thing I am, because he places his hand on the hilt of the knife on his belt. I see Jada do the same next to Tyler.

At this point, I don't think anyone knows what to say to Ester. We all know the truth and what happened to Walter. Asking 'what makes you say that Ester' would be the dumbest words to utter right now. What is troubling me, though, why does she care so much? She wasn't Walter's child, he had none. And her name... she changed it to Samuels. Why?

None of this is adding up.

Ester feigns exhaustion, and cradles her forehead in her hand. "Oh my," she says, laughing, "there's so much to tell. You mind if I come back tomorrow to share the rest? I believe my blood sugar is getting low."

Tyler rushes to get her something for her sugar, but she refuses it and says she only likes this or that. Insisting she's fine and that the house she recently bought is not far away, Tyler lets her leave without further protest. Once her car pulls out of the driveway, I cross my arms and lean against the door.

"Tell me that wasn't creepy."

"What do you mean?" Tyler asks, brows creased.

I roll my eyes. "You trust in people too much."

"Or maybe there should be more people like me who give others the benefit of the doubt." Same line, different day, although I would bet ten bucks he has no idea why he's rehearsing that same old line.

"You don't think she was acting strange? I mean, what was that bit about 'sins of the fathers'.' Who talks like that?"

The others agree and Tyler sighs. "Okay. She was acting a little strange."

Then why the argument? Never mind. It doesn't matter. "Something was definitely off. She referred to the town being quaint, but it sounded like she said it mockingly."

"I think we need to keep an eye on her," Jada suggests.

"I agree," Tyler says, "But she may just be upset. She hinted at knowing what happened, and she did say she lost her cousin. That's a lot to take in and deal with, no matter how much time has passed. And moving back... it brings everything to the surface again."

Kirk and Millie have stepped off into the living room and appear to be having a heated discussion. I start their way when Kirk pulls her to him and tucks her head under his chin. He glances over me, a haunted expression on his face. This is probably a lot for him to take in as well.

Too tired to figure out what our next plan of action should be, Tyler says we can figure it out later, and walks Jada out the door.

"Cooper, you coming?" he asks.

"In a minute," Cooper answers.

When the door shuts, he grabs me by the arm and pulls me into the dining room. He looks behind us to make sure Kirk and Millie are still occupied in the living room.

"Jada is right that we should keep an eye on Ester, but I think she came here for a reason tonight. I don't want to leave you alone. She said you were related to Beatrice, which is interesting, but it's the *way* she said it I don't like." He takes my hand in his. "I know we are only friends, but I don't want anything to happen to you. Do you think Tyler would beat the crap out of me if I guarded your door?"

I laugh, but my stomach twists at the thought of what Cooper is suggesting. "So bad you wouldn't be able to walk for weeks."

His head droops. "I was afraid of that." He pulls a bowie knife from out of its scabbard on his hip. "Keep this, then."

I take the blade from his hand and set it on the table. "If it makes you feel better."

"It will, but what will make me feel even better is if you remember what I showed you today. You were paying attention, right?"

I was paying attention to a lot of things. Things that had nothing to do with combat but a whole lot to do with body movements. Things I feel extremely guilty for.

"Yes," I answer and turn him toward the door. "Now, get going. I'm exhausted."

Opening the door, I find Tyler and Jada standing by her car and embraced in one another's arms. Neither one of them is talking due to the fact that their lips are otherwise occupied. Cooper groans behind me.

"I'm happy for them, I guess, but I really wish I was left in the dark."

"Me too," I say, opening the door wider and waving goodbye before shutting it.

Kirk and Millie are still talking. I debate whether to go upstairs, where I can hear my bed yelling at me, or interrupt them and say goodnight. Lucky for me, I don't have to make the decision.

"Jo!" Millie calls out.

I look up the stairs with longing, picturing my comforter and fluffy pillows waiting for me, and send up a silent apology and promise to be there soon. Doing the best to wipe the sleepy look off my face, I turn and go into the living room.

"Can you take me home?" Millie asks.

I look around for Kirk, wondering where he went and why he didn't take her. "Where's Kirk?"

She shrugs, her eyes red and puffy. "He said he needed to check on something. He told me to give this to you."

I take the wrapped box from her, curious. I'm careful when I open it, afraid that it's some prank. This would be a nice time to play one on me, my nerves are tight and on edge. I'm sure the slightest jolt of noise would cause me to panic, let alone something popping out from inside.

When I see what's inside all my thoughts cease and everything around me vanishes. Tears burn my eyes and I'm quick to wipe them away, not wanting to ruin the gift Kirk has given back to me.

It was the first time it had snowed on Christmas in years, a rare treat in Arkansas. No one dared to venture outside of the city limits for fear of having an accident on the curvy country roads that were now slick with snow and ice. It was the first year without my grandpa, but we had planned to go to his house anyway that Christmas morning to cook our annual breakfast. After seeing how bad the roads were that morning, my parents decided against it, though I pleaded for them to reconsider.

I was sad and upset and allowed my feelings to ruin the breakfast my mom tried to make at our home. It wasn't the same. I began to feel horrible as she cleared the dishes, realizing I was being petty and how hard she had tried, and went to apologize when she looked out the window and smiled. I saw Bryce walking down the street towards the house, presents in hand as mist puffed from his mouth with every breath.

Mom had smiled, saying she understood, and I dashed out of the house to greet him. We opened presents in front of the fireplace, a happy setting. I insisted he open his gifts first, and though he said he liked the sweater, when he opened the next gift and saw the framed picture of us, he kissed me. His hands shook as he handed me his gifts. I figured it was from the cold, but I soon realized it was because he was nervous.

First, there was a silver heart shaped necklace. After he put it on, I opened my other present and found a red sweater. After kissing him, I started picking up our trash when he grabbed my hand and pulled another package out of his bag, his face full of fear. With a wide smile, I opened the surprise gift. I began to sniffle as I looked at the hand-crafted sketchbook he insisted he made himself. It wasn't a typical large scrapbook, but one of the smaller ones that can fit in a purse or bag. It was full of pictures of our favorite times spent together, highlighted moments, with a note written by each photo of what that day had meant to him.

I look up at Millie and a tear slips down my cheek. Whether he knows it or not, he has given me so much, a part of me that I had forgotten and needed back. Each day, as we reveal more and more, and I'm not locking myself away, the more easily I'm able to breathe.

"This means so much to me."

Millie smiles and hugs me to her. "I know," she whispers. "He knows too."

I want to remark that if it hadn't been for Kirk coming to steal it out of my room, I would never have lost it, but I let it go. I have it back and that's all that matters.

I pull away from Millie and wipe the tears from my cheeks with my sleeve. I grab the bowie knife off the table, clutch the scrapbook to me, and tell her I'll be right back. I'm careful to place both items on my nightstand, eager to get back home to look through the pictures again. Now with more inspiration to get settled in my room for the night, I grab my keys and rush Millie out the door.

"I never expected all of this," Millie whispers, hugging her chest, as we pull out onto the road.

"Me neither," I reply. "I've always thought there was something off since that night, but I thought it was my imagination playing tricks with me. I never would have guessed this outcome."

"You think we can trust Ester?" she asks.

I think about her odd comments, and sudden faked rush to leave. "No. I don't trust her." Another thought occurs to me. "She said she became interested in my story when she realized I had survived. That's how she found out I was from Beatrice's line. But what about Jesse? And why would she feel the need to track us down to tell us all this?" I shift gears and shake my head. "It doesn't make sense."

"I'm scared, Jo," she admits.

I reach over the console and grab her hand. "I am too."

"What if my family had a part in this?" She lowers her head, her thumbs circling one another. "I don't want to be a part of some conspiracy."

I stare out the windshield and the lights reflecting off the road signs as we pass. "Millie," I say, my tone compassionate but wanting her to understand me. "If every single stone was flipped in everyone's family history, we would all find things we wouldn't like or agree with. The actions our ancestors made were done in a different time, and were done according to what was relevant during the time. But what we have to understand now, is their actions don't make up the people we are now. Their actions may have formed what we see around us now, but our actions are what shape us from this present moment, and on forward from now."

The headlights swing across her hedges as I pull into the driveway and prep myself for an awkward goodbye.

"You're right," she breathes. "The future is all mine, baby." Her smile is forced, and knowing her, I know it's still bothering her. I imagine it will bother her until the day she discovers the truth.

"Jo, I need you to do something for me," she says and swivels to face me.

"Name it." *Wrong thing to say when you don't know what the other person is going to ask, I know.*

"Quit protecting me. I know I said I couldn't do the ghost thing, I want to help you. I've been by your side forever. I still want to be by your side, no matter how dangerous it gets."

I place my hand over hers, happy. "You got it. Sugarbug and Saucy are back at it."

We both chuckle at the reference of our childhood superhero names. Yes, we were badass.

She asks me what I have in mind next. I'm not sure, but it seems the only two people who know anything about this who will talk to us, Jesse and Mason, is a place to start. I promise to pick her up in the morning before I go to see them again.

A black car sits off on the side of the road and I go around before stopping at the intersection. Seeing no traffic, I look down at my phone for a few moments to pick a playlist, when both doors are pulled open. A person wearing a black ski mask jumps into the passenger seat, while strong arms wrap around my shoulders from behind.

I punch the gas, but the engine roars without us moving because the car is still in neutral. I struggle, hitting and elbowing at both my assailants. The one struggling to hold me instructs the other one to hurry. I notice the voice is feminine. A wet cloth is placed over my mouth and I gag at the penetrating odor, and claw at the hands holding it. I feel my muscles weaken moments later, my body relaxing from the fumes of whatever's on the cloth. I scream at myself to stay awake, to fight, but the battle leaves me and I succumb to the darkness.

Chapter Eighteen

The first thing my mind registers are the voices, a variety of them, all female. The next is how at ease they seem, how comfortable, when they shouldn't. Hello, they're kidnappers. Are they not worried about getting caught? Considering they kidnapped me in the first place, I'd say not.

I open my eyes, ready to glare at my captors and give them what for, but can't make out anything through the cloth bag over my face. I can make out the glow of a fire and the smell of smoke through the cloth, but little else. Feeling around with my tied hands, I find I'm leaned against a tree, which explains the rough lump under my butt. It must be a root.

I take the time to access my body, glad to be conscious again, but am I missing anything? Have they done something to me? Moving all my toes, fingers, joints, and muscles, and with my hearing and sense of smell back online, my only problem at the moment is the cloth over my head and the rope tied around my wrists and ankles.

An important lesson I learn real quick is no amount of television watching, reading, or what if scenarios can actually prepare you for the real thing. Bryce, Millie, Kirk, and I used to sit around all the time watching survivor shows, scary movies, and playing out different scenarios while slamming the idiots who wrote such over the top fiction. What I'm learning, is they had it right all along and we were the idiots. It's sheer panic, the whole live or die senses kicking in and overshadowing common sense, begging you to find a way out, while you claw and scrape at your bonds.

That's what I have resorted to. I dig at my wrists and can feel the sting of my skin breaking open, my nails getting packed with blood and flesh. I don't care. I'll do whatever it takes to get free, no matter how painful. I bite down on my lip to keep from crying out as the ropes rub against my now open flesh. I test the ropes around my ankles, hoping I can at least attempt... something. But whoever's done this is not stupid. My legs are firmly tied, with no wiggle room.

I gasp, loud, feeling as if something is sitting on my chest. Nothing is there, of course. It's my own body suffocating me, believing that I'm doomed.

"I think our guest is awake."

My heart stops, at least that's what it feels like, and I'm sure I'm going to pass out when a fingertip traces a line on the back of my neck, sending a heart pounding shiver down my spine and causing the hair on my body to stand. Good news, I know my heart is still in working order.

"Stop it, Stella," Ester's familiar tone chastises. "Take off the cloth."

The fire's light burns my eyes, the flame too bright after the darkness, and I have to turn my head. Standing next to me is... Ms. Stella. The freaking librarian. She can't be... can she?

I start to ask what she's doing here, why she would do such a thing, but then decide against it. I don't really care. All I care about is why I'm here and what their plans are for me. Looking out at the others, I note there are ten other women, not counting Stella and Ester, sitting around the fire. I am not liking these odds.

"What do you want?" I turn my attention to Ester. I knew there was something off about her. But if this was her plan all along, why did she show up at my house? Why did she talk to the others the way she did?

"Nothing bad, I promise."

Maybe with a little bit more conviction in her voice, and a little less kidnapping, I might believe that line of BS.

"I had wanted to do this a little more smoothly, but your friends ruined my plan. Jo, all I want to do is talk." Her hands are crossed behind her back and her shadow dances through the forest as she walks from one side of the fire to the other. "I wanted your brother to hear what I have to say as well, but you can help me convince him later."

"Good grief, woman, get on with it." If she's going for torture me by yammering, she's doing a fine job.

"You better watch that temper. It can get you into trouble." The glow from the fire casts an eerie shadow over half her face when she turns to smile at me. "But I'll do it your way. We want you to join us, the Daughters of Beatrice."

I know she didn't say what I think she just said... did she? There's no way. With horror on my face I'm sure, and my body tense, I look at each of the women sitting and standing around the fire. Their ages range from my age to the elderly. But they can't be... it doesn't...

"The coven," I whisper, knowing in my gut that I'm right no matter how much I want to refuse to believe it.

"That's right." Ms. Stella rewards me with a pat on the back and the only smile I've ever seen her give.

This can't be happening. It can't. How did I live beside these women, interact with them on a daily basis, and not get any weird vibes from them? It doesn't make sense. How could no one notice? Talk about not knowing your neighbor.

"You said the Daughters of Beatrice, right?"

"Yes," Ester answers.

"What about her sons or men or whatever?"

Ms. Stella huffs beside me. "There's no need to talk about him," she spats.

"Stella," Ester chastises, "I do believe Jo was speaking of Alexandra and Katie's children and those since then, the men who were born right alongside of us. Not those who betrayed us."

I was already confused, but the pointed look Ester gives Stella and the rest of the women pushes that aside for curiosity. *One thing at a time, Jo. One thing at a time.*

"Our brothers help when we need them to, but only so we can continue with Beatrice's wishes."

"Which is?" I prompt.

"To bring Walter back. Her love. He never should have been stolen from her." Ester's eyes are hard as she stares into the fire. All the women nod in agreement. "What William done can never be forgiven and the reminder of what our mother lost is evident every day as the town continues to grow and thrive."

I understand Beatrice's pain, having someone ripped from your life too soon... there are no words to describe the emptiness that is left behind. But as much as I understand that loss, I don't understand this idea of revenge years later after her death. And how about the loss I suffered due to their actions? And Walters ? Why think I would help them after that?

"Not that I think that is possible, but how am I supposed to help?"

"We need your blood. You are one of us, after all."

Speaking of blood, I can feel my face pale as all my blood drains with the horrors filling my mind. Are they going to sacrifice me? Or do they want me to become a coven member and help some freaking evil spirit stay strong until what, he kills the whole town? Yeah, I don't think so. Neither option is going to work for me.

Ester sits beside me, her expression one of hope that I will understand. It reminds me of the look she gave me earlier at the house when she told me I was David's great something or another niece.

"After Walter's death, it took Beatrice some time to move on, but she managed. Of course, she was never able to love her husband wholeheartedly, but she tried. One night, while grieving on the anniversary of Walter's death at the overlook, he came to Beatrice.

"He began to teach her things, things he had only began to learn himself. Teaching her about the energy around us, and how to manipulate it. I'm sure you know what I'm talking about," she says, giving me a hard look.

How could she know about Cooper and what he told me? Instead of answering, I say nothing, not even moving a muscle. Sometimes, being passive is the best way to go.

"Anyway, Walter asked her to do some research for him. In those times they didn't have the technology they have now, but there were theories. Beatrice did what he asked, even going as far as traveling to New York. Her husband didn't understand her strange behavior, but didn't stop her. She wasn't grieving any more and she seemed to be happier, which he was grateful for, so he let her be.

"Little did he know what Beatrice was planning behind his back. They had two daughters, Alexandra and Katie, and one son, David."

She says David's name with a bitter tone, and the others shy away, as if that name can cause them harm. *O-kay.*

"As the decades have passed, our numbers have grown. We are now a strong coven who plans to carry out our mother's wish, which is to restore her love, Walter. To give him the life he never had."

"Why didn't she do it before now, when she could have been with him?"

"We didn't know then," Ester admits, her eyes sharp. "We took an oath on Beatrice's death bed to continue searching, to complete her promise to Walter, and we have. Now, all we need is to finish the deed."

I'm still not following all of this. If Walter came to Beatrice after he died, hoping she could bring him back so they could be together, but she dies before finding a way, why would he still want to come back? Why would her daughters want him to come back? Are they all just crazy psychos doing someone else's bidding without knowing why?

"So… you're going to bring him back because…" I trail off, hoping she gets the hint and explains this nonsense to me.

Ester looks to the others, a wicked secret on her red upturned lips. "Are you suggesting we have other plans other than wanting to fulfill what has been asked of us?"

"Sure am," I answer.

"Well," her eyes sharpen, "we may be benefited afterwards. Walter is a generous man."

Crazy psychos. Got it. "I beg to differ. If you'll remember, the coven and Walter killed my boyfriend."

The women all stand as one. "We have prayed for your healing since—"

"You can cut the bullshit," I interrupt. "You did what you did and no amount of remorse or prayer will ever change that."

"I hate that you feel that way, Jo. It was an honest mistake."

I struggle against the ropes binding me, not from fear this time but from anger. How dare she speak so callously about Bryce's death! The burn from the wounds on my wrists returns, but I ignore the pain and continue to fight, ready to show this bitch the only thing I'm willing to do. Get a little payback of my own.

"You may want to reconsider," Stella whispers next to my left ear.

Ester stoops down next to my right ear. "We would hate for Tyler to suffer the consequences if you didn't."

I freeze. The mere mention of a threat against Tyler has me ready to agree with whatever they want me to do. He's been there for me, taken care of me, even when our own parents wouldn't. No way am I leaving him vulnerable to these crazy women.

"You still haven't told me everything," I say, making them think I've changed my mind though I'm not sure what I will do yet. "You want me to join the Daughters of Beatrice. You know how to bring Walter back. What I don't get is how those two pieces fit together."

"You're right." Ester motions for the women to take their seats again. As they do, I try to get a glimpse of their faces. Some have their hoods raised, making it impossible. The ones I do see, I don't recognize. "We want you to join us because you are one of us, a daughter of Beatrice. We also need you for the next generation, and the generation after that. The more of us there are, the stronger we are."

I'm sure she means Walter as well, and not only the coven.

Ester comes to stand right in front of me and stoops down so she's eye level with me. "We can bring him back without you, you know. But you are of our blood and if you join us, you will reap of the benefits Walter has promised us. I don't want to see another one of our own suffer. There's been too much of that already."

It sucks how my hand is only inches from her face, but I'm not able to deck her like I want. Oh, how I want to. "How, Ester?" I demand, wanting to know what she is hiding from me.

"We need a vessel to carry his spirit."

The missing piece. Once it fits into place, I snap. "You have lost your ever-loving mind if you think I'm going to convince Tyler to sacrifice himself for Walter. That will never happen," I hiss. "And I'll never be one of you."

"I told you," one of the women in the back snaps. "She is David's daughter for sure, not the proud line of Alexandra or Katie."

What does that matter? They are all three from Beatrice. Before I can ask, Stella tells the others to hush and then pins me with her harsh eyes.

"Refusing to join us now will not change Tyler's outcome. It will only effect yours."

Panic begins to swell again in my chest, causing my heart to pick up and my breathing to become short. "Listen," I begin, my voice a little shaky. After clearing my throat, I continue, "What Williams did to Walters was horrible, and I can understand Beatrice's pain, but what about all those lives taken? How is that justice?"

"Greed is what stole Beatrice's soul, greed is what will destroy this town." Ester pulls a knife from under her black robe. "Beatrice made us promise to finish her task. That was her final and only wish. Nothing is going to stop us from disappointing her, or keep me from getting what I was promised."

"Why Tyler?" I ask, desperate to spare him.

The hot logs crackle again, causing embers to shoot from the fire. Stella doesn't spare it a glance as she answers me. "Although it pains us Tyler is from David's line and will be hosting Walter, it is because he has both Beatrice's and Walter's family blood in him, as you do."

All eyes turn to me, expectant. Why, I don't know. Are they expecting me to jump for joy or something?

"You see," Ester continues, "your father is of David's blood and your mother is of Walter's brothers line. It is the first time the two lines have come together and became one since Walter was taken from Beatrice."

"Plus, he's young and stout. We like them stout." One of the women laughs in the darkness and the other follow suit. I don't.

With disgust on her face, Ester leans down with the knife firm in her hand and cuts the ropes on my feet. She doesn't have time to stand before I'm attacking. Well, trying to attack anyway. The others are prepared and grab me by the arms. I jump, kick, and continue to fight but it does no good.

"We don't have time to play games with you," Ester says through gritted teeth, as she holds my face tight in her hand, squeezing my cheeks together. "I always hold out hope we can convince David's daughters to join us, but they never listen, never see what they can have with a little sacrifice. Regretfully, it always comes to this." Ester walks away and the others follow, dragging me with them kicking and screaming through the woods.

Where are they taking me? And what did she mean by the others?

"I don't want you to think all those lives taken were chosen at random," Stella says beside me. "Beatrice's only rule was to sacrifice descendants of those she had breathed life into, and those of Williams. Never would she stoop to killing others' blood."

A and C start to form a B, so that the whole song can be sung without holes. Beatrice had two daughters and one son. The son didn't agree with her, but the daughters did, and would later become known as the Daughters of Beatrice. David's children suffered for his decision by being thrown from the overlook to sustain Walter. *And I thought my family was screwed up. Oh, wait a minute, we are from this family. Damn.*

"Although, we have had to make a few sacrifices over the years. The lines are starting to thin out, after all," Stella chuckles. I sneer at her in disgust. Who in their right mind finds pleasure in killing innocent people? A mad loon, that's who.

The glow from the fire begins to fade the deeper into the woods we go. All is dark until we come upon Montgomery cabin. Something bright bursts inside, causing the doors to rattle and pieces of glass to fall from the window.

Ester laughs. "Foolish old man. You know, I once loved him. I thought of him as my own grandfather. But after that little brats death, I never saw him again. A few years later he committed suicide, hoping to make up for what William had done." She laughs again. "He did nothing but trap himself in that old cabin."

Hmm, guess those stories about strange noises in the woods are true.

Ester's story from earlier comes to mind as I look at the cabin. "What about MaryAnn? Did you not love her?"

Ester wheels around, and the glow coming from the cabin allows me to see the anger in her eyes. "My childhood was a lie. MaryAnn did nothing but make it harder."

"I don't believe that," I challenge. Hands grip me harder, warning me to shut up. But if I'm about to die, that will be the last thing I do. "She was like a sister to you, wasn't she? I could hear the love in your voice when you said her name."

"It was a lie," Ester screams. She straightens her shoulders and tries to collect herself, but I don't miss the gleam in her eyes. "Her mother was an Edwards and her father one of David's sons. She was a traitor of the worst kind."

"Yet, she did nothing but love you, just like you loved her."

Smack. The sting from Ester's hand burns my cheek and causes water to fill my eyes. With hard eyes, Ester turns around and continues the way she was going before I called her out. The windows and doors shake again as we walk by the cabin, as if the old man is begging for Ester to change her mind. *You and me both.*

"He always did cater to MaryAnn." Ester stares at the house. "Guess we know why. Too bad his precious granddaughter wasn't saved like I was."

We continue through the woods, the silence now more oppressing. The few sounds we hear makes me feel like nature is giving me her own goodbye and I start to panic all over again, but the women's grip on my arms is too strong for me to get away. One has enough of my squirming and grabs me by the hair and jerks my head back. I cry out and plead for her to let go. Instead, she tightens her hold and pushes or pulls, I can't tell which at this point, me through the woods.

"You see, Jo, Walter could sense it inside of us, sense Beatrice's blood in ours. That's why he spared us and warned the other daughters not to kill us. You're alive today because of him."

"But Bryce isn't!" I scream.

Ester and the others look away from me, their expressions hooded.

"We had no—" Ms. Stella starts.

"Don't give me that 'no choice' shit. He was a person, a good person."

"Jo," Ester says, her voice soft and a little winded as we start up a hill. "Like it or not, we had no choice. David's line was getting thin. After doing some research, I found that you and Tyler are the only ones left in town. There was no one else to sacrifice."

We reach the top of the hill and I can see the overlook a few yards down the road.

"We saved you that night, knowing who you were so we could offer you a place by our side. We could have let you die then and been done with you, let David's line die out. But we wanted to give you a chance. Walter wanted to give you a chance."

"Plus, you needed Tyler," I scream as they begin dragging me toward the overlook. I do my best to stop them and dig my heels into the gravel and dirt of the road. But no matter what I do, they keep pushing and pulling. My pleas mean nothing to them.

When we reach the rock wall, I'm shoved to my knees in front of it. The mysterious lights, which I know now to be orbs, float and dance among the trees of the hollow. Some burn out, only for another to appear yards away. A tear slips down my cheek as I stare out across the valley. It's a place I used to find so peaceful, so serene. Not anymore. And soon, it will become my home if Ester and the others get their way.

"Ester," I say, my voice calm. I keep my eyes on the orbs below, and refuse to look at her. "Why do you have to kill me? I don't understand. If you had never involved me, I would have never known."

"That's the problem, Jo. You did get involved, even though it was by accident. Walter wouldn't kill you because you are of his love's blood, but by him sparing you, he only prolonged your pain. Beatrice told David, before she killed him herself, that his family would pay for him turning his back on her. She needed his help and he thought she was crazy."

Sounds like I come from the smart side of the family. I agree with you one hundred percent there, great uncle. Bitch was crazy.

"But you don't need to kill me now!" I say with a shaky voice, unable to keep myself calm.

"Oh, but I must, to keep you quiet. You know too much now. Plus, your death will encourage Tyler to give me his soul. What the fool won't know is he won't be giving up his spirit to get you back, he will really be giving it up for Walter."

I scream and try to get to my feet. My bloody hands are still tied behind my back, throwing me off balance and I stumble, but manage to get to steady myself. I'm ready to ram into Ester, when a shot rings out, loud, and a rush of cold sweeps through my body. I freeze and wait to feel the blossom of pain from wherever I've been shot, when I hear another blast from behind me. I turn, my eyes wide, and find Mason Edwards standing in the road, shotgun in hand.

Chapter Nineteen

"Jo, I want you to walk toward me," Mason instructs, keeping his gun aimed on Ester.

I take a step but am yanked back by my hair. I scowl at the woman who has a grip on me, not recognizing her, and start to tell her what for when Ms. Stella pulls out her own gun.

"I don't think that's going to happen," she says, cocking the pistol. "She's fine where she's at."

Figures they'd be packing. Damn the luck.

Mason and Stella glare at one another, sizing each other up, when a blazing horn rips through the tense silence. Seconds later, two vehicles come sliding around the curve, a truck tailing in tight behind a car. Dust flies as they both come to a quick stop. I try and take the opportunity to run, but the wench and her friend holding me aren't loosening their grips anytime soon.

The dust settles to reveal Jada and Cooper getting out of a black two door Chevy Nova. *That's a nice freaking car.* Which reminds me. Where the hell is my Mustang? Tyler and Kirk get out of his truck, armed and aimed. Doesn't look like I'm dying tonight without a good old fight.

"I don't care what you thought you were planning to do with Jo, but you can forget about it. She's coming with us," Tyler demands and signals for them to let me go.

Ester laughs. "You may think because you are holding a gun that this was going to be easy. But I assure you, it won't be."

My attention is drawn from their bickering about who is more badass, as Bryce appears next to Kirk. It's still strange to see Bryce and know he's real, that I'm not imagining him. Although, knowing I'm not imagining him helps make it less strange, just a tiny bit. The sorrow on his face causes me to pause. Why does he look so sad?

"Jo!" Cooper screams, and starts for me, but Jada holds him back.

I look around, confused as to what all the commotion is about, and turn to find Walter closing on me.

Whoosh.

A scream rips from my lungs as he opens his nasty black mouth. The sound that has haunted my dreams and thoughts for over a year fills my eardrums to the point I can't hear anything else around me. The two women holding me let go and step back, covering their ears. I catch another glimpse of Bryce, then, as if by magic, my hands are freed and I cover my ears. I double over and tuck my head between my knees, but nothing helps stop the assault. And just as fast as it came, it goes.

Cautious, I stand back up and search around me through tear-filled eyes. Seeing nothing, I dart toward Cooper, ready to get to safety. Walter appears feet in front of me, mouth open, threatening, but nothing comes spewing out—thank god—as I turn to run the other way. The appearance of Walter has distracted the coven, and my crew takes the opportunity to fight the sisters hand to hand. But Walter keeps me busy. Every turn, every mad dash I try to make, there he is, blocking my way.

I thought he didn't want to kill me. Could have fooled me.

"What are you doing?" Jada yells, while blocking a bat being swung at her head. "He's a ghost, dumbass. Go through him."

Okay, so not my brightest moment.

Walter looks from me to Jada with pure hatred and flings his arm out to the side. Jada is thrown against the Nova, and crumples onto her side in the dirt. When she makes no effort to get up, I panic, knowing they are going to kill us all if they have to, in order to get what they want.

Closing my eyes, I prepare myself to run through Walter and picture Cooper and Tyler on the other side. *I don't see Walter. I will not go through him. I'm just running through cool air.* I keep telling myself these things as I run. It's not until I'm fixing to peek to see if I've made it through when I'm side-swiped. My vision blurs as I topple over and come crashing against the rock wall.

"Child," Ester sneers, and gets to her feet. "Killing you will be a pleasure." She wipes blood from her face before stooping down to get a hold on me.

I bound up on my feet and barrel into her, ready to teach her just what this *child* can do. Dust flies when she lands on her back with me on top. For an older woman she sure is strong. Her fist comes flying at my face and I duck to the side just in time. When she rolls over and comes for me, I notice a brightness around her, as if the air surrounding her body is glowing.

Ester tackles me to the ground again, this time knocking the air out of me. "You cannot defeat us. The power in our veins…" she trails off, laughing, and pulls out two zip ties. "No need teasing you with something you'll never have," she spits and places her knee in the middle of my chest.

Gunshots ring through the air and I see two hooded figures crumble to the ground. Another gunshot is fired, but this time I'm not sure who it came from. To my right, Walter stands watching Ester as we struggle. He knows I'm of Beatrice's line so maybe he doesn't get what she's up to. Does he not get how messed up these women have become? Considering he was just playing cat and mouse with me, he's obviously past the point of caring.

Rocks dig into my back as Ester pushes down harder with her leg, pulls on my hands, and starts to wrap the ties around them. Walter smiles. *Great.*

Swoosh.

"Jo!" Cooper yells and tries to get to me, but is stopped by Ms. Stella who puts the barrel of her gun right up against his chest.

"Drop it," she instructs, indicating his axe.

A flash beside me takes my attention away from them two. Bryce flashes back and forth between Walter and Ester, who still has me pinned. He's the one making that swooshing sound as he flashes in and out. Walter watches him closely, trying to pinpoint his next move I'm sure. I can see the anger in his eyes build with every false guess.

Walter closes his eyes and all the light energy I saw around Ester and the others begins to gather around him. He spreads his arms wide as a cyclone of spirit energy spins around him, making him more human-shaped by the second.

I fight against Ester, feeling stronger than her now, and am able to get her knee off of me. I hear another gun-shot to my right and turn to see Ms. Stella fall to the ground, clutching her leg.

"Jo!"

My heart races as I look from Bryce to Cooper and then back again.

Walter sets his sights on Bryce and I know I have to stop him or he's going to consume all that is left of Bryce. Cooper knows it too.

"Catch!" he yells and tosses me his axe. With a skill I didn't know I was capable of, I manage to catch the axe by its handle and swing my whole body around with the weight.

Ester tries getting to her feet, but I swoop her legs out from underneath her and pop her in the face with the end of the handle. She falls back, motionless. *Get up from that on your own, bitch.*

Energy blasts from Walter and I have to push against it to stay up-right. He starts for Bryce, who looks determined to do what he must to keep the attention away from us.

"Hey, Walter," I yell. "I've got your fucking silver over here."

Walter turns, almost solid now, his eyes red and unfocused. As I hoped, he forgets about Bryce and rushes for me. I stand still and tighten my grip on the damp twine wrapped around the handle. Nice to know Jada had time to bless this thing before it saw some action. Looking at Bryce one last time, I swing around and put all the weight I can behind the axe blow. When the sharp blade makes contact with the transparent outline of Walter, a bright light explodes all around us. The blast pushes me back into the rock wall, the light blinding me.

The last thing I wonder, as my eyes begin to close, is who will I wake up to see? Bryce or Cooper?

Chapter Twenty

"Jo."

What sounds like snapping fingers break through the darkness and pulls me from my sweet slumber.

"Come on, Jo. Please. Don't do this to me."

Confused as to why he sounds panicked, I start to open my eyes when the pain hits. And boy, does it hit me hard. Reaching up, I gently touch the large knot on my head, and find that my hair is coated in blood. I know why Tyler is freaking out. He's glad to see I'm not dead.

"Jo?" Cooper says.

"Quieter," I whisper, with my eyes still closed. "Too loud."

"Tyler, come here. I need you." Kirk's voice comes from a good distance... I think.

"You got her?" Tyler asks Cooper. "I'll only be gone a minute."

"Don't worry," Cooper answers, cradling my head in his lap.

Once I hear the sound of crunching rocks fade as Tyler walks off, I sit up. My mistake. The world spins, and my stomach rolls with it. I close my eyes and do the deep breathing exercises I've seen on television. A few moments later, Cooper cups my face in his hands.

"Open your eyes," he instructs.

Not up for arguing, I do as told. I continue to do as asked, follow his finger, look straight ahead, without arguing. When Cooper is satisfied I'm okay, he sits back with relief.

"You had me worried there for a minute. I was the first to you," he pauses and shakes his head, "and I swear you weren't breathing. It scared the shit out of me."

"Need some toilet paper?" I say, smiling, and after he tries to stop himself, Cooper smiles too. That's when I notice the blood on the side of his face, right next to his hairline and ear.

"Let me see that," I say.

"It's nothing," he says, dismissively, but after getting a glimpse at my 'I don't think so, Mister' face, he turns his head so I can see.

"Looks like you'll need a few stitches." There's a small one-inch gap beside his temple and above his ear, but it's not too deep. "You should be fine," I tell him.

"Told you," he says.

Grabbing his hand, I look up at him. "Thank you."

"For what?" he whispers, glancing down at our intertwined fingers.

"For saving me." I duck under his head so I can make eye contact with him again. "And Bryce. It means a lot to me."

I'm not sure who pulls who in, maybe it is a mutual thing, but we hug each other tight, thankful to be alive. Closing my eyes so tight I see dancing spots, I revel in the moment. The touch of another person holding me, the air filtering into my lungs, the slight breeze ruffling my hair and cooling my damp cheeks. Life. I pray I never forget the feeling of fear I had ten minutes ago when I thought all of this would be gone and remember to appreciate every single second of life. I don't want another near-death experience to have to remind me again.

Cooper clears his throat and pulls away. I try to keep him close, not ready to let go yet.

"Jo," he whispers next to my ear, and I can hear the pain in his voice. Thinking I'm hurting his wound, I go ahead a sit back only to see that wasn't why he sounded upset. He continues to stare over my shoulder, a sense of defeat in his posture. "There's someone here to see you."

My stomach tightens and I'm sure I'm going to be sick. I have a good guess as to who is waiting on me and when Cooper's eyes meet mine, I know for sure. *Bryce.* Guilt slams into me, though so does relief and excitement, when I turn to look at him. The need to rush to him and throw my arms around him overwhelms me, even though I know I can't.

Squeezing Cooper's hand and telling him I'll be right back, I walk over to where Bryce is standing—or floating, whatever it is ghosts do.

"I'm so glad you're okay," he says when I'm mere inches from him. I don't know if it's possible, or if maybe it's the transparent look he's sporting these days, but his eyes shimmer like they're full of tears. "When Walter.... " he trails off, his voice cracking at the memory of what happened.

Instinct causes me to reach out to grab his hand, although it does no good. My flesh goes straight through his energy. Pulling my hand back and crossing my arms over my chest, I bite my lip and struggle to think of something to say. There's so much I've wanted to tell him since he died, but now, now it feels impossible. I don't that I can speak around the lump in my throat without breaking down.

"I'm so sorry, Jo."

His face falls and my heart breaks. I want to hug him and reassure him that it's okay, because it is okay. It's not his fault. It never was his fault.

"I should have done more that night."

"No," I snap, finally finding my voice. "You did everything you could. We both did. The only regret that I have is that it was you and not me. Living without you has been the hardest damn thing I have ever done. The pain... it's unboarable."

His gaze meets mine. "I'm glad it wasn't you. And yeah, the pain sucks. But you've freed me Jo, and the others. So many others. We aren't trapped anymore in this god forsaken hollow." He looks at the trees surrounding us, and shakes his head. "Remember all those times we came up here and said we could stay here forever. Well let me assure you, we couldn't. It's not as great as it looks."

I smile, remembering the longing to stay when it was time to go home.

"I love you, Jo."

"You're not leaving yet, are you?" I ask, panicked.

He chuckles. "Soon, but not yet. I've been wanting to say that to your face for so long. I've whispered it every night, hoping that you heard me."

Damn him. I swore I would stay strong for him, that I wouldn't break down and bawl. But dammit if he didn't ruin all of that. I do my best to hide my pain and cup my face to hide the tears. My shoulders shake from sobbing, and I curse myself over and over to get under control.

"Jo, I do love you and I know you're hurting. I'm hurting too. If there was anything I could do to come back to you, I would do it in a heartbeat. But baby, there's not. Please believe me."

"I do," I mumble through my hands.

"Jo, please look at me. Please," he begs.

I wipe away the tears and through the blur of more that are building, I look at him.

"The others are leaving." He gestures out to the valley that is sparkling with orbs, brighter than I've ever seen them. One by one they begin to ascend into the sky, and disappear out of sight.

"I'm going to have to go soon too. But first, I need you to make me two promises."

I knew this is why he wanted to talk to me. It's why my stomach tensed and my nerves shook. I don't know if I want to hear this, because what happens after is that he says goodbye.

"Bryce, I—"

"Promise me, Jo. Promise that you will always remember that I love you. Baby, I love you so much it doesn't feel like that word is enough. And because of that, I want you to be happy. And promise me that you will move on, that you will find a life beyond your sorrow, and live. I need you to live life to the fullest. Please promise me those two things." His fingers twitch at his sides until he balls them into fists. I know how he feels. I want to touch him too.

"I don't think I can," I whisper.

He feigns being hurt. "You doubt my love?"

"No," I answer, rolling my eyes while my lips twitch into a smile. "I don't think I can move on from you Bryce. You've always been it for me. And I don't..." I trail off, a lump of guilt building in my throat.

"You don't want me to think you don't love me anymore, or that some other guy can replace me."

I nod.

"Please," he says and does a manly posture. "I know there's no guy that can replace this awesomeness. The only person I feel sorry for is you. Finding a guy who comes even close to this package is going to be quite the task."

"Oh, I'm sure there's a few," I tease, but when I do, I'm hit with guilt again. How could I say something like that to him?

"Don't, Jo," Bryce warns. "Don't feel guilty. I want that for you. I swear I do. And Cooper, he seems—"

"Let's not play matchmaker tonight, okay?" I ask.

Bryce digs his hands deep into his pockets. Ghosts have pockets? Who knew?

"I've got to go, babe. I am so grateful that I got to say goodbye. The thought I might not get to is what hurt the most."

"I know," I whisper as tear after tear fell down my cheeks.

"I love you, Jo."

"I love you too, Bryce. Always have, always will."

Waving, with a tear of his own sliding down his transparent cheek, he floats out over the hollow until he becomes a blur of light like the others.

Headlights shine across the overlook and I turn to see Millie pulling in. She hops out of the Jeep and without pause, comes crashing into me. Over and over again she tells me how glad she is to see me alive. It had been her who had seen Ester kidnapping me and called the others. Seeing the orbs and my tear stained face, she clutches me tight and says nothing more. Together we watch as one by one, the orbs of each soul floats off into the sky.

Chapter Twenty One

One month later.

The night breeze is cool against my skin as I rock back and forth in the rocking chair on the front porch. A lightning storm like I have never seen before drew me outside to watch. No strikes have hit the ground yet, but the flashes are coming frequently—like a county-wide strobe light. It's kind of ironic now is the time for such an event. It's as if Mother Nature is giving Cooper and Jada a farewell party of her own.

The thought of them leaving saddens me and I sigh, wishing things could be different. While a lot has changed since we reported the coven and vanquished Walter to the other side, not much has changed in terms of my own life. It's not like I can go around and say 'see, I told you there were evil spirits killing people' to everyone in town. No one knows about Walter and his part in the killings. All of that is being blamed on the coven. So the only ones who know what really happened, are Cooper, Jada, Tyler, Millie, and Kirk. And now, I'm losing Cooper, the one who I can talk to the most. The one person I don't want to leave.

I haven't reduced myself to begging, yet, but when I asked him why he couldn't stay and finish out senior year, he just shook his head and whispered he couldn't. I almost understand why. What he and his sister do is important, more so than the world will ever know, but it still sucks. What's wrong with taking a little break and living a little of your life for youself?

Oh, I don't know Jo, because others' lives could be lost while they lay around.

Damn the truth.

The screen door slams as a rumble of thunder booms overhead, with the lightning stretching through the clouds. The flashes of light illuminates Tyler's face, which is filled with concern.

"You okay?"

No. "Sure. What makes you think I'm not? This storm is pretty awesome to watch."

He steps up closer to the edge of the porch and peers up at the sky. "It is. I haven't seen anything like this."

"Makes you wonder," I mumble, although I'm sure he still heard me.

"Jo, I know with them leaving—"

"What about Jada? How are you taking it?" I interrupt, knowing he was about to go on a spill about their duty, how hard it is for me, and all that good stuff. Yeah, I'd rather not hear it. I would like to know how he plans on dealing with Jada leaving. He hasn't acted mopey or anything. Neither have I, not until tonight anyway.

Once the dust settled with the coven and we dealt with what we faced, Tyler and Jada started spending a lot of time together. And I do mean a lot. Some nights he wouldn't even come home, which forced Cooper to hang out with me more. Not that I was complaining. We visited a lot of my old favorite spots in town and in the mountains, places I hadn't ventured to in a long time. While I sketched a scene, he would read, or practice his fighting routines. Him getting all sweaty as his muscles flexed didn't elicit any complaints on my part. If anything, it only made the attraction I had building up for him stronger.

Now, here we are, facing a moment we all knew was coming but ignored until now. Saying goodbye. I don't want Tyler to lose the smile and light in his eyes that has been there since he started spending time with Jada. I also don't want to lose Cooper. My friend. Someone who has helped me more than he could possibly ever know.

Tyler rubs his hand across the back of his neck, his eyes locked on the wooden slats of the porch. "It sucks," he whispers. Dropping his hand, he looks at me and shrugs. "But there's nothing we can do about it. They have to do what's right for them. And as awesome as Jada is, she's not the settling kind." He shrugs again. "Even if I am." He runs his hands along the porch's railing and up the posts. "I don't think I could live a life like they do. You know she asked me, right?"

I nod. "Cooper mentioned it. He said she figured you would say no, but she wanted to ask anyway."

"I don't know," he says, obviously struggling for words that match his thoughts. He gestures around us. "This is our history, Jo. I could never see leaving it, just like they can never see leaving theirs. I'll never forget her, but this is what's best for all of us."

Is it? I know Tyler can't and won't leave Dover. It's our family home, and he has become a big part of the community. In fact, there's talk of voting him into the City Council next month since a few slots recently came open. *Imagine that.*

But what about me? The only reason I am staying is for him. I may not be that much help, and I know he feels he needs to take care of me, but I'm also all he has of family around here. Well, at least family we knew about and who aren't bat shit crazy. Up and leaving him would be near impossible right now, even if I feel no such connection to this place like he does.

"Did you know mom and dad called?" He says, breaking the silence.

"Nope," I answer. But the lie is obvious. I knew. I just didn't care.

Tyler chuckles. "Well, apparently they have been doing some soul searching and entered into counseling. They realized how crappy it was for them to leave us like they did and after a few sessions, their therapists told them it would be best if they came back home to mend some bridges."

My face falls, as does my stomach. "That's bullshit. What they did was wrong on so many levels, and you know, as well as I do, things were going to crap before my "episodes" as they liked to call them. They haven't been there for us in a long time and you know it."

"I know. That's why I told them no."

"You what?" I say, shocked. Tyler is the one who usually is trying to ease the situation and look for some way for us to be a family again.

"It wasn't easy," he admits. "But I told them they couldn't move back into the house with us. I can't stop them from moving back to town or anything, but the house is now mine—they signed it over. If they want to prove themselves or whatever, they can, but while living somewhere else."

"That's awful... strange of you." I say, not understanding where this is coming from.

Tyler walks over, squats down, and clasps my hands. "I miss them. I can't lie about that. They are our parents, whether we like it or not. But the way mom was talking, I felt like she wanted to do this for her and not for us."

"That's how she's always been," I reply, thinking about all the functions she participated in, trying to make a good name for herself as a caring mother, but how she never had time for the children she said she was doing it all for. Nobody else saw it, but she never had time for us, it was all for her and how she appeared in public.

"It's funny, though," I say, thinking about her oh-so-important status, "that she would come back knowing everyone in town knows they left us here. Not really part of her mom of the year look, is it?"

"I don't understand it, either, but I don't care about that. I'm going to make sure she doesn't hurt you again. Leaving like that, claiming it was too hard on them, was the lowest move she's ever made. And dad too."

It was, but a part of me now wonders if there was more to it than they claimed. "You don't think they knew about the curse, do you?" Why else would they want to come back home after the news broke that the coven have all been arrested in connection with a string of murders? It sure has me curious.

Tyler chuckles. "Funny you should bring that up. I've been wondering the same thing. We know dad is from

David's line, maybe... I don't know, I hate to speculate. We need to talk to him."

I don't hate to speculate. If our parents knew, and we find out they did, then they can write me off as dead. To leave us here, possibly knowing what was going on and what I was dealing with, to run and save their own skin will be the last straw for me. Tyler can do whatever he wants.

We continue to sit out on the porch in silence as the storm continues on around us. I don't know how much time passes, but eventually I say goodnight and head up to my room. I open all the curtains so I can see the flashes in my dark room and lie back on the bed.

It's strange, lying here in the quiet with no worries about what I might see or dream. Adjusting to the quiet hasn't been easy. The first few nights after the attack at the overlook, I had lain here waiting for Walter's transparent flickering image to appear in the corner of my eye again. Each night that I waited, tense and afraid that we weren't as successful as we believed, I slowly began to relax. Now, there's no wondering, only silence. And to be honest, I don't like it.

I feel as if I have nothing to wonder about, nothing to fear, nothing to look forward to. I used to question whether or not what I was seeing was real, feared my dreams, and looked forward to a day when I was normal again, well, as normal as any teenagers life is anyway. Now that day is here and there's nothing. I know I have things I could look forward to: graduation, whether or not I'm going to college, all the inner works of bringing your high school years to an end. The problem is, after all that's happened, those things don't seem to matter to me anymore. They should, but they don't. Now I'm living day by day, sketching my way through the time until I figure out what I do need to concentrate on.

My eyes begin to grow heavy, with the sound of the thunder helping carry me away, when a soft tap comes at my window. At first, I think it's a tree branch or something scraping against the glass, but as it continues I look over to see a dark silhouette. Talk about old days coming back to life. My heart picks up speed and I sit up, debating on what I should do. Am I seeing things again?

"Jo." Cooper's voice is a whisper through the thick pane, and I roll my eyes at myself for jumping to the worst conclusions first.

Opening the newly-installed window, I help Cooper over the ledge. I'm not much help though, considering he lands face-first on the rug.

"Ouch," he murmurs against the plush red carpet before lifting himself up on his hands.

"What are you doing?" I ask, laughing and shaking my head. "Tyler told you the front door works. Did you forget?"

Brushing off his clothes, he shakes his head. "I didn't want him to know I was here."

My stomach does a somersault as heat rises to my cheeks. *Dammit.* Turning away so he doesn't see my obvious blush, I shut the window. "Why? It's only 10:00 pm. He wouldn't mind."

"I know," he says, close, as in right over my shoulder close. "How's the new window?"

"It's a window." Gathering my courage, I turn around to face him. Like I expected, he's mere inches from me. "So... what's going on?"

I'm surprised when he lets me walk around him and I go straight for my chair in the corner. I had expected him to stop me. It's obvious he has something to say, something from the expression on his face that is hard to express.

Running his hand over his face and letting out a deep breath, he sits on the end of my bed. "Not much. Jada was watching the news. They were talking about the council members who were revealed to be a part of the coven, along with Chief Tucker." He shrugs. "I'm just tired of hearing about it."

It had been no surprise to me to hear Chief Tucker was the son of one of Beatrice's granddaughters. It explained a lot, including his creepy stalking, and his ignoring everything I'd told him. The two councilmen, however, had been a shock. For decades, probably since the council was formed, Beatrice's bloodline had somehow stayed on board, whether it was a son or daughter. Explains how they could keep all the so-called 'accidents' labeled as such and never have an investigation of what was going on.

We were all relieved to find that Millie's family had nothing to do with the events of our town's secrets. They were as shocked as the rest of the town.

"I am too. Tyler brought home the paper today and it was all over the front page. I chucked it. As far as I'm concerned, they are getting what they deserve and it's all behind me now."

Cooper nods but his eyes are focused on the floor, like he's thinking about something else that has nothing to do with this conversation.

"Okay, tell me what's really on your mind. And don't you dare say 'nothing'," I warn.

"It's just... I don't.... " his search for words gets the best of him and he jumps to his feet, then starts pacing. "I've never felt this way when leaving a place. I don't know how to handle it."

Biting my lip, I ask, "How do you feel?"

He turns, his eyes searching mine. "I don't want to go," he whispers. "The thought of leaving is killing me. But I have to."

My eyes begin to sting and I turn to look out the window to try and keep myself from crying. "I don't want you to leave either." I hadn't meant to say it, but it's how I feel. I never thought saying goodbye to Cooper would be this hard. We've gotten close over the last two months and the thought of never seeing him again hurts.

"You understand why I have to, don't you?"

Closing my eyes and wishing the tears away, I nod. "I do. It's the same reason I have to stay."

Tyler doesn't know it, but Cooper did ask me to go with him as well. The same night Jada asked Tyler to go with her. Of course, I told Cooper no, not because I didn't want to go but because I knew Tyler would stay.

"Jada and you need each other, just like Tyler and I need each other."

It gets quiet, neither one of us knowing what to say, or how to deal with what we are feeling. I wish things could be different, or perhaps there was another job for them to do that is close. But there's not. Worse yet, they've been called to Georgia to investigate a plantation home that is being haunted, with several deaths occurring inside the home since the people who built it in the early 1900's passed away. Every time someone purchases the home, someone in the family that moved in dies. Creepy. But there it is. They're needed.

"How have you been dealing with seeing Bryce move on?" Cooper asks. His unease in asking is obvious but I have to wonder if there's motive behind the question.

"I'm handling it a lot better than I was before."

Cooper looks around the room. "I can see that." He steps over to the closet where the door is halfway open. He points inside. "Did you wash those before you hung them up?"

I flip him off but laugh. "Yes. I may have been a mess, but I'm working on it." I think back to his question about Bryce, while I stand and go over and sit on the bed. I feel restless, like we are dancing around each other, and around something we both feel but don't want to admit.

"I'll always love Bryce, you know?" He nods before I continue. "But getting to say goodbye, no matter how hard that was, gave me some peace. *He* gave me some peace. I'm not saying I'm ready to go off and get in a serious relationship anytime soon, but it's getting easier every day to accept what is and to know that I can live and remember him at the same time."

With slow steps, Cooper comes to stand in front of me. He peers down at me with curious, yet intense eyes.

"That's good. I hope some day you can find a person to share your life with and who understands you love them but that you will always love the person you lost as well."

I wet my lips, struggling not to fidget under his gaze. "Me too," I whisper.

Not taking his eyes away from mine, Cooper kneels down in front of me and rests his weight on his knees while placing his hands on the bed on either side of my thighs.

Wetting his lips, he says, "I came here tonight to say goodbye. I don't want Jada or Tyler watching and I didn't want you to be the last thing I see in my rearview mirror. I wanted to be alone. So when Tyler asks if you are coming to meet us at the diner in the morning before we leave, please say no."

"Why?" I ask, hurt that he wouldn't want to see me one last time.

"Because if you're there," he whispers and brings his hands up to cup my face, "I don't think I will be able to leave."

The desire in his eyes is clear and I know he is going to kiss me. This also happens to be the time my tears decide to build and break without given me a chance to stop them. Cooper catches the tears with his thumbs and wipes at my cheeks. Concern and a lot of hurt fills his eyes.

"I'm sorry. I shouldn't have...." his voice catches and he starts to pull away, but I grab his wrists to keep his hands where they are.

I can only imagine what he's thinking. I'm sure the name Bryce is floating in his head, along with the words 'not ready'. But I am ready for him to kiss me, to hold my hand and understand why I'm going so slow, to be the one who makes me smile, but who also understands why I'm sad at times. What I'm not ready for is to say goodbye. And that's what this is, a goodbye kiss.

Another tears slips down my cheek and he's quick to wipe it away as his eyes search mine for understanding.

"I don't want to say goodbye," I whisper.

He leans in and kisses my forehead and then rest his on mine. "I don't either," he breathes. "God, I wish it was me who could stay here and be the one you need."

Pulling back, he pauses only for a second before inching forward until our lips meet. It's a slow exploration at first, a testing to make sure it's okay, as our lips sweep over one another. Feeling the desire rise, Cooper deepens the kiss and pulls me closer so that our bodies are together.

The guilt I had expected the first time I kissed another man doesn't come. All my thoughts are centered on Cooper and the bond we have shared over the last few months. I'm focused on his touch, and the feel of our lips together.

It isn't until he pushes me back against the bed so that he's lying on top of me that I freeze. My lips stop moving and I swear so does my heart. *This, yeah, I'm not ready for this.*

Cooper looks down at the terror on my face and his eyes soften. "That's not happening. I promise. If I did that, I'm sure there's no way I would ever leave." He smirks.

Smiling and feeling relieved, I relax and let him know it's okay.

Hours pass as we lie there and talk, kiss, talk, and then kiss some more. Our topics range from movies to fighting to ghosts to college. Cooper admits he's always known he would never go to college, and that whenever a person mentions so and so college or university, he has no clue what they are talking about. I open up about how I don't know what I'm going to do with my life. He reassures me that it's okay, not everyone does. I know he's trying to be helpful, but that doesn't do the trick.

Before we know it, the sky starts to lighten, with the first rays of morning peeking over the horizon.

Here it is. Goodbye. God how I hate goodbyes.

Cooper stands in front of the window, his face torn with sadness. "Keep in touch, okay? If my number changes, I'll let you know."

"I will. I promise. And you too. Send me pics of the house in Georgia. I'm kind of intrigued."

He nods but swallows hard. "I'm going to miss you," he whispers.

"I'll miss you too."

Hefting one leg out the window, he sits on the sill and looks out over the yard. "Hey, you know, I could fall from the window and break my leg or something. It would delay my leaving."

I roll my eyes and smile. "I advise against that. You may crack your skull open."

He shrugs, a smirk on his lips. "I've got a hard head."

Wrapping my arms around his neck, he rests his head on my stomach and we both sigh. After a few more stolen seconds, he turns with a hard expression and climbs down the tree. For the second time in a month, I watch as another guy I really care about fades from view.

~

Despite only getting two hours of sleep after Cooper left, I'm surprised when I wake up full of energy. The bittersweet promise of coffee wafts through the hallway and I'm quick to get dressed. Tyler sits at the table sipping a cup while looking over the paper. I pour one for myself, grab two muffins, and join him.

"Want one?" I ask, holding out the muffins.

"I thought you were going with me to meet Cooper and Jada before they left."

My face falls, my hatred for this day rising. "Nope. I changed my mind. I'm going to school."

"What about Cooper?" he asks, confused.

I picture us lying in bed last night, our lips locked, and have to fight to keep the smile off my face. "I've already said goodbye to him, no need to keep dragging the inevitable along." I say this, even though I don't mean it. I do want to go see Cooper, but I made him a promise that I wouldn't, and I'm going to stick to it. No matter how much I hate it.

Tyler fumbles for something to talk about. It's obvious I'm upset. Ready to go, I finish off my muffin, tell Tyler I'll see him later, and head out the door.

My phone beeps with a message from Millie asking if I need a ride. I text her back saying I'm going to walk and then put my phone on silent before tossing it into my bag.

The walk to school is peaceful—well, except for car after car passing me as they hurry to drop their kids off to get to work. Another normal day for our small town.

"Hey!"

I jump, almost screaming, and turn to see Kirk laughing behind me.

"You're such an ass."

He shrugs. "Never said I wasn't."

I roll my eyes and take deep breathes to calm my racing heart. We walk in silence after that, and I almost expect him to start walking faster before anyone can see us. While he no longer blames me for his brother's death, he still doesn't acknowledge me in public. Shitty? Yes, but I'm past the point of caring. I know he's only trying to deal with all that's happened, just like I am. Plus, how can he one day go from hating me to being my BFF.

"You been doing okay?" he asks, breaking the silence, and staying in pace with me.

"Good as I can be. You?"

"I'm dealing. Still wish things were different."

I nod, but say nothing.

"So…. I've been wanting to talk to you," he rushes out.

Really? Because I've seen you every day and yet you make no gesture to acknowledge me. "About what?"

"I know I've been a real jerk lately."

He bows his head. Is he embarrassed?

"And I'm sorry."

I stop and brace myself against a tree, fearing I might faint. "Say what?"

"Come on, Jo. You heard me."

"No, I don't think I did."

Kirk kicks at the sidewalk, his hands deep in his jacket pockets. "I'm sorry, okay? I've been shitty, and I shouldn't have been that way."

"Thanks Kirk." I take in a deep breath, hold it, and let it out fast. "I'm sorry too," I mumble, knowing I owe it to him.

His shock shows only for a second before he masks his face with a smirk. "You never could stand being mad at me for long."

"Yeah, but I think a year is a new record for us."

"True," he says. "Let's make sure it never happens again."

We toss jokes at one another as we finish our walk. When we round the corner onto school property, the sound of a rumbling engine catches my attention and I look to see a familiar Nova driving away. I wave for Kirk to go on and watch the car until it fades around the corner of the main road. A slight breeze ruffles the oak leaves over my head and I lean against the trunk for support.

The days ahead aren't going to be easy, the memories and longing I carry for not only Bryce, but also Cooper, will be hard to boar. But for the first time in a long time, I feel lighter and stronger. I know I can deal with the pain now, and that I have a strong support system of people that love me. Smiling and wiping away a stray tear, I turn and take my first step toward my future.

Epilogue

I clutch the bouquet of red and white roses tightly in my hand and take a seat on the rock wall. The sun has just begun to rise over the mountains behind me, keeping the valley below encased in shadow. I sit there for a moment, having had all these things to say but unable to find my voice to say them.

A hawk flies out over the hollow, its cries echoing as it dips closer to the creek below.

"Remember that one time we went swimming at the bluff and you found that injured hawk?" I smile, recalling the memory. "I screamed and begged you not to touch it, but you were fearless. The hawk had opened his mouth wide, warning you to stay back, but you scooped it up anyway and picked the twig from its wing." I chuckle. "As a reward, it pecked at your arm before flying off. What was it, three stitches or four?"

The wind blows my loose hair around, a few strands cross over my face and I have to tuck them behind my ear.

Clearing my throat, I continue. "Kirk has been doing good. I know he comes up here, but I figured I'd let you know that he's quit drinking. He's dominating at Northwest. I bet you anything he'll have offers coming from everywhere in the next year to go pro. You'd be proud of him."

My vision begins to blur as my tears begin to build. I do my best to try and fight them, but it does no good. They fall, one after the other, to soak into my shirt.

"God, I miss you. It seems so unreal that it's been a whole year since we said goodbye. And damn, two years since the accident." I shake my head. "It still doesn't seem real to me at times."

Unable to hold it back any longer, I break down and sob. My shoulders shake from the force of my grief.

The sky becomes brighter as I sit staring down at the hollow, my cheeks cold and wet.

"I know you're no longer stuck here in this valley, and I thought I would never come back, but as time passed I realized I was allowing Walter to take something away from us. This was our spot, our favorite spot. It's also the place where I got my wish, a chance to say goodbye to you.

"It's also a memorial to all the lives lost here due to the greed of one man. I'm not going to allow them to steal from anyone else again, so that includes remembering each one of you. I won't be here, but starting next week construction workers will be up here to build a memorial I've designed with the names and pictures of each person who was killed and trapped here for so long. It's not much, but I wanted to do something."

"It means a lot to me."

I gasp and jerk around to find Jesse Ford. Next to him is Mason Edwards.

"You guys scared me," I gasp. "What are you doing here?"

"We came to pay our respects." Mason nods. "Same as you."

I glance down at my flowers and smile. "That's nice of you."

"It was a mighty fine thing you did, Ms. Vanguard," Jesse says. "A mighty fine thing indeed."

I blush, hating the attention. I've never been one who likes getting compliments. "I didn't do much." I shrug.

"Are you kidding me?" Mason huffs. "You put together a whole campaign and worked until you had every dime collected to cover the cost of the memorial wall. That's honorable, young lady."

"Thanks." I blush, and tuck my hair behind my ear.

"You up here to say goodbye to Bryce?" Jesse asks, his face curious but understanding.

"Yes. I'm leaving soon."

"We know. Your brother has become a regular around the house," Jesse says. "Poor sap. I hate that I beat him like a lamb the other night."

I laugh. Tyler came home pissed that night because he lost every cent he had to Jesse and Mason in a game of poker.

"We tried to warn him." Mason shakes his head, a bit of mischief on his face. But no matter what kind of tough guy exterior these two try to put up as a front, I know they have kind hearts. Proof is from the sack of groceries and extra money that was left on the front porch the next morning after Tyler lost. The same exact amount of money he lost in the game. Coincidence? I think not.

Looking at my watch and seeing it's almost nine, I ask the two for a few more minutes of privacy. With solemn expressions and nods, the two walk on down the road, out of earshot. From what Tyler has told me, the two often walk these old roads together, keeping an eye out for mischief.

I turn back to the valley and take a deep breath. "Like I said, I'm not letting this place, our place, be taken from us. I'll be back here, every year, until the day I die. I love you, Bryce."

I place the flowers on the rock pillar in the middle and walk away. As I'm getting in my car, I wave at the two elderly men and yell for them to be good. They wave back and tell me not to worry about them. *Oh, how I am going to miss them.*

An hour later, I'm placing my last duffle bag into the passenger seat of the Mustang. Heaving a sigh, I turn to see four sad faces staring out at me. Great. Here come the water works.

Kirk, Millie, Tyler, and Anna all come out onto the front porch together, then stop. Kirk is the first to come forward, while the others stay up on the porch.

"I'll tell you this. We've had quite the interesting relationship over the years," he says, and crosses his arms as he leans against the car.

"Tell me about it," I say, chuckling.

"I'm not going to make this awkward or anything, so I'll get to it. We're gonna miss you around here."

I flick a glance up to Millie, who is leaning against the porch post.

"Something tells me you will manage."

He gives me a quick hug and walks back up to the porch, giving Millie the go-ahead. She bounds down the steps, and I can already see the tears in her eyes.

"I hate that you're leaving."

I open my mouth, but she waves me off.

"I know. You need to do this. And I'm happy for you. I just wish it didn't require you leaving."

"I know, but I'll be back. I'm not saying goodbye forever."

She sniffles, and looks up at the sky. I know she's trying to fight to keep her tears from falling but it does no good. One slides down from the corner of her eye anyway.

"Dammit. I'm sorry. I just love you and I hate saying goodbye."

"It's not goodbye. It's see you later."

She makes me promise to call and text a million times a day before she agrees to let go. I laugh and promise to do my best. When we hug, I don't know who finds it harder to let go, her or me. Reluctantly, we both squeeze as hard as we can one last time and then step back.

After joining Kirk back up at the house, Tyler and Anna are next. They walk hand in hand down the driveway. Anna pauses but Tyler pulls her along. The two met eight months ago, after Anna moved to town and started working at the diner. They hit it off pretty quick. When I told Tyler I was leaving, I suggested that Anna move in with him to save her from struggling to make rent. I want to say it was a selfless act, but it wasn't. It helped with the guilt of leaving my brother. I know Anna will take care of him and he won't be alone now, which gives me reassurance about him being okay.

"I still can't believe you're leaving," he says with a sigh.

"If my empty room and packed car hasn't convinced you yet, maybe me driving off will help it sink in."

Tyler shakes his head. "What am I going to do without your wit?"

"Probably stay sane for one." I smile and nudge him in the shoulder. Anna laughs beside him, but tries to hide it behind her hand.

Clearing her throat, she tries to tame the smile. "We are going to miss you around here, Jo. I don't know what I'm going to do with myself on those lonely nights when your brother is working."

"Enjoy it. God knows he's needy when he's home."

She chuckles again. "I'll remember that." She gives me a quick hug and goes back to the house to give me and Tyler a moment.

"She's a keeper. You know that, right?"

"I do," he answers, a smile tugging at his lips. It soon falls and his concern makes my eyes sting. "Please take care of yourself, Jo. Jada assured me that she would watch out for you, but still, I'm—"

"Worried. I know." When I told Tyler I wanted to go join Jada and Cooper in Louisiana, I thought for sure he was going to have a stroke. His face turned fifteen different shades of red before he could figure out the words he needed to express his outrage. We went round after round about it for days before I finally made him realize this is what I wanted and he couldn't stop me, but that I loved him and didn't want to hurt him. He had relented, but it wasn't easy.

"Have you heard from Dad yet?" I ask.

It was no surprise to either of us when our mother backed out of coming home. I'm sure whatever guilt she had been feeling was suppressed the more she began to think about what people would say about her behind her back once she returned. Two weeks ago, though, we were surprised to receive a phone call from our dad saying he had had enough of our mother, and was coming home without her. It was all kinds of crazy, and to say I'm glad I won't be here when he arrives is an understatement. I've had enough of the family drama.

When we asked him if he knew about the coven and hinted about Walters death, his answers were evasive and gave us nothing to go on. His admitting he's made some mistakes in his life kind of confirmed it for me, but not for Tyler. Tyler has to hear it or see it before he will ever believe it. One piece of closure I did get was finding a letter tucked under our parents mattress that stated if they didn't leave town, they would pay. The letter was left unsigned, but Tyler and I both think the coven had threatened our parents, and maybe even us, so they could get to us. Their tactics worked, but thank god the outcome was in our favor and not theirs.

"Yes. He sends his love and wishes he could be here to say goodbye, but he has a few final details to finish with the divorce before he can leave."

Bullet dodged. "I'm going to be okay, Tyler. I promise. I'm not going to do anything stupid. I want no part in fighting the spirits."

"Then what *are* you doing?"

I bite my lip. "I don't know. I've told you. This feels like what I'm meant to do. Maybe that's why I survived, I don't know." Tyler opens his mouth, no doubt to spout something off about Cooper, *again*, but I hold up my hand. "And yes, Cooper has a little to do with, but he's not the only reason. I want to do this for me, Tyler. Please understand that."

After learning everything we did about Walter and William and the feud that followed, I became, I guess you could say obsessed, with history and mysterious facts. I started looking into other legends and the history of the area around it. When I became tired of reading about it, I would draw some of the old sites I found or pictures from the internet and bring them back to life. It has become a part of my life, something I love. I may not be fighting spirits, but there are other ways to help.

Tyler grabs me by the shoulders, pulling me to him, and hugging me tight. "I do understand. I'm just going to miss you, turd."

Many tears and sniffles later, I get into my beauty and start the engine. The rumble of the engine calms my nerves and sends a tingle of excitement through my veins. As I pull away from the curb, I look in my rearview mirror to see the others waving at me as I drive out of their lives.

I don't know if I'm making the right decision, who does? For now, whether I'm following my heart or my mind, I know this is where I'm supposed to be headed. Turning onto Main Street, I set the GPS for the address Cooper gave me in Louisiana, and start my journey to a new beginning.

Acknowledgments

There is a lot of credit I can give for the creation of Deep in the Hollow, but I think the biggest acknowledgment needs to go to the spirit of the legend in my small town. It is because of the people where I live that The Lights has continued to be a legendary story. Way to keep the story and speculations alive guys and gals!

I'd also like to thank Jesse, Jay, and Edward for allowing me to interview you and share your stories. It was a fun and amazing time!

To my husband and kids for their support and excitement for this book. I love you guys to the moon and back.

J. Cameron McClain, you are the man and I will be forever grateful for your editing and teaching skills.

To Penny, who always has my back and keeps the hype alive. You are the greatest.

Last and most important, thanks goes to you, the reader. Thanks for taking the time to read my twisted version of The Lights. It's a legend I have grown up fascinated with and am thankful I got the chance to write about it. I truly hope you enjoyed it.

Other Books by Brandy

The Shadow World Trilogy:
Uniquely Unwelcome http://amzn.to/1Agvthr
Blood Burdens http://amzn.to/1JSSmMS
Sacrifice: A New Dawn http://amzn.to/1ER6Xus

The Spiritual Discord Series:
Broken Faith http://amzn.to/1DKrESS
Raging Storm http://amzn.to/1Ku1kBi

Connect with Brandy

Website: www.brandynacole.com
Facebook: www.facebook.com/authorbrandynacole
Twitter: www.twitter.com/authorbnacole
Goodreads: www.goodreads.com/BrandyNacole

Made in the USA
Columbia, SC
08 June 2020